Dancing to a Dangerous Tune

By R.A. Carter-Squire

Copyright 2015 Rick Carter-Squire

License Notes

To my greatest fan.

Thank you

[signature]

Chapter 1

Michael Eldridge gazed out his office window, the fingers of his left hand mindlessly rubbing the palm of his right. Memories of a day thirty years ago plagued him as he neared the solution to his current problem.

The company was developing software for a NASA mission to Mars. He needed one more solution and the project would be complete. This project could mean the end of the company, unless they finished on time. Eldridge Computing was the largest commercial software and hardware developer in Silicon Valley. Everything was riding on this contract. He could also complete another task he'd been working on for the last fifteen years.

He sighed and wiped a hand down his face. The trouble lay in a section of the program dealing with the transfer of data over long distances in real time. An algorithm to manage the problem should be obvious, but time kept getting in the way.

His mind envisioned the probe streaking towards the red planet. "Twenty minutes to send radio signals at the speed of light. How do I get the signal to move faster?" He closed his eyes.

Once he had the solution to the Mars program, Michael could solve a thirty-year-old mystery. He had a plan to go back to his childhood, but the time sequence issue was the same. He'd started thinking about a solution to this problem twenty years ago, which led him to where he was today. This last piece would make time travel a real possibility.

"Time is the road block in each case, not the sending or receiving data," he said to the window and leaned back in the leather chair. "Ground controllers need instant feedback from the probe at every stage and machines in my lab need the same from whatever time I'm in at that moment. In both cases, adjustments may be necessary, especially to keep the probe and me from being lost or killed." He sighed once more and opened his eyes.

A knock sounded on the door. Turning away from the window and taking a second to compose himself, Michael sat forward and said, "Come in."

Billy Dunsten strode across the plush carpet and flopped into the high-backed chair in front of Mike's desk. His six-foot body sagged into the cushion while he stretched his legs toward the front of the walnut desk. The remaining hair on his head had gone grey. Michael remembered the boy he'd grown up with as a friend, kind, happy, and yet many people saw Billy as depressing. The boy had grown into a man who frowned a lot.

"Hi, what's up," Mike asked.

"I'm exhausted," Billy sighed and rubbed his face with both hands. "All I've done for the past two weeks is put out fires and kiss the asses of those NASA engineers. Are you close to finishing the program? We only have two weeks to complete this project, or they cancel and we'll be screwed." Mike opened his mouth to say something, but Billy interrupted. "No, change that, we'll be so fucked it'll take the rest of our lives just to be able to walk straight again."

"You sound just like you did in high-school. Even as the quarterback, you'd get overly dramatic when there was a problem. Would I lie to you? There's only one thing left to finish which shouldn't take more than a couple of days. After that, all we need to do is run a few simulations to prove the system works." Mike leaned back in the chair. He forced a smile.

"I'm glad one of us is so confident. I might be less anxious now, if I knew more about this technical mumbo-jumbo. Since I don't have half your smarts, please tell me we aren't going to fuck this up." His voice went from a baritone to an alto as he spoke.

"There's nothing to worry about, Billy. I was working on the final problem when you came in. All I need to figure out is the time shift equation, and the puzzle will be done." His eyes dropped to the blank pad in front of him. Wrinkles appeared between his eyebrows.

"You've been working on this same problem since high-school? I may not know how to program a computer, but I can still see where this is leading. There's no way that you going back in time will change what happened to Joe in that drainage sewer."

• • •

Michael strode confidently along the sidewalk. He's been anticipating this day for a year. Today is going to change his life forever. It's Friday, June 2, 1957 -- sports day.

Most of the other kids treat the day like a holiday, but for some, the day is a chance to shine as they show off their physical abilities in track and field events. Mike has imagined himself as the next

Olympian, even while racing against other boys his age. Billy Wanger, his best friend and neighbor since before they started school always wins the hundred yard dash, but the distance between them gets smaller every year. Today will be different; he's energized, and his feet seem to float over the concrete.

His gaze drops to the sidewalk. The only things keeping his mood from flying are the shadows. They scare him. Mike knows there are spirits waiting to steal his soul in the darkness, at least that's what his older brother told him. If you can't believe your brother, who can you believe? What's an older brother for if he can't look out for his little brother? These and many other sayings come frequently from the twelve-year-old Scott. Darkness doesn't scare him. That would be silly because everyone would be taken at night; Mike has reasoned it all out. No, the shadows hide the evil spirits, and they can only get you in the daylight.

Mike moves to his left, hugging the picket fence while tiptoeing around the shadows of leaves and branches on the sidewalk. He sees them clutch and grab for his feet in the light breeze; each time they move toward him, his heart skips a beat and he jumps high into the air to avoid their grasp. Clear of the shadows finally, he senses he's safe and moves forward again with confidence. Nothing is going to stop him from winning the races today, not any old shadows at least. There are three more trees reaching out over the sidewalk between him and the school.

He remembered walking this way with his parents. Dad laughed when he saw his son skirting the shade on the way to watch the summer fair parade on Main Street. Michael jumped and dodged the shadows. Mom hadn't said anything. She must have been upset though because she didn't seem happy when he turned around on the other side of the shadows. Ever since then, his parents wore their unhappy faces if they saw him jumping shadows. Don't they know about the soul stealing spirits? Maybe there's a day when kids reach a certain size or age and their souls aren't as tasty, but that day can't be soon enough.

The schoolyard, another two houses, and he'd be there -- safe for the rest of the day. Billy stood waiting at the gate; really just an opening in the chain-link fence, but everyone called it a gate.

Billy was wearing a pair of gym shorts in the school colors of blue and yellow with the crest of the Eagle mascot on the side. He had a new pair of black-and-white high-top running shoes, tied together by the laces and slung over his shoulder. His Dad managed the bank. Michael overheard his Mom on the telephone last year talking to someone about the Wangers. "They can afford to pay for anything he wants. The boy is going to grow up spoiled rotten and probably in jail." She didn't know he'd been listening. Holy crow she would have flipped a lid if she'd caught him; he smiled at the thought. Billy was standing at the gate with his new clothes and a smug expression on his freckled face, Mike understood then, what she meant by spoiled and his young mind yearned for a better life.

"It's about time you got here, slow-poke," Billy called from the gate as Mike passed the last house. "Try running past the shadows instead of tiptoeing, you might get faster and beat me some year." This good-natured jab still stung. Billy was three months older and two inches taller, which made Mike wonder if there was a combination of age and size before the shadows didn't want your soul anymore. Maybe they only want the good kids, his mind whispered, or maybe Scott is just full of shit.

"I'd get here sooner if I got a ride to school too. How come you need a new pair of runners every sports day? Mine were new last fall and they're still fine for running." Not being quite as good as his friend nagged at him and made his stomach flutter.

"Dad says new tires on the car give it a better grip on the road so it makes sense to have new runners to race with." He shrugged and scraped the ground with his toe.

"Well, this year you're gunna need 'um. I'm feeling as fast as a rabbit. Let's go watch some of the older kids run; maybe we can get some Kool-Aid."

"Yeah, maybe we'll get lucky and see Fred Stoddard trip over his laces like last year. Cripes, his face was a mess after falling on the track. I think he nearly tore his nose off by the way it looked." Billy puckered his face in disgust.

"He's too old to be still going here, but seeing all that blood made some of the girls upchuck behind the bleachers. There's Joe," Mike trotted off without waiting for Billy. The three boys were like peas in a pod, his mother said. They sat together in class, played together at recess and nearly always agreed on how to have fun.

Their parents were fine with the boys being friends; they were good students. Neither caused a problem in class and they got

5

excellent report cards. The teacher this year, Miss Belfridge, was kind and she was pretty too. A sweet young thing with ta-tas out to here, Michael heard his Dad say to a friend at a barbecue last October before giving the other man an elbow in the ribs and they laughed. Michael didn't know what was so funny. Sometimes, when she was trying to show him how to print or pointing out a mistake in his arithmetic, she would reach her arm around his shoulder and her chest would press into the back of his head. He'd go all goosy and lightheaded, between her perfume and the soft pressure of her breasts.

"Hey guys," Joe called. "Your Dad got ya new tires again this year, eh Billy. Boy that must be nice, I wish my Mom wasn't so cheap." He stared over at the start line even though nobody was there yet. Mike could see they shared the same sense of embarrassment. Don't let the shadows get you drifted into his thoughts.

"Here, they'll fit you," Billy handed the new runners to Joe. "I wish Dad didn't keep buying me stuff like this, it feels," he shuffled his feet and stared down at the ground, but still held the shoes toward Joe. "It makes me feel yucky around you guys. I don't like it." His face had gone red as he spoke with his heart.

"Naw, I couldn't take your shoes Billy. You might finally lose to Mike and I'd stand a chance of catching you too." He laughed and pushed the shoes back. Billy laughed too, but his eyes were sad.

"We're best friends right, no matter what. We'll always be friends because we're the Three Musketeers -- all for one and one for all," Mike shouted and they clasped hands over their heads holding imaginary swords. When Joe was sick two years ago, Mike had visited his house every day until his friend recovered.

"Wanna' get some Kool-Aid and go watch the grade eight girls high-jump." Joe moved without waiting for them to answer.

The sun shone down on competitors and spectators alike, baking them like Sunday hams. It was only nine thirty, but already 85 degrees; the temperature was supposed to rise to 102 F his Mom had warned Michael as he left the house. Unusually hot for June in New England, this would be a record year some said.

Mr. Fredrickson the Principal had taken off his coat and tie; the sleeves of his white shirt rolled up to his elbows revealing the pale skin of his forearms. He stood by the bleachers with a clipboard in

6

one hand and a megaphone in the other. The loudspeaker would come up to his mouth and he'd shout for groups of people to go to the broad-jump pit or to the starting line for upcoming events. Other teachers herded children trying to assist in completing the events in a timely fashion. They seemed to be enjoying their time outside as much as the kids.

The three amigos spent the next few hours together, watching their friends and classmates compete, sometimes cheering, often laughing at the failures of the athletes. The bell rang to signal lunchtime. Most of the students ran for the bleachers or toward the school to find some shade while they ate their bag lunches. Joe and Billy were headed toward the school until Mike saw an empty spot next to the bleachers. There was only enough shade for two of them, so Mike sat in the sun keeping an eye on his friends to see if their souls would be stolen by spirits.

"What did you get?" Joe asked Billy.

"Cold beef I think," he wasn't sure yet as he pulled the sandwich from the bag.

"Peanut butter and grape jelly," Mike said softly. Being poor nagged at him again.

"Yeah, me too," Joe chimed sadly. The friends ate in silence, wolfing the food like starving animals. Their meals were gone in a few minutes, but they remained quiet for another five each boy thinking about the afternoon race. "Ya wanna do something after school? We could go by that new drainage ditch on Maple Avenue and see what's happening. They've got some really big equipment over there," Joe said. Mike knew his friend would go whether he and Billy went or not. They all knew that getting into trouble was better with friends.

"I can only go for a little while. My Mom said we were going out for supper to celebrate." Billy shifted a little more into the shade, but the heat wasn't making him feel uncomfortable.

"What are ya celebrating?" Mike asked with a grin. Joe laughed.

"I don't know. I'm just the kid and I do what they tell me."

"I'll go," Mike agreed while ignoring the obvious lie from Billy. He knew Billy only got angry when he was embarrassed. "As long as I'm home by five, my parents don't worry about where I am." He lifted the baseball cap with the Yankees logo off his head and wiped his forehead with the sleeve of his T-shirt. His Dad had bought him

7

the cap last summer. The Yankees were his favorite team and he only took it off when he was in the house or in school.

"All seven-year-old boys competing in the hundred-yard dash, to the starting line now. If you're running the hundred-yard dash, and you are a seven-year-old boy, you need to be at the starting line now," Mr. Fredrickson shouted through the megaphone. Mike, Billy, and Joe scrambled off the ground and trotted across the playground. There were always enough boys to make up two races, so they didn't hurry. As friends, they tried to run in the same race.

When they approached the area of the race, a teacher neither of the boys recognized was sorting boys onto the start line. She turned and grabbed Mike by the arm and pulled him into the only empty spot available. He looked back at his friends with an expression of fear and sadness. This was the first time he'd run the race without them.

Another teacher shouted, "On your mark," and he instinctively bent into his starting position. When the gunshot sounded, his arms and legs pumped his body down the track. He felt like he was flying. Wind whipped past his face; the ground flew by under his feet so fast the stones seemed to melt together into a smooth surface. He saw the finish line, a white strip of chalk with another unknown teacher standing to one side with a stopwatch. His shadow crossed the track mere feet before the white line.

Mike couldn't see anyone else running on either side of him; he was winning the race. He leaned forward, just a bit to make his legs move faster. There was no way he would lose this time. This would be his year to take home a blue ribbon.

Two yards from the finish line, just four more strides at most, he saw another boy coming up on the right. A moment of blurred color and motion out of the corner of his eye, but he saw him. His mind made the next few seconds pass in slow motion. Two steps to go and Mike turned his head. The boy was red-faced and moving as hard as he could, but he was tired. Mike smiled inside. He was at least a step ahead still and didn't feel the least bit tired. His head snapped back to the front and he tripped on something.

The forward motion carried him over the finish line, but tripping hadn't reduced his speed. His hands shot out to save his face from becoming spaghetti like Fred Stoddard. Sharp granite stones cut into his hands as he slid across the chalk line lifting dust into his face and eyes. Memories of beating the blackboard erasures against the side of the school came back to him. Pain shot up his arms; tears came to his eyes, but from the dust not the pain. *'Remember, big boys don't cry,'* his brother's voice said in his head.

Cheering sounds drifted into his consciousness as he looked around, embarrassed and bloodied, but sure, he won. He was also sure the teachers' shadow had been what tripped him. Gentle hands jerked him off the ground and the face of Miss Belfridge appeared. She was smiling and wiping the dust off his face and then held his hands leading him to the side of the racetrack.

"I'll just clean out these cuts on your hands and knees before you go home. We don't want your parents thinking we abuse you. This is going to sting, but it'll feel better once I'm done." Her hands were soft and warm. He watched her tip a bottle of some clear liquid onto a cloth and dab his cut and bleeding palms. Each touch of the material sent fresh glass shards of pain shooting up his arms. Her eyes reflected her compassion letting him know she cared. For some reason, knowing she cared eased his suffering and by the time she finished dabbing his bloody knees, the pain was gone. When the last bandage was applied, she reached around him and gave him a tight hug; he was pressed firmly against her chest. His Dad's comment about ta-tas on a woman surfaced in his mind; he blushed.

She let him go and smiled at him. He mumbled his thanks and turned to find his friends. Something stirred in his head and tingled on his chest where her breasts had pressed against him. He smiled. A girl in his class was going in the opposite direction and returned his smile. Nancy Allen was her name and he kind of liked her. He'd catch her staring at him almost every day any time he looked out the windows in the classroom. The idea of having her as his girlfriend didn't seem gross anymore.

The second race, which included Billy and Joe was lined up and ready to start. He glanced down at the finish line in front of him and noticed the smudge in the chalk where he'd slid through. Shadows of those around him reached across the track. The gun sounded and he turned to watch the race.

Billy came off the line first. Joe was always in third or fourth place when the three friends ran together. Today though, he was even with Billy all the way down the track. No way, Mike giggled. Joe was wearing the new high-tops Billy had brought to school. The shoes really were making a difference. They were close at the line, but the result was never in doubt. Billy won as usual. He collected his blue ribbon from Mr. Fredrickson with a sheepish grin.

"Michael," Mr. Fredrickson hollered across the track. "Come and get your ribbon." How is he able to keep everybody's name straight in his head, he wondered as he walked toward the Principal. "How are the war wounds," he asked kindly as Mike stopped in front of him.

"Not bad, Miss Belfridge did a good job of patching them up."

"Well, you ran a heck of a race, young man, and deserve this ribbon. Wear it with pride." Mr. Fredrickson reached forward and pinned the brightest and most glorious blue ribbon on Mike's shirt he'd ever seen. His chest swelled with pride. The pain in his palms was gone, and all around him was silent. He bent his head trying for a better view of the ribbon.

"Thanks," he managed to mumble and walked away still gazing at the prize on his chest.

"Hey, you finally won, way to go buddy." Joe came running to catch him. Billy joined them and they went to sit on the bleachers.

"That was sure one hell of a spill you took at the finish line, me and Billy thought you were gonna look like Fred for certain."

"Me too, all I could think of was keeping my face off the gravel. Jeepers, I only needed a couple more steps and it would have been perfect. Oh well, I won and that's all that matters now. I've got war wounds and a ribbon to show for my efforts." He hoped they wouldn't say anything about Miss Belfridge's chest. "Who was that kid running beside me?"

"Don't know," Billy shrugged. "He's in the other class, you know, the brainy kids." His lip curled.

Michael nodded. Those kids were a bit snotty just because they thought they were smarter. It didn't seem right to separate kids like that. They learned the same stuff and read the same books in both classes.

"Why don't we leave now? There isn't any reason to stick around and nobody is going to miss us," Joe asked.

"What about the ice cream?" Billy whimpered. "We always get ice cream after the races. Let's wait 'til then and we can still go over to the ditch before supper."

Mike nodded, considering all options. He was the leader and the choices were up to him. "We'll go see if we can get some now, tell them I'm not feeling too good and you guys are taking me home." He smiled at them.

They had to wait until three for the ice cream, but twenty minutes and a quarter mile later, three young boys stopped at the edge of a gravel and dirt slope leading to the bottom of a drainage ditch.

"What are they doing this for, anyway?" Michael asked.

"Dad said the city needs to drain water from the north side of the city to the river on the south side. I can't remember how many miles it is, but he said they'd take months to complete the job." Work had ceased for the day, but they saw a man in a truck parked among the heavy equipment.

The boys stood together, looking down at the maw of the unfinished end of the drain. At first glance, they figured the tunnel was big enough to carry a train. They took tentative steps toward the opening, tense with anticipation and dread at being stopped any second. When no shout came from above, Mike led them single file into the darkness of the tunnel.

"Torches, we're gonna need torches if we want to go further," Michael decided, his voice echoing down the pipe. The smell of concrete and damp earth filled their noses after walking a few yards into the drain. Strange noises echoed out of the darkness.

"How far do ya think it goes?" Billy wondered, his voice quavering back to them as he stared into the gloom.

"Probably all the way to the ocean," Joe said. "If they've got that end finished, we should be able to hear the waves like when you hold a shell up to your ear."

"Maybe we're too far away, 'cus I don't hear any waves. I'm not going further without some light. Who knows what's living in here? We could come face to face with an alligator if it does go all the way to the ocean."

"Don't you know anything Billy?" Joe scolded from behind. "Alligators don't live in the ocean. Besides, that's gotta be at least a hundred miles away. There wouldn't be any way out for an alligator and it sure as hell wouldn't be hangin' around where there isn't any food."

"Where did you learn to swear like that Joe?" Mike asked. His voice was a mixture of awe and contempt.

11

"Mom's always talking like that. It's sure as hell this and it's sure as hell that. This morning she told me to clean up my room because it sure as hell wasn't going to clean itself."

Maybe they were afraid or because of how normal the words sounded coming out of Joe's mouth, but they laughed. The sound rippled down the tunnel into the solid blackness. The noise of a vehicle engine starting came to them from the open end of the pipe.

"Let's get out of here and get some flashlights or something, so we can see." Mike turned around as he spoke. Once they'd scrambled back up the slope of the ditch, he noticed the truck with the man had gone.

"There isn't anybody here now. They've probably all gone for the weekend. Either of you two got a flashlight at home?" Joe acted very determined to explore the tunnel, nodding his head eagerly, frantic almost.

Mike and Billy shook their heads no.

"I do, two. They were ones my Dad had in the army. It'll take me about ten minutes to run there and back. You guys stay here." He didn't wait for them to answer. Michael stared at Joe running away.

"I'm supposed to be home by five, what time is it?"

Billy looked at the watch on his left wrist. "Aw, shit," he moaned. "I forgot to wind it this morning. It stopped at two o'clock." He shook his wrist as if that was going to change the time.

"It had to be almost three o'clock when we left the school grounds," Michael reasoned. "That was about an hour ago, so it's gotta be almost four by now. If it takes me half-an hour to get home, it'll be four thirty. I've gotta get going, Billy, and so do you." Mike cringed as he stood from sitting on the ground. The scrapes and bandages on his knees were tight.

"What about Joe? He's going to be mad when he gets back if we aren't here," Billy whined as he brushed the dirt off his legs.

"Yeah he'll be mad, but I'd sooner he was mad at me than my Mom. We can always come back tomorrow. You can wait for him if you want, but I'm leaving." He turned and started walking toward home. A sense of guilt kept him looking over his shoulder in a vain hope that Joe would return before they went too far.

Chapter 2

"I know, but if I could just figure out what happened, then I'd get some peace. I've blamed myself all these years and nothing anyone says is going to take that away."

"You," Billy sat up in the chair and leaned forward, anger darting from his eyes. "You weren't the only one responsible. I'm just as guilty as you for not being there to stop him when he got back. I didn't need to be home that night...my parents were working late or something. Anyway, he was old enough to know better. What do you think you're going to accomplish by going back there? If you stop him, the whole history of the planet could change. We'd certainly change and never be where we are now. You've always been a determined guy, even before Joe disappeared. The closer you get to actually traveling in time, the more selfish you've become. You're pushing everything and everyone aside. Nothing matters anymore, except what happened thirty years ago. I'm afraid, Michael, afraid of what might happen to you -- to us. God, Mike, we might be poor and living on the street."

He finished with a smile as he poked at Mike's old insecurity about having been poor. The opulence of the office surrounding them showed the anxiety was still there. Billy watched his best friend return a weak smile, which quickly faded into a frown as his eyes dropped to the blank pad on the desk. Billy had been a partner in this business since the beginning in high school. They maintained a relaxed and casual dress code since then.

Suddenly, the scowl disappeared as Mike snatched the pen and started scribbling on the pad. His hand moved back and forth making chicken scratches, which only he could read. Billy watched fascinated at how Mike worked. Four minutes later, he put the pen down, and picked up the notes, reading each line. His eyes brightened. Looking over the pad at Billy, he beamed. "We need to test this, but I think it should work."

"Great, do you want to do that now or wait until morning?" Sarcasm tinged Billy's voice. "Aw screw it, let's go get a drink and celebrate." He chuckled and stood up.

"Yeah let's take the night off and relax. Starting tomorrow, the next two weeks are going to be the toughest fourteen days of our lives." Mike threw his arm over Billy's shoulder as they walked out of the office.

An elevator ride and two blocks walking in silence, and they were seated in a booth and had their drinks, Billy lifted his and proposed a toast.

"Here's to finishing the project on time."

"I'll drink to that," Mike grinned back as their glasses clinked. "But I still need your help to complete the other project."

"I haven't forgotten about that, but you better promise you won't do anything until the code is perfect. No kidding, Mike, if there's even one thing wrong you could be trapped or killed in another time. What happens then? How do I explain that to the press? Oh, he's just on an extended vacation, but he'll return in thirty years or so. That's if I had some way of knowing for sure you were trapped back then, but what happens if you're killed somehow. Mr. Eldridge died today in 1957. I'm not sure of the details because there's no way of knowing what happened. Yes, he was here up until the time he disappeared and then he died. How do I know he died? An obituary notice appeared with cards of condolence in the paper at my house that morning in 1957; all of them had Michael Eldridge as the person who died." He gulped his drink and waved to the bartender to bring them more.

Mike stared down at his glass, nodding his head slightly in agreement. Billy didn't think Michael understood how angry and frightened, this personal project made him feel. He squeezed his eyes shut trying to hold back angry words boiling in his mind. His concerns were far greater than he could ever say.

Other groups of people were laughing and talking or watching basketball on television. They all seemed happier and carefree compared to him and Michael.

The drinks arrived and Billy grabbed his, tossing it back in one gulp. Mike stared up at his friend. Billy could see emotions drifting across his face, and the hard swallow before his friend spoke.

"I'm sorry Billy. I didn't realize how much this was affecting you, but you know I can't quit. I don't intend to take chances with my life, and nothing will happen until I'm certain the program is completely safe. I give you my word. I would never lie to you." His fingers twirled the glass on the table.

"What's the point, Mike?" Billy hissed and leaned forward. "You can't change what happened that day or any other day. If you're trapped back then, you'll be reliving the rest of your days repeating a history you already know. Which means you'll need to bury your Mom again, hear about your crazy brother being sent to prison, everything that hurt you in the last thirty years. Ultimately, you won't be here to make a difference in what happens from this moment onward. I can't run this company without you, if there is a company without you, because you're the brains of this outfit. You were the one who came up with a program to detect missile launches on the other side of the world by monitoring deep earth sound waves. The military said your software was a stroke of genius. Eldridge Computing wouldn't be where it is now, without you. There won't be any new inventions or groundbreaking discoveries unless someone else makes them. What happens to me?"

"You have nothing to worry about there, but I promise I'm not willing to live my life over again. I've made provisions for the company in the event of my death or disappearance, Billy. Nothing is going to go wrong if I can help it, I promise." He raised his right hand to make the promise official, and smiled.

"Yeah, I know, you've taken care of all the details you always do, but if anything bad happens, I'll be waiting for you with an axe when you reappear." He chuckled and ordered more drinks.

Heather Sykes walked through the door. Silence descended as all eyes turned appreciating her. The sultry redhead strolled through the bar, her eyes locked on Mike. His heart beat a little faster as he watched her. '*I shouldn't be having these feelings for my director of marketing, but she doesn't do anything to turn me off,*' he thought.

She slid into the booth next to Billy. Her perfume wafted like a cloud over Mike adding to his arousal. Her red lips parted and she spoke to him. "I thought I'd find you two in here, so, unless you're talking secrets, I'll join you. Are we celebrating or drowning our sorrows?" There was a sly sparkle in her eyes and a sexy growl in her voice.

Mike waved at the bar to order more of the same. "We're celebrating," he said, adding a forced smile. "I finished the computer code. Once we've completed the testing, the launch will happen on schedule."

"That's wonderful Michael, don't you agree Billy?" Her eyes never left Michael's face. Drinks appeared on the table, set in place by a disembodied hand from out of the gloom. Michael stared as her slender fingers, with nails lacquered to match her lipstick, gripped the glass, lifting it toward her mouth. The ruby lips closed around the straw in her drink. Her throat moved as she swallowed, then the delicate hand set the glass on the table and she began to wriggle out of the suit jacket buttoned to her throat. As the coat opened, a low-cut blouse revealed lovely cleavage, even in the dim light of the bar. Once she'd finished peeling away the coat, she leaned her elbows on the table.

Michael's eyes went to the swell of her breast for a second, even though his mind tried to stop them. He glanced at Billy, but his friend was ogling shamelessly. '*I can't be doing this. She's an employee.*' His mind whirled with thoughts of lust while his eyes remained on her breasts. He remembered Miss Belfridge. Heather's warm hand on his wrist broke the sexual fantasy.

"I'm sorry, what did you say?" he stammered and sat back in the seat.

"How long will it last?" There was a leering grin on her face as she slowly licked her lips. Michael knew her teasing was working, but he was determined to ignore it.

"The testing will be finished in the next two weeks -- has to be." A cheer went up from the group watching the game.

"Is there anything I can do to help? Should we put out a press release?" The teasing stopped as her mind shifted to her work.

"We should hold off releasing any statements to the press until we get closer to the launch date, -- just in case something goes wrong." Billy blurted.

"Nothing is going to go wrong Billy," Michael snapped and instantly regretted his tone. "What I mean is that the testing will find the errors in the code and let us know if there are any other issues to consider. Tomorrow we'll find out if it works and we'll move forward from there." He raised his glass and all three clinked in agreement.

An hour later, Michael entered his house and dropped the keys on the table by the door. He flipped on the lights in the living room, discreet illumination set behind a mahogany valance around the ceiling. The drapes were open on the floor to ceiling windows, allowing him a clear view of the city spread out through the valley below. Yellow, red, green with a few blue lights thrown in, twinkled, and glittered to the mountains. Moving toward the windows, he slid out of his suede jacket and dropped it over the back of the leather sofa. Folding his arms across his chest, Michael stared out at the lights and sighed.

Somewhere among the glowing dots there were people having a party, someone was sitting in the dark thinking about ending their life; one of those houses had a couple making love. His mind shifted trying to imagine how the valley had appeared thirty years ago.

Silicon Valley was a virtual wasteland when he'd started here ten years ago. A few houses and smaller factories, but nothing compared to now. Once news of his success and the move to the valley hit the media, every computer-related business on the planet set up a shop here.

His thoughts were interrupted by a soft beeping sound. As he moved away from the windows down the hallway to the bedroom, the sound grew louder. He opened the door to the spare room and flipped on the lights.

A computer filled the wall opposite the door. Metal frames held boxes filled with circuit boards; wires connected them together to make a thinking machine. Lights flashed on and off while processing information, the noise was the computer's way of saying a solution had been found to yesterday's problem. He sat at the desk and punched the button to turn on the monitor.

Michael assembled this computer with more thinking power than anything else in production. NASA's capability didn't come close, and they were ahead of most companies on the planet. The screen brightened, showing several lines of text.

'Error line 36589 code missing or corrupt'

'Please enter code and try again'

I don't know if this is going to work, but I have to try.' His fingers tapped at the keyboard entering the six lines of code he'd written earlier. When he finished, the middle finger of his right hand hovered over the enter key as he reread the lines of text. Finally, with a deep breath filled with hope, he pressed the key. The computer beeped once and the screen went blank except for a blinking cursor in the top left corner.

The doorbell rang. Michael turned off the monitor and the lights before closing the door. His nerves were on edge about the project and he wasn't expecting nor needing company right now. When he opened the front door, Heather Sykes was standing on the step, her suit jacket slung over her right shoulder, and her high-heels suspended from her left hand.

"Can I come in?" She asked softly and smiled slyly, but didn't move. She seemed uncertain of his answer.

Michael took a deep breath while letting his eyes run from her face to her stocking feet. *'Should I let her in and risk my urges getting the better of me,'* he wondered? *'Is there an upside to sleeping with her? Is that what she really wants?'*

He smiled, not quite a happy effort, and stepped back to let her pass. She moved like a cat toward the living room, dropping her shoes by the door and jacket next to his before flopping on the sofa, pulling her feet up beside her. There was nothing left to his imagination about what she wanted. Her eyes sparkled in the light from the recessed bulbs and he could see her breathing rapidly. She held out her arms, reaching for him.

"Heather," his tongue seemed too large and he nearly choked. "Heather...ummm, I don't think this is such a good idea." He wanted her, but now that he'd put the words into the air, he couldn't take them back. Her expression became shocked, hurt, and angry in that order. She sat up and adjusted the blouse to hide her chest.

"Are you saying I'm not good enough for you?" Her voice sounded angry, but her face said relieved.

"No, that's not what I'm saying. I'm thrilled you want me and I want you, but I can't get distracted right now. I need to concentrate on finishing this project. After I'm done, we can try this again." Hoping he'd smoothed any hurt feelings and left the door open for a night of passion soon, he smiled.

Her mouth twitched in an effort to smile back, but she didn't look at him.

"Would you like a drink?" he offered, trying to change the subject and dampen his growing sense of guilt for hurting her.

"Well, since I drove all the way out here, I guess I wouldn't go home empty handed." Her smile said all was forgiven, for now, and the sexual glint was back in her eyes. He opened a bottle of red wine, expecting they could talk like friends over several glasses.

18

She accepted the drink he held toward her. They sat in silence for a minute before she began to tell him about the schoolgirl crush she had for him. Her older brother hated Michael for being smart and because Heather liked him. Tonight was a spur-of-the-moment thing, but something she'd been dreaming of for many years.

"I've wanted to have sex with you since I was fourteen, Michael." She was staring into her glass, while her face became the color of a ripe apple. He wondered if her open honesty was the booze talking. "I'd lie on my bed at night and imagine us together, and then you graduated and left me. When I finished college, your picture was plastered on the front cover of every magazine in the country. I remembered those adolescent feelings for you, and became determined to get close to you again." She stared into her wine for another moment, her words spoken barely above a whisper. He shifted in his chair. She took a deep breath, her eyes focused on him. They were sad and needy. "If we just had sex Michael, I'd be fine with that, but I really want a longer relationship. I'm not shallow, or a slut screwing for easy money. If you can find a spark of love for me, that'd be wonderful because I know it would grow. I'd do everything in my power to fan that spark into a flame."

'My God, she's proposing to me. What the hell am I going to say? Marriage is the last thing I want right now,' he thought.

He smiled broadly, staring out the window, trying to organize his thoughts. *'She'd be great to make love to, I'm sure, but is that all I want? Could I live with her for the rest of my life? Would she still want me once she finds out what I'm like? God, I'm so useless around women. I wish I'd spent less time with computers in high school and more time dating girls.'*

"Thank you and I need to be honest with you too." Mike stammered. "I remember thinking the first time I saw you in school that you were cute and I'd like to get to know you better. The day I saw you at the office, I couldn't believe you were the same girl. All my feelings for you, rushed back into my mind. The school-boy images about being able to get into your pants." He blushed and slid forward on the sofa, holding out his hand in panic. "I'm sorry I shouldn't have said that. As for a relationship, let's see what happens after this project is finished. I won't promise anything, but maybe after a date or two we'll know if we can stand each other's company. I have no doubt the sex will be great and you are gorgeous to look at,

19

but as I said, I'm not able to focus on anything but my work at the moment. Am I being too blunt, talking about sex? I am and I'm really sorry. Oh God I've made a mess of everything haven't I?"

She set her glass on the table and moved to the arm of the chair beside him. Holding his face in her hands, she pressed her lips to his. They were warm and soft. He gently moved his free arm around her shoulder and pulled her close. Her head moved back and the scent of her perfume enveloped his senses; her green eyes sparkled and tears welled up.

"That's the nicest thing anyone has said to me in a long time. I'll accept that for now, but I'll want more, later," she breathed.

He smiled and kissed her again. Before another word was spoken, she stood, grabbed her jacket, and moved quickly toward the front door. She stooped to grab her shoes. "I'll see you tomorrow at work. Thanks for the drink," she shouted over her shoulder as the door closed softly.

Michael stood, staring at the dark wood of the front door for a minute, wondering if he'd done the right thing and if his refusal would affect their future. A beep from the computer down the hall ripped his mind away from her. He frowned, walking toward the bedroom. The computer shouldn't be finished. Something must be wrong, or the program worked perfectly, but he didn't feel hopeful.

He turned on the light and he sat at the desk pressing the button for the monitor again. The blinking cursor was below a single line of text.

'Program complete, please go to results.exe for outcomes'

Michael frowned and typed...results.exe.

The screen went black and then brightened filling with lines of text. At the bottom of the screen, 'hit enter to continue...' was followed by the blinking cursor.

He scanned the results for error messages. Nothing on this page, so he hit enter. A new page appeared which had the same results. Frustrated, he hit the enter key several times and waited. The screen filled only half way this time, the last line read, 'Program complete, ready to send and receive.'

His heart beat faster. *All I need to do is attach the relay node and find out what happens.*' He couldn't stop his fingers trembling as they plugged wires into the computer. Several times, he needed multiple tries to fasten the correct lead, but finally, everything was attached. The node was a four feet by two feet wide stainless steel table in front of the computer. *'Now what,'* he wondered in a panic. *'I was so concerned with getting the program right I didn't think about sending something.'* The first object he saw was his father's old coffee cup full of pens. Printed on the side was: 'World's Best DAD'. Deciding an old coffee cup appearing in the past wouldn't create too many concerns; he dumped the pens on the desk and set the mug on the table. Rushing to sit at the keyboard, he banged his hip on the corner of the desk, yelping with the pain, but ignored it. Typing in the date, time, and location, he pressed enter and realized there was going to be a problem.

'How will I know if it went anywhere or not?' He watched the cup become transparent, but not completely disappear. The program had a built-in four-minute window of operation, which would give him a quick look around, but not enough time to get into any real trouble when he went into the past.

Keeping track of the time, at exactly four minutes the cup became opaque once more. He stretched over his desk and grabbed the mug off the table. The pottery was warm in his fingers. Not too hot, more like his father just finished drinking coffee. *'This mug went somewhere, but how do I know that was the right time and place?'* A mental image of a tiny camera came into his mind followed by a clever smile.

"Yeah I could attach a video camera and record what happens." He felt giddy, elated as he dug through the closet. Moving one of the boxes on the shelf, he found the tiny black camera, a battery pack, and video receiver; he nearly burst out laughing. The devices had a six-hour battery and storage capacity, which would be perfect, and they fit neatly into the mug. *'A self-contained time spy,'* the idea makes him laugh.

Clipping the camera to the rim of the mug, arranging the rest of the device inside, he placed the unit on the table once more. His finger came down on the enter key and he watched the mug almost disappear again. Four minutes later, his excitement rose, making his fingers tremble, trying to pull the receiver out of the mug before making the attachments to the computer.

Typing the command to download the video had to be repeated twice before he managed to hit the correct keys. Once the words were in the precise order, the machine crunched the data and spit a command back on the screen.

'To view images, press enter.'

He held his breath and pushed the key. The screen went black, and for a moment, he thought there hadn't been nor was there anything to see. Suddenly, an image of the kitchen in his old house appeared. Everything was exactly as he remembered even the same cupboards and curtains. The cup must have been sitting on the table. His chest hurt and he thought he might faint as he stared at the monitor.

A bird flew by the window on the screen, but otherwise, Michael was becoming anxious for something other than the cupboards and curtains to appear. As if by command, a face shot onto the screen, scaring Michael. His father was peering into the camera; his eye so close it was a blur.

Tears began to stream down Michael's face as he watched a younger version of his   father moving about the kitchen in the old home. He was right there obviously intrigued by a cup full of spy gadgets, which hadn't been invented yet. A moment later, there was nothing but cupboards and curtains again, and then blackness as the mug traveled back through time.

Michael backhanded the tears off his cheeks while staring at the mug on the table. He had proof that leaping to another time and place was possible, but the cup's partial disappearance puzzled him. Obviously, the mug went back in time, but didn't completely disappear. Would the same thing happen to him? What would happen to him if something went wrong? Would he be stuck halfway between worlds? How could he keep his body safe in this time?

There wouldn't be much trouble on this end. Billy had agreed to be here when the time came, but he couldn't say the same for the other end. Did the mug only partially appear to his father? Was that why he seemed so confused? How would a living breathing human appear to someone on the other end?

"I must figure this out before I try to jump. Jesus, imagine showing up as a ghost. Not only would I scare the shit out of everybody, but also I might affect time in ways that I don't want to happen. How, how can I be certain what happens at the other end?" Talking aloud always calmed him, and usually brought out the correct solution, but not this time. He felt further from an answer than before. A thought floated along the edge of his mind, something to do with the past and his childhood, but he couldn't snatch the moment.

Leaning back in the chair, he closed his eyes. Images of his father staring at the strange mug filled his mind. *'Dad never said anything about seeing a cup full of spy stuff; at least not when I was around. Still, he didn't seem too interested in using his favorite coffee mug after the weekend Mom and I went to Aunt June's in Detroit. Now that I think of it, he never used the cup after that weekend. No wonder -- he'd seen it full of gadgets; probably seemed like a bad dream. I have to find out how visible I'll be when I travel back. I'd rather be totally invisible than show up like a ghost or a hologram. Tomorrow, I'll think more about it tomorrow, but right now, I'm too tired.'* The unclear thought tickled the inside of his head again, and this time he saw shadows moving over the ground. Effort wasn't helping...the harder he tried to bring the image into focus, the less he could see clearly.

He switched off the monitor, stabbing at the button in frustration, and then the light as he went across the hall to his bedroom. The overhead light shone down on a king-size bed, a dresser, and a television on a stand in the corner. A set of floor to ceiling curtains covered sliding glass doors to the two-tiered deck at the back of the house.

Slipping out of his shirt and jeans, he slid under the covers before flipping on the television with the remote. His favorite twenty-four-hour news channel appeared. The minutes before going to sleep were the only time in the day he could learn what was happening in the world. A tornado struck the mid-west United States last night, the reporter talked over the scenes of destruction. Michael heard and saw their pain and made a mental note to donate to the relief efforts.

Chapter 3

Heather Sykes drove away from Michael's house with tears streaming down her face. The kaleidoscope created by her weeping blocked her vision and she nearly missed the turn at the bottom of the driveway. Twice more, there were narrow escapes with vehicles on the way to her house on the other side of the valley.

"You're such a stupid slut, Heather," she shouted at the road ahead. "He probably thinks you're nothing but a gold digger. Way to go, flash your tits and he'll ask you to marry him on the spot. How did that work out for you?" For a moment, the shouting cleared her vision in time to see the curve ahead, but she immediately went back to blubbering.

"How could you be so wrong about him? Why didn't you know he's timid around women?" She giggled and sniffed. "Why didn't you know he'd be absorbed in finishing the project? You've been with the company three years and you didn't notice he's compulsive about seeing things through to the end. Fuck, you're stupid!" Full-blown bawling followed for a minute, but dwindled to sniffling. The familiar shape and glow of the 7-11 on the corner of her street appeared in the darkness ahead. She pushed the brake pedal and turned the corner. Her house was the third on the left. She reached up and pressed the garage door opener on the sun visor. The big door opened and the overhead light was on as she pulled into the driveway and parked carefully inside the garage.

Her blubbering stopped for the thirty seconds while she switched off the motor and pressed the button once again to close the overhead door. She watched it come to a stop and then buried her face in her hands against the steering wheel. Self-pity drained her of tears for the next five minutes. *'I should go in the house,'* she thought. *'Sitting here isn't doing any good, he's probably going to fire me tomorrow, and I wouldn't blame him.'* Grabbing her purse, she opened the car door and clumped up the two steps to the door separating the garage from the house. None of that mattered now as she blinked through her tears trying desperately to see the keyhole. The light in the garage went out as she opened the door to the house.

She lived alone in a two-story condominium. Heather kept a cactus in a shallow pot on the windowsill, a sofa she'd rescued from a thrift shop, a kitchen table with one chair, and a few pictures on the wall, but otherwise, the main floor was empty.

That's how her life had been until now. The less there was to tie her down, the easier it was to move on. Her wardrobe was another matter. Clothes filled two closets in the two-bedroom house. She'd had another closet renovated to accommodate her shoes. Three racks, which pulled out of the closet with shelves on both sides.

The dark entrance greeted her, but she didn't turn on any lights. With a deep sigh, she slipped off her shoes and walked in her stocking feet toward the stairs to the second floor. There were only ten steps and three more to her bedroom, but they seemed to take an eternity. There was nobody in her life to talk to about her crumbling world. Parents long dead and her brother absorbed by his own life. The pale glow from the street highlighted the bed. She closed her eyes while sitting on the edge of the mattress.

The phone rang. She jumped and reached for the receiver on the nightstand beside the bed. Michael spoke softly to her left ear and her heart melted.

"Good morning, Miss Sykes."

"Morning," she said. Her stretch ended with a shout. "Morning, oh my God, what time is it?" She realized the room was very much brighter. Her eyes turned to the clock on the nightstand. "Oh shit, I slept in! I'll be there in half an hour, I'm so sorry it won't happen again." She hung up, stripping off her clothes before she realized what she'd done. "I hung up on him, oh my God, what the hell was I thinking?" Anger and a need to hurry propelled her through the shower. Twenty minutes after the phone call, she was headed into the garage. *That has to be a record, for not only me but all women, to get ready in twenty minutes,'* she thought. A satisfied smile crossed her face. *'Women can be fast if we want to, but we'd rather take our time and do it right the first time. Now, I just have to get to work in one piece.'*

Michael smiled, replacing the receiver. He hadn't expected to wake Heather. Her proposal last night had taken him off guard. Obviously, she'd been disappointed, but he couldn't tell her about his plans. He wanted to apologize and make her feel better. Only Billy knew the details, and the chances of success were less than fifty percent. If he was killed or was trapped in time, he didn't want her to suffer, now that he knew her feelings.

Billy called up from the lab to say they were ready to begin trials on the software. "I'll be right there." Michael said. He stopped on the way to the elevator. "If Miss Sykes calls or comes looking for me; I'll be in the lab with Billy. She can join us there," he told his secretary.

After a ten-minute walk, he entered the lab. He remembered when he and Billy started the business. They worked out of Mike's basement apartment. Now, they had a four-story building sprawled over two hundred acres. There was a thirty-acre 'clean' room where components for the space program and the company's hardware were assembled. Offices, testing and further assembly took up much of the rest of the acreage. A relatively small area was tucked in the corner of the massive building, five thousand square feet, reserved for the building's computer room. Most of the space housed the hardware running the business. The machines in this room were designed and programmed by Michael to be technically more advanced than anything else invented. He built them from custom-designed parts, many of them manufactured in house. No other computer company had the same level of technology. He walked toward an office set in the corner big enough for six desks, computer terminals, and the people to work them.

Billy was hunched over a desk beside three other technicians as Michael entered.

"How's it going?" he asked Billy.

"We're just programming the last of the code." Billy swiveled away from the desk to look up at Michael. "Five minutes and we should be ready for testing." The smile on his face didn't hide the fact he was worried, but trying to be enthusiastic at the same time.

"It'll work," Michael said. "No problem Billy, I'm certain." He gave his friend a wink and a smile.

Billy's face sagged, the color drained away and his mouth fell open as he realized what Michael was saying. Michael held up his left hand to cut off any further comment.

"Ready sir," another man at the desk looked up waiting for confirmation to continue.

"Go ahead, Randal." All eyes turned to the monitors mounted on the wall above the desk. Cameras had been focused on the probe at the far side of the 'lab'. A finger punched the enter key and immediately streams of words -- code, poured across the monitor. Thirty seconds passed as the words scrolled and they held their breath. When the cursor stopped at the bottom of the screen, three seconds ticked by before anyone reacted. Lights on the probe activated. Cheers and backslapping erupted. The process would be faster when commands were sent to the probe because the program would run continuously.

26

"We did it," Billy yelled and jumped around the room. The tech guys shook Michael's hand and said, "Well done sir, congratulations."

"Thank you, but you men did the most work the praise is all yours."

"Ok, so we know the code is fine, but how do we test the system under space conditions?" Billy chuckled with relief and draped an arm over Michael's shoulder.

"We'll begin with more in house tests. If those go well, then we can move outside." Michael was talking to Randal.

"Outside, what do you mean outside? I thought this was supposed to give NASA the ability to talk to the probe in real time. How is taking the probe outside going to tell us if the software does the trick?"

"We'll move the probe to the other side of the country, certainly to another time zone, so we can gauge the results. If that works, there shouldn't be any delay in connectivity between the probe and the computer." Michael had explained all of this to Billy before.

"How is this going to benefit NASA? They want to be able to communicate instantly for whatever reason, but I don't see how this is going to work. Forgive me Michael, but I'm just a little slow today, and the truth is, I never listened when we started planning this project. I figured you were the brains, and all I had to do was schmooze with the buyers at NASA."

"The onboard computer can steer the probe out of harm's way while traveling through space, and even maneuver the craft into orbit. They need to be able to see what the probe sees and instantly control the machine on Mars. Imagine yourself going on a road trip from here to New York. Before you start, you have to figure out what's going to happen each foot of the distance you're about to travel. Not only that, but you need to imagine every second of the time you spend in the Big Apple. Can you do that?"

Billy thought for a moment, "No, but they already know how to do that, what difference is this going to make to them?"

"They can't possibly program every detail of what the probe is going to encounter into the onboard computer. First, they don't know everything that could happen, second, what if the probe lands and there's a Martian waiting with a club to bash it to bits? The signal normally takes twenty minutes to get there. They must be able to make instant decisions and react to any situation that occurs. This is going to do that for them."

"Oh now I see. Not the part about Martians waiting with clubs, because they aren't real, but the twenty minutes waiting for the signal to go from here to Mars, would make swift action difficult or impossible for them. So, they need a way to stop the thing instantly or turn to avoid a problem, makes sense now." Billy was becoming calmer and Michael could see that the previous discussions were coming back to him.

"We'll ship the probe across the country, if the program operates correctly, the machine should instantly receive the command from here. Normally, there's about six seconds between this coast and the east coast, so twenty minutes will be the same. This program proves Einstein's theory about bending time and space. We've eliminated the problem of traveling faster than the speed of light."

The techs left the control room to set up the probe. Once they were out of the room, Billy turned to Michael.

"You're one fucked-up bastard, you know that? You said you weren't going to try to time travel without me there. Obviously, anything you say can't be trusted because you went ahead with your personal agenda last night didn't you?" Billy's face grew red as he moved menacingly toward Michael.

"No, I didn't. At least, I didn't go myself. I sent my Dad's favorite mug with a keyhole camera back to our old house. Dad was there. He looked like he shit his pants when this weird thing appeared in the kitchen. All I got were shots of the cupboards and him, but something else is just not right."

Before they could say anything else, Heather Sykes entered the computer room.

"How'd it go?" She was being passive; her face didn't show any emotion. Her sweater matched her eyes, he noticed.

Michael glanced at his wristwatch and was pleasantly surprised she had taken less than an hour to travel here.

"Fine, the tech guys are moving the probe, so we can do the first obstructed short distance test. Once that's done we can go outside, for a longer distance trial." He stared at her with an expression of amusement and pride.

"Shall I prepare a press release then? Initial success with further testing to proceed over the next few days," her face reddened under his scrutiny, but a smile tugged at the corners of her mouth.

"I think that'd be fine, what do you think Billy?"

He shrugged, "Yeah, but keep the wording low-key. We don't want to sound too hopeful just yet."

"The distance trials will be the critical point. If they go well, we can announce our success." Michael added. She nodded her understanding and turned without another word. Michael smiled as he watched her walk away.

"You know she wants you, right? All you need to do is relax and let it happen." There was nothing snide about the remark and the smile was open and warm when Michael turned toward his friend.

"I might be ready to settle down, but not until I'm able to go back in time. Safely, of course," he added quickly, seeing Billy frown.

"What happened last night? Why aren't you satisfied?"

"The mug didn't completely disappear. I know that traveling through time is possible, because I have the video from the camera as proof. Did the cup fully materialize in the past or not? Would I be the same?" Michael was walking back to his office with Billy by his side.

"How are you going to find out? Sounds like there's a plan, which better not include you lying on that table yet."

"No, I'm not going myself. How many times do I have to say that before you believe me? I sent a camera in a mug. Maybe I could send a cat with the camera on a mast to get a picture of how the animal appears in the past. The trouble with that idea is keeping the cat in the same place long enough to bring it back." Mike looked away hoping Billy wouldn't see the frown on his face.

"Which brings up another concern for me, what happens to you if you move or aren't back when the clock runs out? There has to be some kind of fail-safe to protect you, or I'm not going to let you try. Can't we put some kind of beacon on you somehow, maybe a switch that you can activate the computer here and bring yourself back?"

"Definitely, but the signal would need to travel forward in time to start the program. Without the computer, I don't see any way of..." His voice trailed off as they entered Michael's outer office. They walked past the secretary and when the inner office door was closed, Michael finished his thought.

"The program is what makes everything happen." Billy watched Michael pace while thinking aloud. "The object travels when the program activates the time distortion. Technically, this should be like the transporter on Star Trek, but either something isn't working right or the computer can't let go of the object completely. Damn, I didn't think about that. Even if I send myself back, I won't be able to travel, Billy. All I can do is stand there and look around." He pounded his fist into the palm of his other hand in frustration.

"Too bad we don't have the same kind of devices as they do on the Enterprise and then the computer could find you anywhere."

Michael's face brightened like a child's on Christmas morning. "You're right again, Billy," Michael shouted. He felt like dancing. "There has to be something that will communicate with the computer in this time, something small too. Perhaps I can rig one of those cell phones to ping the computer. I'll work on that while you manage the probe testing. This will be great, Billy. Everything's going to work out perfectly."

Billy shook his head, smiling. He left the office. Michael ignored him, too focused on scribbling notes on a pad.

Chapter 4

Robert Eldridge sat heavily into his easy chair. He felt older than his seventy-one years. Everything in his life had changed. Irene, his wife, died. He retired six years ago, and ended up in this senior's home. All that remained were memories, and a famous son who didn't visit any more. His gaze fell on a rumpled magazine on the coffee table. "She is you know," He remembered the day they were sitting in the old kitchen, the father at one end of the table, the son in his usual spot at the side. They'd returned home in the evening of Irene's funeral. Robert was looking sadly at the cupboards he'd never gotten around to replacing and the curtains that Irene had stitched with her own hands. "Still by your side, making sure you stay out of trouble. I wish she could tell me how to run that damn washing machine in the basement though." He chuckled at the quick look from Michael. "I miss her too, son. Without her, I feel as if somebody came along and chopped off my right arm." He swallowed hard to keep from bawling like a baby. "She did everything for me and you while she was alive. You were her pride and joy, no matter how much you succeeded." He fumbled at the papers on the kitchen table and pulled out a rumpled Time magazine. "When this came out, I was afraid she'd buy up every copy at the store. This one almost went to bed with us the first night after she brought it home." Another soft chuckle, this time from both men. "She read your story every morning and last thing at night until the day she died. I got home from work that day and found her lying on the floor holding this magazine." Tears were streaming down the older man's cheeks and Michael was close to crying too. The tap dripped in sympathy.

"I know, Dad. I came by earlier that day to see how she was doing. She never let on there was anything wrong. She seemed happy. All she talked about... was how proud she was to see my picture in Time magazine."

Robert reached across the table and patted the boy's hand. He looked up at the old curtains and remembered the day he saw his mug on the table with the gadgets sticking out of it. *'Never could touch that cup after that,'* he thought.

That was then. Today, his favorite chair sat in a single room of a nursing home in California, not in the house he'd lived in with Irene for thirty years. A few pictures and his clothes were all he'd been allowed to bring with him. His stroke last year had partially paralyzed his left side, which made walking and dressing difficult. He smiled, but he could feel the left side of his face sag. *'I guess my son being rich and famous doesn't matter. The fact is putting me in here is easier than hiring a nurse. I can't blame him though. He's busy and doesn't have time to take care of an old man.'*

The vision of the mug on the table drifted into his mind again. *'What the hell was that thing? That was my favorite cup, but I've never seen anything like those things stuck all over it. Where the hell did those come from?'* "Must have been a trick of my imagination," he muttered, instantly afraid that someone might hear him. *'Piss on them if they can't take a joke'*, he thought and continued his one-way conversation. "I could see right through it, but the damned thing seemed real enough, not a reflection or trick of the light." His hands twitched and rubbed together on his lap; a nervous habit that started years ago. "Wish I'd said something back then, but my family would've thought I'd gone nuts. I thought I WAS going crazy. Maybe I did, perhaps this whole time I've been living in a nut house drooling on my pants and this is just some kind of fantasy in my mind." He groaned as he shifted his backside in the chair. His eyes scanned around the room peering at what his life had become. "Nothing left, but a place to die. Michael hasn't been to see me in months, my friends are all dead, and I can't do anything physical. Oh Irene, I wish I'd died that day instead of you. She was better than I was at seeing the bright side of life. I miss her so much." He buried his face in his hands and sobbed.

The door to his room wasn't closed. Two nurses standing at the station across the hall gave each other looks, which said they thought the old man was senile. This wasn't the first time they'd heard the elderly talking to themselves, but this conversation was about weird mugs and wishing he could die. The senior nurse picked up the phone and dialed the doctor on call. He was going to have to contact the family and let them know their father was failing.

• • •

There was a knock on the office door and it opened. The assistant Michael called an hour ago stepped inside. "I've got your cell phone sir, but there was a problem." The young man wearing a lab coat over a pair of scruffy jeans nervously stepped up to the desk.

"What kind of problem?"

"They wouldn't let me buy it without activation like you wanted." He laid the phone box on the desk in front of Michael.

"That's alright. I didn't know if they would or not, but that could work to my advantage. Thanks, Trefor, for doing this for me. How're they doing down there?"

"Fine so far, the probe is at the far end of the lab and they should be running communications now, or at least by the time I get back."

"Good, tell Randal to call me when that's finished."

Trefor gave a short nod and left.

Michael turned his attention to the red and white carton before him. The phone inside was heavy, the size of a typical telephone receiver but thicker. A number pad on the front and a retractable antenna on the top were the only distinguishing features that separated this thing from a brick.

He stared at the phone in his hand for a minute, wondering how its signal would help or hinder the trip through time. A picture was starting to emerge in his mind when the telephone on his desk rang.

After setting the cell phone down, he picked up the desk receiver. "Hello, Michael Eldridge here."

"Mr. Eldridge, this is Dr. Caraway at Central Park Manor."

"Is something wrong with my father?" Michael demanded expecting the worst.

"No, not really, I'm just concerned that his mental state is deteriorating. He's talking to himself more than other patients his age." The doctor's voice had a greasy, snakelike quality, which made Michael's spine crawl.

"I do that all the time Doctor, but I'm thinking out loud. Does that mean my mental state is slipping?"

"I'm sorry to bother you Mr. Eldridge; I thought you'd want to know about your father."

'Fuck, I've hurt his feelings,' Michael thought. *'I can't deal with this right now.'* "I'm just in the middle of a critical project for the government and I took my frustration out on you. If you wouldn't mind telling my father I'll be up to see him tomorrow, I'd appreciate that." *'Hopefully, he won't think that's too much trouble.'*

"You can count on me, Mr. Eldridge. What time should I tell him to expect you?" Michael could almost see the forked tongue flicking between the other man's lips. *'I don't know when I'll get up there for sure, why can't he just leave Dad a simple message? Shit, now I have to make time.'*

"Tell him I'll visit after lunch to take him for a ride." *'Now fuck off you snake and let me get back to work.'* He saw his Dad sitting in the chair waiting for him and he felt guilty.

"That will do nicely, Mr. Eldridge. I'll let him know and make sure he's ready when you get here. Goodbye," The click on the line happened before Michael could respond.

"Prick," he snarled as he put the receiver back in the cradle. "I should just go take Dad out of there. He'd probably be fine at my place if I hired a full-time nurse." *'Yeah, but you know that would cause more problems,'* his mind said. *'What if Heather and I start dating, Dad would be in the way.'* He heard his mother's voice for the first time in many years. "Your father is more important than any woman you meet. He looked after you all those years when you were

33

younger and paid for your college education, the least you can do is take care of him now that he's not getting around so well."

"I know, Mom." His whispered voice seemed suddenly loud in the office. "I've lost track of time and he's paid the price." He reached over and pushed the intercom button.

"Christen, can you make a point of reminding me to go see my father tomorrow afternoon?"

"Yes sir," the sultry voice of his secretary replied.

"No matter where I am or what I'm doing, don't take no for an answer please."

"Even if I need to drag you there myself sir." He could hear the smile in her voice.

His mind returned to the cell phone. He picked up a small screwdriver and began to twist out the screws on the back of the casing. Five minutes later, the top of the desk was covered with all the separate parts that made the phone. Circuit boards, battery, speakers, and the case lay in front of him.

He picked up the circuit board and examined the wiring pattern. The incoming radio signal activated the call. The phone stayed in ready mode, until the call came in and the phone made the bell ring. Computer code was the same. All he had to do was modify the computer to send a signal for him to return. "What the hell, being able to call the computer to bring me back would be even better. I could stay there as long as I wanted." He smiled happily and dumped most of the telephone parts into the garbage can at the side of the desk.

His office phone rang. The button next to the name of his chief technician was lit.

"Yes Randal, how are you doing?"

"Complete success sir, we're packaging the probe for transport to New York. The truck should arrive there by Sunday and they'll be ready for testing first thing on Monday morning."

"Well done." Michael was going to hang up, but thought of something else. "Randal, I've just decided to fly out to meet the probe in New York. Could you let the team there know I'm coming please?"

"Very well sir." He hung up.

He'd decided to take his father. The old man would enjoy the trip and Michael would have an opportunity to get him out of the retirement home for a few days. They'd spend some father-son time together -- that's if his mind can keep up. The dementia had gotten worse since he'd moved his father to California.

He looked down at the electronic pieces on the desk. '*What if I had convinced Mom to see a doctor? She'd still be alive; maybe Dad wouldn't be in that retirement home. I'll rethink taking him out of there after Joe,*' he thought.

· · ·

Randal stared out of his office at the crew sliding the probe into a crate. The space machine looked like a giant caterpillar in a cocoon. There was enough plastic wrapped around the contraption to stop a bullet, but better safe than sorry. The real probe, the one going into space, was already at the launch site in Florida waiting for the clearance to load it onto the rocket. This one was the Guinea pig, the stunt double, built to do all the hard work.

He was proud to be part of this company and the work they did for the space program and for technology in general. Before Michael had found him, Randal remembered the mind-numbing days at another company, building home computers. Personal computers they called them, but they were nearly the size of a sofa and the user had to type in particular lines of code to make them work. The technology changed faster than normal people understood and they kept paying thousands of dollars for junk.

His own creation became part of the system here at the lab. Michael had taken every suggestion Randal made and built the juggernaut that ran this place. He smiled. There wouldn't be any acknowledgement of his contribution, but some day he'd be able to design and distribute a machine that could truly revolutionize the personal computer business.

He sighed. The men were moving around the crate surrounding the probe. Michael was going to New York. He hoped that didn't mean he'd screwed up somehow. His eyes focused on the men in time to see the crate lid being lowered onto the hand of one of the crew.

"Watch out!" He shouted. All eyes turned and the man whose fingers were about to be crushed moved them in time.

"Didn't you see his hand up there?" He demanded rushing out of the office toward the crane operator. "If I hadn't shouted, the lid would've crushed his hand. Jesus H. Christ as if there isn't enough pressure with this project. Let's be careful, but hurry up and get that thing loaded on the truck. They need to be there by Sunday, so the technicians can set up for the tests on Monday." He walked away, shaking. '*I shouldn't have shouted at them. They don't understand how important this project is to the company...to me. If that man had lost his hand, the days of paperwork would have delayed the crate here until the investigation was over.*'

Randal slumped into his chair behind the desk and ran a hand down his face. '*I need a drink,*' he thought. '*I do, but I can't,*' he reminded himself. '*I'd only need to have one to send me back to that other company or worse. All you'd be is a drunk with a screwdriver. You've come a long way since then and there's too much to lose so forget the booze and get back to work.*' He sighed and let the last of the adrenaline slip out of his system. Pulling open the file folder closest to him on the desk, he began making notes on the current progress for readying the probe for space.

Chapter 5

Michael stared down at the cell phone circuit board in his hand. A plan was forming in his mind, but until all the details were clear, he wouldn't know if they were correct. Similar to a jigsaw puzzle, you have the picture of the finished product, but getting all the pieces to fit takes patience. He worked out every problem the same way. Once he'd started thinking, he needed to let his brain do the work.

He shrugged and set the part on the desk before reaching for the telephone. Punching in the number for his private hangar at the airport, he waited and listened to the ringing on the other end of the line. Someone answered on the third ring.

"Hello, this is Sam." A burly voice growled.

"Sam, its Michael, how is my plane today?"

"Champing at the bit, sir, just waitin' to fly." The chuckle that followed sounded like distant thunder. There was even an echo in the background.

"Good, I'll be heading to New York on Friday. If you can file a flight plan and book me a car, that would be much appreciated. I'm taking my father with me, Sam, so no loops or rolls on the way."

"Me sir, I'd never do anything like that," this time there was a hearty laugh.

Sam had retired as a navy pilot ten years ago, still a young man age wise, but too old for military service. He was ten years older than Michael was, but had the temperament of someone half that age. Mike had been at the airport inspecting a possible private jet for the company. Sam was there, working on the tow truck hauling planes out of hangars. The laugh caught Mike's attention; deep, infectious, rumbling sounds. When he looked around, he saw a stocky man with a crew cut driving a service vehicle away from a corporate jet. Sam was hired the same day the jet was purchased.

"A Hawker-Siddeley 800B is not a toy," Sam said before they took to the air for the first time together. "She's delicate and temperamental. There must be plenty of attention paid to her or she'll give you nothing but grief." He was serious, or at least Michael thought he was.

"I know about calling a plane she, but is this one really that much trouble?" He was having second thoughts about buying a troublesome airplane.

"This is the best corporate jet in the air these days and that's saying some, I'd stake my life on it." The mischievous twinkle in the pilot's eyes made Michael hesitant about asking any further questions, but he had to know for sure.

"Well, you wouldn't be risking just your own life; you'd be putting mine at risk too. Is this a good plane or not, Sam?"

"Mr. Eldridge, of all the jets in the air today, I can tell you with certainty that this is the closest I've ever come to flying a fighter plane. She cuts through the air like a knife, responds quickly and purrs like a woman having the best sex of her life. This aircraft is perfect, but all I'm saying is that she needs to be cuddled once in a while." He laughed loudly at the shocked expression on Michael's face.

"I'm glad to hear that, Sam. You can do all the cuddling you like and I'll ride inside." Since then, they'd been all over the world together; Sam treated him in a casual manner, but their relationship didn't extend to Sam using his boss's first name. Michael accepted the formality of being called 'sir', but he didn't believe it was necessary.

"Christen, could you please book me my usual room in New York for four days starting Friday night. I'm taking my father, so there'll be two in there and Sam needs a room for the same time."

"Yes sir," she purred.

"Thank you." He replied. Her voice always made his stomach flutter like a teenager in heat. Swiveling his executive chair, he gazed out the window at the clear blue-sky overhead. The valley climbed from the parking lot toward the hills and mountains. If he squinted, he could just make out the roof of his house on the hillside twenty miles away.

He'd work on the phone tonight and reprogram the computer to listen for the signal. The processer needed to send something that sounded like a radio tone to the phone, but that shouldn't be difficult to duplicate. His mind was already envisioning the work being done in the computer room at home.

He glanced at his watch...four o'clock. His stomach rumbled in complaint at missing lunch. Inspiration struck him and he reached for the telephone, punching the number for Heather Sykes' office.

"Yes sir," she answered sweetly. A tickle ran down his spine at the sound of her voice. He wasn't used to dealing with women on an intimate level. They were a complete mystery to him; dating had always scared him. Heather was someone he had to deal with at work and if all went well, on a close personal level soon. He wanted that relationship to become a reality more than ever before in his life.

"What are you doing for supper?" He was suddenly nervous about her answer.

"I'm not doing anything, what did you have in mind?"

"I was thinking maybe we could eat together. Do you have any preferences?" He was beginning to relax.

"There's a new place on Grover I'd like to try, it's a Greek place I think. Do you want me to call and find out if we can get in tonight?"

"Yes please, and if they're booked then anywhere else you like is fine with me. I'll pick you up at your office at five-thirty sharp." He emphasized the last word from habit and also to remind her about being late that morning.

"I'll be ready," she sounded delighted.

Michael sat back, smiling. '*Small steps Michael,*' he thought. '*She wants a relationship not a one-night-stand.*' Trying to imagine the rest of his life alongside Heather seemed like a dark tunnel filled with needs and desires he had never allowed into his life. '*Is that a bad thing,*' he wondered, '*or maybe I should just become a monk. I don't know, but once I get the time machine running, I'll take a trip forward and see how my life ends up.*' That might be a bad idea, some unknown voice said in his head.

He walked into the advertising department at five-thirty, nodding to several of the faces he recognized. Heather came out of her corner office to meet him half way. Her whole face lit up as she saw him, her smile gave his stomach butterflies.

"I told you I'd be ready," she breathed and slipped an arm through his as they turned to leave the office.

"Yes you did, but waiting wouldn't have been a problem. There are lots of other pretty girls to talk to here." He tried to keep a straight face, but she punched his arm and he giggled. Emotionally, he felt fourteen again.

Half an hour later, they entered the restaurant, a family-style place, casual dining. Plenty of Greek pictures and fake sculptures peeked out from among the plants; male and female waiters dressed in traditional costumes hustled food and people to tables; Greek music or whatever passed for it belched from hidden speakers around the room.

A tall man with an accent and a drooping moustache, dressed in a dark suit met them and showed the couple to a table near the window. There was a candle in an old wine bottle wrapped in string or jute or something in the middle of a blue and white checkered tablecloth.

'*Tacky,*' Michael thought, '*but if the food's good who am I to judge.*' Heather was arranging her purse and jacket on the chair beside her. He looked at her face and decided that being with her couldn't possibly be the worst thing in his life...now or in the future. An unconscious smile crept across his face.

She caught him. "What?"

"Nothing," he stammered, trying to hide his embarrassment.

"You were sitting there smiling like a circus clown and I'd like to know what was so amusing." Her lovely green eyes were turning black and her mouth was held tight in a thin red line.

"Ok, I was thinking about how lucky I'd be to spend the rest of my life with you." He smiled brightly, but her expression didn't change. *'She must think I'm lying to her. Why would I do that?'* "Honest, that's exactly what I was thinking." Now his anger flared a little, concerned that he'd misjudged her intentions last night.

Her face softened into a sexy smile. God, he loved her smile.

"Alright, I'll believe you this time, but what changed your mind?"

"My mind hasn't changed about getting serious before the project is finished, but I'm changing my attitude toward being involved in a long term relationship. Up until now, I've never needed or wanted someone to share my life. I wasn't looking for anyone when you came to the door last night. Your openness took me by surprise, Heather. I didn't know what to do." *'Why am I saying this to her? I've always been tongue-tied around women, but this is easy.'*

Her hand touched his, stirring up the butterflies in his stomach again. *'This is crazy, I'm about to leap into a relationship with this gorgeous woman and she doesn't know anything about me or what I'm going to do. I've got to tell her about the time travel before it's too late.'* He was about to open his mouth when she spoke.

"You should know something about me before we go any further." She cleared her throat and pulled her hand away. Just then, the waiter came to take their order for drinks and food. Michael ordered a beer and personal sized Greek pizza; she wanted white wine and Souvlaki. They sat in silence until their drinks arrived. After a sip of her wine, she began her story.

"You already know my brother was the big bully in school, but what you don't know is the reason he picked on you in particular." She smiled, but there was sadness in her expression. "He didn't like the fact that I had a crush on you back then. I think he picked on you as a way of defending me. After high school, you went off to college. For a few years, I forgot about you, and went to university in Boston to get a degree in advertising and political science. I know," she smiled. "They're a strange combination, but I didn't know which one interested me more. Anyway, about then you started the company. I was in Europe when you first made the cover of Time. You wouldn't believe how excited and homesick that made me feel when I saw your face on the newsstand in a dingy lobby of a Belgium hotel. Your gorgeous blue eyes staring up at me from that front page and I knew right then where I needed to be. I spent a year trying to get past the hordes of people who think they need to protect you, but eventually I was hired. The rest they say is history and I've been watching and dreaming of you every day since." Her hand trembled as she lifted her glass to her lips. Embarrassment colored her face a brilliant red.

Their food came at that moment. He carefully lifted a slice of hot pizza to his lips and bit into the tangy sauce, cheeses, olives and more. Her dainty fingers lifted a skewer of meat and vegetables off the bed of rice. His eyes watched her open her mouth, her tongue caressing the meat, her lips closing and then pulling the chunk of food off the stick. He stopped chewing.

"Oh this is soooo goood," she purred. "How's your pizza?"

He gulped. "Good, really good, I don't think I've ever had Greek pizza before. I'm not sure what this white stuff is, but it's tasty."

"That's Feta cheese, made from goats' milk I think." Her smile was driving him nuts; the beer wasn't helping keep his emotions in check. He'd never been a heavy drinker, but he liked to be sociable.

"I had a crush on you in school too," he said between bites. Her fork clattered on the table. Shit, she's going to be upset now; he thought and rushed on without looking at her. "I was a shy gawky kid back then. I got all tongue tied whenever I had to talk to a girl or a woman. Do you remember Miss Belfridge? Even she made me weak in the knees." He heard her giggle. "I knew your brother Brad was trying to keep me away from you, he told me so one day in high-school. By then, I was only interested in going to university. Dating wasn't a priority." He picked at the tablecloth for a moment. "Sad isn't it? All those years we both wanted the same thing and pushed away any relationships because we thought we'd lost our chance. We could have had different lives together, if we'd seen the signs. I hope we're not too late."

Heather had been smiling until then, looking excited and happy. When he said the words 'too late', her face went ashen and sagged.

"What do you mean, too late? Are you seeing another woman?" Her face reddened with anger; her eyes turned a darker shade of green. The effect seemed to make her hair turn the color of flames. Before he could calm her down with the truth, she gasped, "You're married aren't you?"

"No, no, no, nothing like that, listen, I can't tell you anything at the moment, except that this project we're working on and

41

something that happened a long time ago, are more important than my personal relationships. You need to trust me, I'm not married or anything else. This has nothing to do with you." For some reason, he found himself pleading for their future. Losing her was no longer an option.

Her face became less ablaze, and her eyes went back to their normal green...slowly. She reached for the wine glass without taking her eyes off him. After taking a sip, she held the glass, with her elbow resting on the table.

"I suppose I can trust you, but if you think I'm going to roll over and accept what you say without some more information, you better think again. I've waited all my life to be with you and nothing, no matter how secret or life threatening, is going to keep me away. Especially something life threatening," she added as she set the glass back on the table.

He looked at her face, that lovely face. There was no way he could go back in time, risking his life, without telling her the whole truth. "I'll tell you after we've eaten. In fact, I'll take you back to my place and show you." This time, his hand went on hers in a gesture of hope and pleading. She gave him a weak smile and picked up another skewer.

They ate quickly, skipping dessert, both needing to get to his house for different reasons. The drive out of the city to Michael's place took thirty minutes, time he used to tell her about his life and how he'd become successful. She didn't seem interested, staring out the window at the passing houses and businesses. Occasionally, she would make a noise, which he took to be her way of showing interest in his story. After shutting off the engine, he leaped out to open the door for her. She seemed pleased with his manners at least, smiling up at him and offering her hand in a mock debutante fashion.

Inside the house, he took her coat and led her down the hall by the hand. He didn't notice her rapid breathing or the sweat breaking out on her hand as they neared the bedroom door. He did notice the gasp of surprise when he flipped on the light.

"This is my home lab," he announced with pride and turned to see the disappointment on her face. "You didn't think we were going to...," he pointed across the hall knowing instantly that she had been hoping for something more intimate.

"Oh no, that was the furthest thing from my mind," she quickly replied trying to sound innocent. "I just don't understand what this has to do with why we can't be more serious in our relationship."

Michael pushed the table out of the way, pulled out a chair from the corner for her and sat at the desk. He gave her the short version of Joe's disappearance. She listened, but he could tell she still didn't understand. His fingers tapped the computer keys, and then moved the monitor so she could see the screen, before he told her to watch.

She saw the images of a strange kitchen appear, but in the end, she was still puzzled.

"So, what has seeing an old man in what I can only assume is a kitchen got to do with anything?"

"That old man is my father as he appeared in 1957. I sent a mug and camera back in time to that day in my house." He watched her face, waiting for a reaction, some indication that she grasped the significance of his words. At last, her brows arched.

Michael continued. "What I want to do is go back to the day my best friend disappeared, and find out what happened to him. I've got the technology and almost everything's in place. Until I'm finished with the current project, I haven't got time to devote to this or to you." His words spilled out in a rush of relief and anxiety. He desperately wanted her to understand.

"You're going back in time?"

He nodded.

"I thought that was impossible."

"There are laws of physics that say we can't move through time, but I've cracked the problem. With this equipment, I'm almost certain that I can go back and find out what happened and return safely. There are a few glitches that need fixing first, but I'll be fine."

"Uh, huh," she frowned. "So I assume one of the glitches is what happens to you if you get stuck back then."

"Well that's not really a problem. The biggest problem is being able to move around and communicate with this computer, but I think I've figured that out too. Never mind how this is all going to work, just trust me that on the day I go, everything will be perfect." He smiled. She smiled back, but the uncertainty still showed in her eyes.

"I don't understand your need to find out what happened to your friend. He's gone and you've moved on to a new and wonderful life. How will you knowing his fate change anything?"

He looked down at the desk, remembering the day thirty years ago. His guilt rose in his throat while tears welled in his eyes.

"Most families, back then, were hard working middle-class, but still thrifty after the lean war years. Some lost husbands and fathers during the Korean War; Joe's Dad was one of them. The boy was only three at the end of the war, so he didn't remember his father. His mother worked two jobs to keep food on the table; fortunately there was just the two of them. The VA insurance had paid off the house mortgage, but the other bills seemed to keep piling up, she'd always say. I abandoned my best friend and he disappeared. It's my fault, I should have stayed there, and he'd be fine today." He saw the confusion in her eyes. "Whatever happened to Joe was my fault. I was the one, Joe and Billy looked up to. I made the decisions, and I could have told Joe to wait until the next day, but I didn't. I abandoned him the same as everyone else in his life."

Chapter 6

The next morning, Michael awoke, but didn't open his eyes as he stretched. He felt better, more rested, than he had in years. Images from the night before played across the inside of his eyelids and then he yawned.

He sat up and looked at the left side of the bed wondering if he'd dreamt the previous night. The pillow was dented as if someone had slept there, but vacant now. They'd started kissing last night, in the computer room after he'd unveiled his plan. Her mouth was warm, hungry. He grinned, remembering what came next.

They abandoned their inhibitions, and within seconds, they were tearing at each other's clothes. He tried to carry Heather here, to the bedroom, but he stumbled and started to laugh. Reality wasn't as sexy as the movies.

Their first love making session had been quick, frantic, and definitely not his best effort, but she sighed when they were done. He'd held her close, listening to her breathing. The smell of her perfume rose up from the pillow next to him. Her passion surprised him. He was drifting off to sleep when her hands began roaming over his body.

The second time, he'd taken his time, been more focused on her pleasure. He could still feel her body shudder, as she climaxed. They were both finished, this time. Her head nuzzled into his shoulder as they relaxed. The warmth of her body and her slow breathing lulling him to sleep.

He heard a noise in the kitchen, followed by a "Damn." Flipping back the covers, he pulled his robe off the back of the closet door. The kitchen was a room he rarely used unless there was a party. He couldn't remember the last time he'd eaten at home.

His bare feet made little noise on the hardwood floor and he stopped next to the table. Heather was standing in front of the stove with her back to him. She had on one of his shirts, but he could tell there was nothing underneath. The smell of frying bacon filled the room as he watched her crack eggs into the pan. Where the food came from didn't cross his mind then. He waited until she was done with the eggs before speaking so as not to frighten her.

"Good morning," he spoke softly moving toward the coffee pot. She jumped and let out a tiny shriek of surprise. He poured a cup of coffee and looked for hers.

"I'm good," she said, keeping watch on the eggs. "How did you sleep?" Her grin was crooked and there was a mischievous twinkle in her eyes.

"Fine, thanks to you that was the best sleep I've had in years." He moved close and kissed her cheek. She dropped the spatula and kissed his mouth. There was a slight flavor of toothpaste on her lips and he realized he hadn't brushed yet.

"How do you like your eggs?"

"Hot," he smiled. "As long as they don't drip I'm happy. By the way, were did the food come from?"

"Grab a couple of plates and we can eat. I called a grocery store and had them deliver. The guy looked surprised, when I answered the door dressed like this." She chuckled.

He reached into a nearby cupboard and pulled out two plates. She dished out the bacon and eggs, handing him one of the plates, and turned to sit at the table. He watched the shirt slide up her thighs. For a second, he wanted to forget the eggs and repeat the night before, but decided he needed to eat instead.

45

The first mouthful seemed to energize him as if someone had plugged his body into a wall socket. He moved the fork between mouth and plate as quickly and neatly as his manners allowed. Until he finished everything, Heather was forgotten.

"Oh that was sooo good, Miss Sykes," he leaned forward to kiss her. "I'd ask for more, but I'm afraid that might be construed as sexual harassment." He gave her his best sly grin.

She licked her lips slowly gazing at his crotch. "You can have more of whatever you want, Mr. Eldridge." Her fingers clasped the buttons on the shirt and began to open each in turn. Three buttons down and he was panting like a dog. She stopped and stood up. Reaching forward, he thought she was going for his robe, but she picked up his plate and set them in the sink. When she turned back to him, the shirt was completely open.

"Dessert is my pleasure Mr. Eldridge. Would you follow me please?" She moved sensuously down the hall, her body smooth and luscious. His heart and mind reacted to this moment as if he was a teenager again. Damn, he thought, for somebody who didn't want a relationship yesterday I'm sure willing to rut like a dog now. He saw her lovely ass turn into the bedroom and a second later, his shirt fell back out the door. His feet moved just a little faster.

• • •

Michael arrived outside Central Park Manor at one o'clock and went straight to his father's room. Robert Eldridge was sitting in his chair, head back, mouth open, seemingly asleep. He was dressed in a faded pair of white and blue plaid pants, a dark-blue dress shirt under a faded brown cardigan with worn brown slippers on his feet.

A wry smile crossed Michael's face. He wished his father had better fashion sense, but wondered why the nurses weren't more helpful. His mind decided that they likely didn't care. There wasn't time to worry about that now.

"Dad, it's me Michael; are you ready to go?" His father snorted awake and sat forward.

"Michael, oh yeah, I'm ready. Help me out of this chair, and oh damn, I don't have my shoes on yet. They're over there on the other side of the bed. Fetch them for me please and just let the nurses' station know we're going out while I put on my shoes." His hands trembled as they patted at his head and fumbled nervously with the buttons on the sweater.

Michael put the shoes in front of his father. There was only one person at the station when he stepped up to the counter. The woman was dressed in a tailored business suit.

"Hi, I'm Michael Eldridge."

"Oh, Mr. Eldridge. I'm Gloria Thera, the managing director. How can I help you?"

"I'm taking my father out for the weekend. Actually, I won't be bringing him back until Tuesday at the earliest."

Her mouth dropped open and her eyebrows rose in surprise. "You can't do that. There are rules for taking a family member out of the facility. They're on a schedule. A doctor has to authorize any extended outing. We haven't been given authorization for that length of stay away from the facility. You'll need Dr. Caraway's permission." She'd taken two steps back as the words spluttered out of her mouth.

"Is he in the building?" Michael's temper was rising with his impatience, but he kept his words under control.

"No," she snapped. Stretching her neck trying to elevate her authority by looking down her nose at him. "He's gone for the weekend."

"So, you're telling me that my father doesn't have the right to come and go as he pleases?"

"He can do anything he likes within the rules," she barked. "We aren't holding him prisoner."

He wanted to reach across the counter and wrap his hands around her throat, but decided his life would be easier having his Dad live somewhere else.

"Please ensure my father's things are packed and ready to move out on Tuesday when I return. He won't need the room any longer. Is there any medication he needs that I can take with me?"

She fumbled in the filing cabinet and pulled out one slim folder before laying it on the desk. Michael saw his father's name across the top. The woman flipped over several pages and studied one before looking up at him.

"There's nothing in his chart about medications. He's able to travel, but he can't get too excited, or he might have another stroke. We'll have everything packed by the time you return," she sneered, hunching like a troll over the file. Michael turned and went back into his father's room.

Robert was struggling to stand. Michael pulled open the closet searching for a jacket. There was only one shirt and a pair of dress pants hanging on a wire hanger inside the closet, but no jacket.

'*Breathe Michael, relax you can get Dad a new wardrobe in New York. He'll probably be happier with a new set of clothes anyway.*'

"Let's go, Dad. I'm taking you to New York." He held his father's arm gently as they walked out of the building.

The Cadillac at the curb seemed nearly as big as the house where Michael grew up. His Dad made approving noises and then touched all the dials and buttons inside.

"This yours?" He wanted to know as Michael sat behind the wheel.

"Yep, all mine. The plane we're taking to the Big Apple is mine too."

"You must be doing pretty well with that computer fad."

"Not bad, we do a lot of government work and for the Space Agency." He'd told his father before, but understood what a stroke could do with a person's memory.

"Space, we should never have started that race with the Russians. Can't have a race anyway if one side doesn't play by the rules." His tone was grumpy, but Michael knew he was busting a gut proud of his son. "When are you going to get married and start a family? This foolishness with computers can't last. You need to get into banking or insurance. You'd be good at selling insurance. My brother-in-law, Bernie, in Philly, made a good living. Put his two kids through college and bought a new car every year."

"I do alright Dad. This car is paid for and so are my house and the plane. If you add that all up, I'm probably worth a few dollars more than Uncle Bernie." He smiled and his father smiled back. They went through the same conversation every time they were together. Dad ragging his son about being a success; son constantly saying he was a success, but not wanting to brag.

Michael pulled the car up to the hangar, turned off the ignition and went around to the passenger side. When his Dad was out of the car, they moved slowly toward the boarding stairs beside the private jet. The surrounding blacktop intensified the heat of the day.

"This yours?" Robert Eldridge demanded at the bottom of the steps.

"Yes, Dad, this is mine. We're going to New York remember? I bet Uncle Bernie never had his own jet." Reminding his father that he was richer than Uncle Bernie was, becoming enjoyable, and bordering on bragging.

"Damn right he never had a jet. I've never flown in a private plane. I bet my son could have his own plane if he used his head. Help me up these steps young fella and we can take off. The other passengers are probably hopping mad about being kept waiting."

Until that minute, Michael had never considered the possibility that a stroke could cause dementia. He'd heard the illness affected elderly people, but never considered the disease would attack his Dad. The worst part would be if his father deteriorated to the point, he forgot his son. The old man was always joking and saying crazy things, but you could tell he was kidding. This didn't feel like one of those times; his gut sensed this was more serious.

Wearing jeans and a dress shirt, Sam was standing just inside the hatch, smiling and waiting for the senior Eldridge to come up the ladder. He reached out to shake hands and help if he could.

"Who the hell are you? Where's the pilot, isn't he supposed to be standing here?"

Sam's smile never faltered, but he glanced at Michael before responding.

"I am the pilot sir. We don't wear uniforms on private aircraft."

"Private plane you say? I thought we were going commercial. Seems kind of funny my son didn't tell me about this. He should be here to see me flying in style. What's your name, sonny?"

"Sam, my name is Sam and it's a pleasure to meet you, Mr. Eldridge." The old man's hand was pale and blue as he reached to shake with Sam. Michael shrugged and rolled his eyes before guiding his father to a seat in the middle of the cabin.

After connecting the seat belt around his father, Michael sat in the chair opposite, facing the rear of the cabin.

Robert sat staring out the window as the plane taxied away from the hangar. There was a worried expression on his face. Michael suspected his Dad didn't like to fly, or there was something else troubling him. *'Maybe he's just feeling lost. I shouldn't have taken him out of the Manor. This can't be good for him if he's confused.'*

49

"You okay, Dad?" He leaned forward and touched the older man's knee.

"Fine, Michael, why wouldn't I be?" Any hint of fear was gone, replaced with the confident features of his father.

"No reason, I just wanted to make sure you enjoy the trip." '*Okay, I'm officially freakin' out here. If he's pulling my leg, he's doing a great job of it. Ha, ha, Dad you got me. I'll need to get someone to watch him when we land in New York, just in case. Sam could stay with him while I take care of the testing on Monday. No, I don't want to burden him with my father all weekend. I wish Mom were here.*'

"Did you say we were going to New York?"

"Yeah, Dad. I'm working on a project for NASA that needs to be tested on Monday. I thought we'd have some fun together for the weekend. Want to take in a Broadway show or something?"

"Christ, I don't know if I'd like all that singing and jumping around. Your mother tried to get me to a show once. Are the Yankees playing this weekend? I've never been to New York before so we could see a ball game together. I remember they're your favorite team." He looked out the window, a sad expression pulling down the corners of his mouth. "We'd have more fun if your mother was here." He turned away from the window as the plane stopped at the entrance ramp to the main runway. His eyes were serious, but gentle at the same time.

"I know I've been hard on you, Michael. Maybe I could have spent more time at home, learned more about your job. There was always something at work to pull me away and suddenly, you were all grown up. Always remember I'm proud of you son, despite the little I gave you. Your mother was proud of you too. Maybe someday you can be a better father than I was." He smiled a sad smile. His eyes grew bright as he looked up. "First you need to find a woman and settle down."

Michael couldn't help but grin. He wanted to jump up and hug the old man, but the plane had already started to move down the runway.

"I'll do what I can Dad. You might be a grandpa sooner than you think." '*If he doesn't lose his memory completely before then,*' Michael thought. The enormous weight of losing another parent pressed on his mind. They hadn't been close, ever. Still, there had always been a sense there'd be more time, a chance that tomorrow would be better. '*How do I go on without him? Whom can I turn to and who understands me well enough to listen to my problems? Even if he's still breathing in a few years, will he know who I am? I'm not really close to anyone. Haven't been since Joe disappeared. I could have turned to Billy, but instead, I pushed everyone away. Now I'm alone or will be soon. Is that all there is to my life? A billion dollars and nobody I'd call a real friend and no one to inherit when I'm gone. Who will remember me? A few people might stumble across a musty copy of Time magazine and see the article on the 'boy genius', but they won't care. I ought to change my life, become a better friend.'*

He glanced out the window -- they were already flying above the clouds. The sun glinting off the white cotton field below them hurt his eyes. *'First, I need to let people get close to me,'* he thought. You need to open your heart dear, his mother said to him. The only way people will be close to you is if you love them and let them see the real man inside you. Give them your heart to cherish and they'll remember the real you long after you're gone.

He didn't know what she meant, but some part of him understood she was right. His chest hurt and he couldn't swallow for the lump in his throat. The clouds became blurry as tears welled in his eyes. He pressed the button and reclined the seat, pretending to take a nap, trying to hide his tears. If his Dad saw any moisture on his face, he'd make some idiotic comment about being tougher. If he looked at the old man right now, he'd start blubbering. He couldn't imagine what his father would say about that.

Scenes from his boyhood, people he'd done business with and girls he'd known over the years drifted across his mind. *'Strange how I only remember the happy times,'* he thought. *'I need to force myself to remember the sad moments, the times I got hurt or hurt someone. If I hadn't been so self-absorbed with my career, I wonder how many of those people would have become my friend. They all seemed genuine and I liked them, but neither of us clicked.'*

"Gentlemen, we're at cruising altitude. If you'd like a snack or drink, please feel free to help yourselves," Sam's voice rumbled from the overhead speakers.

Michael sat up and found his father doing the same. "Do you want something to drink, Dad?" *'Do you know who I am?'* He added in his mind.

"I'm fine with whatever you're having, son. Something to munch on would be good too. I don't remember having lunch today."

Michael unbuckled and moved to the rear of the cabin. A kitchen area built into a space too small to change his mind opened on the right of the aisle. Cupboards and a fridge were stocked with cold soda, booze, and snacks of all kinds. He opened the fridge taking out two sodas, pulled down two glasses from an overhead cupboard, and grabbed a bag of plain potato chips on the way back to the seat.

A small table, roughly the height of a coffee table, separated each row of forward and backward facing seats. Michael sat down and then put the drinks, glasses, and snacks on the table. His father opened the can of soda with some effort, and poured with his right hand. The pale bony hands trembled slightly, his left hand was used like a stop for the glass, but nothing spilled. Once Michael had done the same, Robert raised his glass toward his son.

"To the finest son a man could hope for in this life."

"I'll agree to that if we can say to the best Dad of all time too." They smiled together and touched their glasses.

Michael took a sip and then picked up the telephone intercom beside his seat. Sam answered immediately.

"Yes sir, what can I do for you?"

"Could you find out if the Yankees are playing this weekend and if they are, do you think you can get me three tickets to the game?"

"Hmm," Sam's deep voice replied. "I'll see what I can do and get back to you."

"Thank you, Sam," Michael said, remembering to put sincere gratitude in his voice. There wasn't much effort required, he realized, especially when you were being sincere.

"Do you want to watch a movie, Dad? There's time before we get to New York."

"Sure son, you got anything in mind?"

"You like Clint Eastwood, right?" His father nodded with an uncertain smile. "I don't know if his latest movie is onboard yet. I think the title is, Heart Break Ridge, and the reviews were great last year." He went to the rear of the plane and found the cassette for the movie. Sam did a good job of keeping the plane stocked with the latest releases in case the passengers had time to watch. Once the cartridge was in the machine, Michael pressed play and went back to his seat. The screen was double sided and pulled down from a slot in the ceiling. He took a sip of his drink and settled back to watch the movie. The intercom buzzed as the opening credits finished so he whispered when he answered.

"Yes Sam,"

"I've found us three seats behind the Yankees dugout. I had to promise them you'd throw out the first pitch, but I didn't think you'd mind -- do you?"

"No Sam, I'd be honored to throw out the first ball, just make sure we get there in time." He was already imagining the roar of the crowd and the feel of the ball in his hand while he replaced the phone. In his mind, the pitch was a perfect strike.

"I'm assuming he got us tickets to a Yankees game."

Michael nodded and smiled proudly at his father.

"How come you get to throw out the first pitch?"

"I guess they think I'm a celebrity or because I'm rich. Either way, we're going to be at the game behind the Yankees' dugout. We'll get to meet some of the players after the game too."

"Should have been me doing this stuff for you, not the other way around," his father grumbled. They did not say any more until after the plane landed.

Chapter 7

Randal Chesterwick scratched his head, a nervous habit for most of his life. He sat in front of his computer terminal at the 'lab' in Silicon Valley, sweating even though the air-conditioning was running full blast.

As the Director of Development for Eldridge Industries, he was responsible for overseeing every project to conclusion. He took his job seriously. He'd heard the whispers that he was a fuss-budget, maybe he was too meticulous, but millions of dollars were being gambled on every venture. If he wasn't scrupulous, lives could be lost and he didn't want that on his conscience.

The Mars probe was their most important project. Even though no lives were at stake, people depended on him to make sure the endeavor was successful. When the probe left for New York, he began running the communications program to make certain nothing could fail.

A glitch appeared almost immediately. Halfway through the thousands of lines of code, one asked for a time and place, but quickly continued when no information was entered. He'd never seen the line before. As far as he knew, there was no need to enter any data into the program. He scratched his head again; sweat trickled down his back. *'Mr. Eldridge must have put that in there,'* he thought, *'but why? Should I take out the line? No, you can't without getting his permission first, Randal. He's very particular about his programs. If you change anything without his approval, you'll be in so much shit you'll never get the stink off for the rest of your life.*

He turned his eyes from the computer screen to the telephone and then looked at his watch. They wouldn't land for another half an hour. He needed to find out what hotel they'd be staying at and leave a message.

The receiver weighed a ton as he dialed the number for Michael's secretary.

"Michael Eldridge's office," Christen's voice came through the line.

Randal never went up to the big office, so he didn't know what the woman looked like, but his mind created a picture for him, a vision that seemed real enough for him to reach out and touch.

"This is Randal Chesterwick in development," he tried to sound macho, hoping she'd envision him as a hunk rather than a geek. "I need to contact Mr. Eldridge, about an urgent matter." He didn't like dealing with people. His brusque manner shocked even him sometimes.

He heard her breathing on the other end of the line.

"He's staying at the Park Regency, I can connect you if you'd like." Her voice was pleasant and he could see her smiling.

"Please." He drummed his fingers on the desk waiting for the connection. He left a message with the desk clerk and hung up. His right hand scratched the back of his head. "I need to figure out what to say to him when he calls. 'Hi Boss, you screwed up the program.' That'll get you fired Randal, but if I just tell him what the line says he'll tell me to delete it. I don't need to know why it's there; that's none of my business." He burst off the chair and walked out of the office into the 'lab'.

The enormous building stretched away from him. Several technicians were busy around the room, carrying out tasks for minor areas of the Mars project, but otherwise, he was alone in the vast space.

His eyes flicked nervously from the ceiling to the walls, and then followed one of the technicians while his mind scrolled through the problem. He was the only person who knew about the problem. Leaving it alone would be sloppy. If he did nothing, the probe could travel all the way to Mars before that one line caused a problem. NASA would point at him. Blaming Mr. Eldridge for writing the program wouldn't save him. Michael would blame him for not saying anything. Claiming ignorance wouldn't work, either. He scratched his head with both hands in growing anxiety.

'You're not a good liar Randal. They'll see the truth on your face. There has to be a reason for that line to be in there, so I'll ask him when he calls later. I ought to know why the words are there.' His hands twisted together trying to wring away nervous energy and keep them from scratching. With nothing else to occupy his mind, he started walking toward the far end of the 'lab'.

• • •

The plane touched down at Teterboro airport as the final movie credits began to roll. He'd enjoyed the movie and by the smile on his father's face, Michael knew the old man had too. They stepped down the ladder carefully, Michael in front, and then into a waiting limousine. Both men fixated on the sites as the car traveled toward the hotel, and then pulled up to the front of the Park Regency. A short elevator ride later, they entered their suite.

The porter left the room. Robert had picked up the remote for the television, and was trying to figure out how to turn on the television.

"Like this Dad," Michael took the remote and pressed a button. Instantly, a picture appeared on the screen.

"What the hell is this? I wanted to watch the news."

"Just a second," Michael snapped with the same tone as his father, and pressed more buttons searching for a menu.

"No need to get sore, you're the genius in the room. I figured you'd be able to find a news channel," the old man grumbled and dropped onto the sofa.

"Well I'm trying to do that, Dad, but if you want California news you'll have to wait. They're three hours behind us at the moment."

"What the hell are you talking about son? We're in California aren't we?" That expression of fear was back on his Dad's face when Michael turned toward him. He pressed the menu button and found CNN, hoping that would be enough to satisfy his father. The old man muttered under his breath, but seemed fine with the selection for now.

I need a drink,' Michael thought, '*not a soda but a real drink.'* He found the bar and poured some scotch into a glass without ice. He'd had better whiskey, but this was still good as he tossed the liquor back. The warmth of the liquor spread quickly and he poured another. This time, he sipped at the drink and stared at the back of his father's head. Equal measures of fear and anger swirled in his mind.

He realized that his father would need constant attention for the rest of his life. It wouldn't be enough to move him into Michaels' house, he'd need a nurse, medical care, and in the end, he'd need to go to a hospital. How could he do that to his Dad? The old man would be better and safer in a facility equipped to care for people with dementia.

A knock on the door made him jump. Robert looked away from the television as Michael went to open the door. Sam stood in the hall with a porter carrying three suitcases. He smiled and stepped into the room. The bellman set the cases down and left.

"Hey Boss, how're you doing Mr. Eldridge," Sam asked brightly in his rumbling voice.

"God damned pilot isn't staying with us, is he?" Robert demanded from the sofa, turning back to the television. Michael glared at him, feeling more and more as if he was dealing with a spoiled child.

"No Dad, Sam has his own room. He brought our luggage and he'll be with us when we go to the ball game tomorrow. You don't have a problem with him looking after you on Monday when I'm at work, do you?" The old man didn't say anything. Michael rolled his eyes, tilting his head in the direction of his father. Sam smiled to show he understood.

"Got one of those for an exhausted pilot and friend?" He was ogling the glass in Michael's hand.

"Sure, you don't mind my taking you for granted do you? I'm only going to be there for a couple of hours." Before they could say anymore, the telephone rang. Michael answered. "Hello," He listened. After the other person said something, he said, "Thanks," and returned the receiver. A frown creased his face.

"A problem?" Sam asked.

"There could be, Randal, the head technician back at the lab wants me to call him right away. He doesn't usually need my help, so I hope there isn't anything serious. Help yourself to a drink while I make the call."

He picked up the phone again, punched the number to get an outside line before dialing the number for the lab. It took a couple of seconds to make connection, and then another couple for the rings before anyone answered.

"Yes, this is Randal," the breathless voice of the Chief Technician gasped.

"Randal, this is Michael, catch your breath, and tell me what's wrong." He could see the scientist standing at the desk, scratching his head nervously. Sounds of deep breathing and exhaling came through the line as Randal tried to relax. Papers shuffled in the background as if Randal was searching his desk for something. Finally, he came back on the line.

"Mr. Eldridge, I sent the probe to the east coast and decided to run the code to make sure everything was perfect for Monday. I was watching the software run and found a glitch." He inhaled sharply as if he'd sworn or just seen something frightening.

"What kind of glitch?" Michael demanded, trying to keep the fear out of his own voice.

"The code stopped for only a second on a line which read 'insert place and time to continue,' and then continued. I don't remember needing to give any instructions like that in the program. Mr. Eldridge, is this going to cause any problems for our tests?"

Michael could almost see the tears in the man's eyes. That particular line was meant for his time-travel experiment. Randal was right, that didn't need to be in the probe code. He felt sorry for the technician having to deal with a problem that wasn't his fault.

"Randal, you can delete that line without any harm to the program. I was playing with an idea and forgot that was still there. Thanks for finding the problem. I don't know what I'd do without your help. I'll do the same on this end when the probe gets here and we'll be good to go. Is that all you found?" He held his breath, expecting more bad news.

"Yes sir that was all I wanted. You have a good time and I'll talk to you on Monday." He hung up without another word. Michael could easily imagine Randal hanging up and then cringing for not saying good-bye. He smiled.

"There, all better now. Do you want another drink Sam? Dad, do you want a drink?"

Chapter 8

The next morning, a men's clothing store brought a selection of pants and shirts for Robert. He objected to trying on the clothes, but he finally chose several outfits. In the afternoon, they piled into the limo and drove out to the stadium. An usher met them at the ticket window, escorting them to their seats. He even stayed nearby to attend to their needs. Robert became a kid again, looking around at the crowd and marveling at the size of the stadium. Michael was glad and just a tiny bit sad. He hoped his Dad wouldn't become disoriented. The old man deserved to enjoy the day.

A voice boomed and echoed over the public address system announcing the teams and welcoming the special guest. Their faces appeared on the massive video screen high on the outfield wall. Michael saw the usher move toward him and knew they were ready for him to throw out the first ball. His name was announced as he stepped onto the field. Cheers and clapping followed him onto the pitcher's mound.

He waved at the crowd and shook hands with the Yankee's catcher. The home plate umpire handed him a game ball and wished him luck.

"Yeah, I'll be lucky to reach home plate," Michael moaned. His hands trembled as the crowd went silent.

"All you gotta to do is throw in the general direction of home and I'll do the rest," the catcher advised. "Just imagine yourself as a kid and you're playing catch with your pals."

"Thanks, I can do that." Michael waited until the man was ready and then hurled the ball toward home plate. The throw wasn't pretty, but the ball did get to the plate and into the catcher's mitt. The crowd cheered and he waved to them on the way back to his seat, happy to be another face in the crowd again.

His father was beaming. Sam thumped him on the back so hard he nearly knocked the wind out of Michael. Several people leaned over and congratulated him on the throw. At the end of the second inning, the batboy for the Yankees brought the game ball to Michael, signed by all the players and coaches. The pinnacle of a glorious day.

When the limo drove out of the stadium parking lot, they went to a steak house recommended to Sam by someone he'd met at the stadium. All three men had eaten very little during the game so Michael suspected his Dad would be hungry. The old man ordered a T-bone with all the fixings, diving in as if he was eating his last meal. They laughed and drank beer with the food, like three friends out for a good time.

Robert seemed quiet when they returned to the hotel, but didn't complain about any problems. He said he might've had too much excitement, and past his bedtime. Michael gave him a hug.

"I hope you had a good time, Dad. I know I did."

"That was the best day, son, and thank you." He smiled and shuffled into his bedroom closing the door.

"Well, I think I'm going to bed too." Sam announced as he headed for the door to the hall. "I'm planning on doing a little shopping tomorrow. There are people back in California who want me to buy them a few things. Good night, sir."

Michael smiled and said good night. He woke up on the couch, his neck ached, he'd drooled on his shirt, and his bladder hurt from all the beer the night before. One thing at a time, he thought as he hurried to the bathroom. The toilet flushed, making a noise louder than his jet, and he cringed imagining his father waking up angry at the sound. Mentally, he shrugged and brushed his teeth before stripping off and stepping into the shower.

Feeling refreshed and ready for the day, he got dressed before returning to the living room. The television was still on and he switched channels to a local news report. His effort to throw the first pitch yesterday was being shown. Not a bad wind up, he thought seeing the throw go straight into the catcher's mitt. A proud but self-conscious smile appeared on his face.

The announcer said, "Eight thirty, and time for the weather." He frowned. *'Dad never sleeps past seven; he must be exhausted after yesterday.'* Mike went to check on him.

He opened the bedroom door slowly until he could poke his head between the door and the jamb. Peering into the gray light, he could see deep shadows over the bed. The old man lay on his back, mouth open and Michael thought he heard snoring, so he pulled back and closed the door. An uneasy feeling settled into his stomach as a faint memory clawed around the edges of his mind. He pushed the fear away and went to make coffee.

Sam came by at nine to say he was heading out to shop, but he'd be back around noon, and asked if Michael needed anything. "No, I don't think I need anything before then. You have a good time, Sam, and don't spend too much." They chuckled and Michael shut the door.

He ordered breakfast for two from room service. His father would never sleep this late. Breakfast arrived forty-five minutes later. The waiter pushed two covered plates on a cart into the room, placing the trolley between the two sofas. Michael gave him a ten-dollar tip and went to see if his father was up yet.

This time, he didn't open the door slowly, but just walked into the room. A stale odor of rotting meat greeted his nose, growing stronger as he approached the bed. The old man was still in the same position, but there was no snoring. Michael touched his neck to find a pulse, but the skin was cold and lifeless.

Dead, his mind told him. The thought shocked his system and his legs went limp. He slumped to the floor beside the bed. Tears flowed, but he made no sound. His mind was numb and empty. The wrinkled hand lying on top of the covers seemed foreign as he touched the skin. Maybe he was looking for comfort or trying to give some, he didn't know. The once strong hand was now bony and purple, the skin so thin he could see the veins clearly. Stroking the back of his Dad's hand like a cat, Michael's tears poured onto the bed in despair.

Later, he would figure out that he'd spent only a few minutes beside the bed, but right then minutes seemed like hours. *'You need to call someone,'* his mind said, which seemed logical, but who? Michael forced his legs to stand and move him into the living room. *'What am I supposed to do now,'* he wondered, but really, he hoped the voice in his head would just take over. Phone, the voice told him, call the front desk, and ask for the manager.

The voice must have control of his hands too, as they picked up the phone and punched the numbers without his eyes. A female voice answered his call and he heard his voice ask for the manager.

"Is there anything wrong with the room, sir?" She asked.

"I need to speak with the manager," he said mechanically. The line clicked and canned music started to play. He didn't laugh when he recognized the song as 'My Blue Heaven' and his eyes started gushing again.

"This is Mr. Cranston, can I help you Mr. Eldridge?" The man's voice sounded the same as Dr. Caraway at the senior's home. *'Is that some sort of requirement to be in management,'* Michael wondered.

"I asked to speak with you personally because my father has died during the night. I'm sorry, but I don't know what to do now." He choked and his throat tightened. I can't fall apart, he reminded himself.

"Don't concern yourself with anything sir, I'll make a few phone calls and be right up. Can I get you anything, sir?"

"No," Michael sniffed. "I'm fine." He dropped the receiver into the cradle and sagged into the sofa. His mind shut off again until a knock sounded on the door. Pushing himself to stand, Michael numbly walked to the door. The manager, a tall man in a black suit, was standing in the hall with three men in uniforms. Michael let them into the room.

"I'm Mr. Cranston," the tall man in the suit said softly. "These men are from the Medical Examiner's office. They're going to take your father to the morgue if that's alright with you."

Michael nodded and shuffled back to the sofa. Cranston stood by the door wringing his hands as the other two pulled a gurney into the spare bedroom to collect the body. Someone asked questions, and Michael answered, but he couldn't remember who or what was said. Hearing the clatter as the wheeled bed came back into the main room, Michael stood up. Cranston held the door and the attendants disappeared into the hall.

"I'll take care of the preparations for you, Mr. Eldridge. We can arrange for the funeral home to prepare your father to return to California as soon as you wish. I'll maintain simplicity as much as possible so you can make your own arrangements for the funeral.

Someone from housekeeping will be here in a few minutes to take care of the bedroom. My deepest sympathy for your loss and if there's anything else I can do for you, please don't hesitate to ask." Michael saw his mouth twitch as if he'd remembered this wasn't the time to smile.

"Thank you, Mr. Cranston, you've been a huge help already. I'll pay for any damages and obviously, this is beyond your job description, so I'll see you're compensated. I have a meeting tomorrow that I can't cancel, but I'll be checking out as soon as my father's body is ready to travel. Thank you again for all your trouble."

Cranston smiled. Michael noticed the greed in his eyes. He ignored the obvious ignorance because he needed the man. The men from the ME's office wheeled the gurney down the hall. One of them handed Michael a sheet of paper before leaving the suite. Cranston followed them with a bow as he closed the door.

The television was still talking, making the only sound in the room. Michael moved to the windows and looked out at the buildings towering into the sky. Glass and steel reflected the sunshine deep into the concrete canyons below. His world had just ended, but the people below didn't know that. They went about their days oblivious to his pain. *'I'm alone now,'* he thought. *'There's no one left in my life. If I jumped through this window, would anyone miss me? Would anyone cry for me? Heather might, but for how long?'*

He sighed and shook his head. "Get your shit together, Michael," he scolded. "You can feel sorry for yourself some other time. He had a good life and you gave him the best day he'd ever had so be happy." Someone knocked on the door.

Sam stood smiling back at him as Michael opened the door. The smile quickly faded as he saw Michael.

"What's wrong, Boss?" His big voice was soft, kind and concerned all at once.

"Dad died sometime during the night." His bottom lip trembled again. "They just finished taking him out a few minutes ago." He couldn't hold back the tears. Somehow there was a pump in his face that switched on and blasted water.

"Christ, Michael, I'm sorry for you. Let me get you a drink. Go sit down." Sam suddenly changed from a strong gregarious giant into a gentle nursemaid. Michael didn't care and didn't notice the use of his first name. Having someone around was comforting, anyone to talk with about what happened.

A glass of amber liquid appeared in front of his blurred vision and he watched his hand tip back the glass, feeling the fire from the whisky.

"So, what happened? Everything was fine when I left." Sam settled on the sofa opposite.

Sam listened to Michael as he relayed the events of the morning. He could tell the younger man was having difficulty controlling the tears. Sam kept quiet. He'd been in situations like this before in Vietnam. His flight wing lost plenty of good pilots; some of them were friends of his. Most of the guys accepted the deaths, but some of them went to pieces and had to be sent home. The worst was a young guy on his first tour in action. He watched his wingman get shot down in flames. Poor bastard barely kept himself controlled back to the airfield before he cracked. The ground crew dragged him out of the cockpit blubbering and screaming. He never came back.

Sam's father had died while he was overseas. There had been tears yes, but the relationship with his father hadn't been as close as Michael's had. Sam joined the air force against his Dad's wishes, maybe to spite him. The senior Worthy was a tank commander in WWII. He'd seen hell and didn't want his son to go through the same shit. They never really talked much after that. Anytime they got together, the conversation was about the weather or Sam's brother Travis an accountant in Wichita.

Yesterday was the first time he'd met Mr. Eldridge Sr. He felt bad for Michael about the old man losing his memory, but that was then. Now his father was gone forever and he could see how painful that was.

"Are you going to the test tomorrow?"

"I'm obligated to, Sam," Michael reached for a tissue and blew his nose. "I need to fix the program and be there in case something else happens. The hotel manager said he'd call me when the funeral home has Dad ready and we can leave right after that."

"Okay, I'll come with you tomorrow. All I need to do is get the airport to fuel the plane so that's ready when we get there. Flight plan is already filed so there won't be anything else."

Michael was nodding his approval, but Sam could tell he was struggling to focus his mind and wasn't really listening.

"Let's get out of this room, Michael, you need some fresh air."

"Oh I couldn't," Michael protested.

"Either you come willingly or I'll carry you down to the lobby -- your choice." He tried to lighten the mood with a tiny joke. Michael's shoulders sagged in defeat. Sam could see he didn't have the energy or will to resist.

On the sidewalk in front of the hotel, Sam asked the door attendant for a cab. Michael stood nearby, leaning against a no parking sign. The man in livery blew a whistle and a second later, a yellow cab pulled to the curb in front of the two men. Sam leaned forward and held the door for Michael to enter.

"Take us to Coney Island," Sam ordered as he shut the door.

"That's in Jersey," the cabbie whined. "I gotta charge you extra for the round trip."

"Don't worry about the fare, here's a twenty to get you started, now go please." The driver took the money while eyeing the wad of money in Sam's hand and put the car in gear. Sam figured Michael could use a distraction. They wouldn't go on any of the rides, but there were other things to see and do in the famous amusement park. Even if they only went for a walk to the end of the pier, that would be better than sitting in the hotel room.

The ride was interesting, to say the least. Traffic was miserable for a Sunday, bumper to bumper in some places, especially on the bridges exiting Manhattan. Several times the cabbie had to slam on the brakes, throwing his passengers forward against the front seats. When they finally arrived, the driver shut the meter off and turned slightly in his seat.

"That'll be one-twenty-five for the time and another fifty for the return." He seemed anxious, as if he expected the men to stiff him. Michael looked like a drug addict, even to Sam. Pale skin, sunken red eyes and dressed in worn jeans and a sweatshirt. Sam at least had on a dress shirt with his jeans. He pulled money out of his pants and handed the driver two one hundred-dollar bills.

"Keep the change, but if you want more you'll be back here in exactly two hours." The driver smiled and said he'd be there as Michael and Sam left the cab.

The air was chilly as they stood at the south end of the boardwalk. Dull grey clouds whirled overhead and gusts whipped across the ocean, pushing salt spray over everything. The fine particles of water stung Sam's eyes as he searched the area for shelter. He noticed the lights in front of a bar three doors from where they stood and pulled Michael toward the chance of warmth.

Further down the boardwalk, a sign announced a clothing sale in front of another store. Deciding they needed jackets more than booze at this point, he dragged his boss toward the clothing store.

There were only two racks of outerwear in the place, most of what they sold being T-shirts and souvenir hats that said 'I was at Coney Island'. Despite the slim pickings, Michael found a gray jacket to fit. Sam had to settle for an extra, extra large when he normally wore an extra-large. Surprisingly, the bright red bomber jacket fit not too bad, but he didn't like red. By now, Michael had perked up a little as they went back to the bar.

Only two other people were in the pub, one of them the bartender. The other guy was seated on a stool, hugging a bottle of beer. Both men turned toward the door as Sam and Michael entered.

"Gents, what brings you two out on a day like this?" The bartender was dressed in a 1930's style. The handlebar moustache completed the effect. A first glance suggested this place was supposed to give the impression of stepping back to the time of prohibition.

"Nothing special," Sam replied as they walked toward a booth in the rear. "Had some time to kill and decided to see the sights. Too bad, the weather sucks. We'll have a whisky each -- neat please for both."

A minute later, the drinks sat on the table between them. The walls of the bar were covered in oak panels, some kind of dark stain, applied to make them appear old. Imitation gas lamps with electric bulbs inside hung from the walls and black-and-white pictures of gangsters from the '30's plastered the walls. Shelves ran along the top of the wall, holding books and mugs of every description filling the space. Glass cabinets, with obvious locks in the front, displayed sub-machine guns, revolvers, and photos of dead gangsters. The place smelled of old cigarette smoke and stale beer, but they were warm.

Sam took a sip of whisky and looked at Michael smiling back.

"What's so funny?" He rumbled.

"Not funny," Michael said. "You were right; I did need to get out of that room. This is my happy face."

Sam grinned. "I don't know why this little adventure would make you happy. Bloody cold outside and this is a real shit-hole of a bar," he whispered.

"No argument there, Sam, but where else could we go today and have this much fun." Sarcasm was not Michael's biggest attribute, but he was right.

"Ok, we'll have a couple of drinks to fortify our bones and then go for a walk on the pier. By the time we get back that cabbie should be waiting for us." He raised his glass in a toast. "To ugly jackets and cold walks on the pier. May one never be needed again and the other never happens again."

"Amen," Michael said, as they touched glasses. They didn't go for the walk, staying and drinking instead. When the time arrived for them to meet the taxi, they wobbled out the door, leaning against each other for support.

The yellow cab was waiting for them. Sam held the door while Michael crawled inside. Their driver was all smiles as he drove back to the hotel, chattering about the city and the weather.

"Thanks Sam," Michael said, as he flopped on the sofa in his hotel room. His words were a little slurred; sounding more like 'thanksh Sham', but Sam got the gist and smiled.

"It was my pleasure sir."

"You know you don't need to call me sir," Michael said, trying to stand. He didn't succeed and fell back against the cushions. "Call...you can call me Michael," he burped and put his hand to his mouth. "Scush me," he chuckled through his fingers.

"I'll do that from now on, Michael. I think you need to eat something before you pass out. Anything in particular you'd like?"

Michael was having trouble focusing as his head drooped, the slurred words an obvious indication the man was drunk. His response was a dismissive wave of the hand. Sam called room service and ordered two burgers and fries before getting a large glass of water for Michael.

He carried the glass to the sofa, thinking about their conversation in the bar -- well, mostly Michael had talked while he listened to the story of Michael's life. How he'd lost his best friend one summer and his mother a few years ago and now his father. Sam could understand the emotional weight of the situation, but not the loss. He'd never suffered over the loss of his parents; maybe that made him an emotional cripple, but he wasn't worried. He felt pity for the young man he called Boss; he could even feel a growing friendship, but they didn't have anything more in common. Maybe one day, but not yet, he sighed as their food arrived.

Michael finished his burger and picked at the fries. The water helped rinse the booze out of his system, but until the food finished the job, he was going to continue to be drunk. At one point, he flopped sideways and passed out. Sam let him sleep for an hour and then gently slapped his face to wake him up. By eight-thirty, Michael was coherent and moving normally.

"I can't believe I got that drunk," he moaned, remembering everything he'd said and done.

"You have nothing to be sorry for, Michael. Anyone in your situation would have done the same. You'll sleep like a baby tonight and be totally normal tomorrow."

"Oh shit, I almost forgot about tomorrow." He jumped off the sofa and dashed to his bedroom. A minute later, he came back into the living room, carrying a piece of paper. "This is where we've got to be at eleven o'clock tomorrow for the test. Do you know where that is?" He handed the paper to Sam. Scrawled in Michaels' messy script, below the address was, 'Thanks for a really great day, Sam. Your generosity and friendship will not be forgotten. You're my new best friend, Michael.'

The big man looked up with a startled expression on his face. "You don't have to do any favors for me. I did what any person would do for you."

"Umm, maybe, but you weren't obliged to, and I was there remember. I'm not very good at saying what I feel Sam, probably why I don't have any friends. I was heading into a heap of self-pity and you stopped me. That is what a friend does for a friend and I'll never forget. I won't ruin my gratitude by offering you money, but if there's anything else I can do all you need to do is ask. Who knows, maybe I can return the favor someday. What you did today means more to me than any amount of money." He was standing there, beaming.

Sam understood friendship. There weren't many as he grew up; one or two, but they were precious. He smiled up at Michael and then stood up and gave his Boss a hug. A man's hug to be sure, but the sentiment was there.

They separated; both men's faces glowing red with embarrassment.

"Well," Michael cleared his throat. "What shall we do the rest of the evening? I have tickets to see 'Cats' on Broadway -- interested?"

"I'm not a Broadway kind of guy, but there's a new Star Trek at the theatre down the street."

"Perfect and we don't need to get dressed up either." Michael smiled. He glanced at his watch. "The next show might be starting in an hour. Want to play a few hands of poker until then?"

"Oh you don't want to do that with me. What are the stakes?" Sam asked as his face fell into a mask of emotionless stone.

"So, that's how you want to play," Michael grinned. "Well, I think we can manage a dollar ante and maximum raises of five dollars."

"Cheap shit. You still owe me for the taxi and the booze at the bar, but you're on." He rummaged in the desk and found a deck of cards.

"Cheap shit," Michael said trying to sound hurt. "That's no way to speak to your Boss."

Sam sat on one side of the coffee table shuffling the cards. "We're friends now, remember, and that's how I speak to my friends. Now sit down and prepare to take your punishment." He dealt out five cards each after declaring they would play Texas Holdem.

Forty minutes later, Michael stuffed twenty dollars into his jeans. As they rode down in the elevator, he pulled a wad of cash out of the other pocket and handed Sam four hundred dollars.

"This should cover the afternoon expenses."

Sam ignored him and stared at the changing numbers over the door. "I told you before, that's what friends do. I was giving you a hard time before when I mentioned the money, but you don't need to pay me back, Michael."

"I understand, but I'm paying for the movie and the popcorn."

"Deal," Sam muttered.

Several people in the theatre lobby did double takes as Michael walked up to the refreshment counter. They'd obviously seen his picture on a magazine. Sam saw the question in their eyes. *'What's a rich guy like him doing here? I'm trying to ignore you people and I want to see a movie,'* he thought. *'Why does anyone go to a movie theatre? Oh yeah, I forgot; billionaires all have their own movie theatre in the house. Maybe Michael should put one in at home, but he's not home, so we had to come here.'*

They found seats in the middle of an empty row in the middle of the theatre. Scattered groups of people took up some of the seats, but the theatre was not busy. When the lights went down, he briefly wondered if the movie was going to be any good.

Darkness surrounded them as they exited the theatre. Well, to be honest, blazing neon lights surrounded them in the darkness. People crowded the sidewalks heading in both directions, even at almost midnight. Michael felt drained, but energized too. He no longer needed to cry, but he still hurt. Having a friend made the difference, something he'd been missing for thirty years.

"Not bad," he said to Sam.

"Yeah, but the movie was really all about saving the whales. I mean, can you imagine traveling back in time to save whales. The Enterprise has all of this wonderful technology and they had to pretend to be ordinary citizens so they didn't contaminate the local inhabitants. Why not just use the cloaking device?"

Michael went silent, Sam didn't know him well enough to make a judgement, but he suspected he was thinking about something.

They stepped off the elevator. "I'll see you tomorrow, Sam and thanks again for saving me today."

"Good night Michael, I'll see you tomorrow." He was already walking down the hall to his room.

Michael wanted to give him another hug, but resisted. All this gushing about friendship was starting to get a bit weird. He unlocked his room and went inside. The movie had keyed some questions in his mind. Why hadn't they used their cloaking device? What harm could they cause if they were invisible? How would he affect time when he went back, invisible or otherwise?

"I'm not going to touch anything, so there shouldn't be any change in time. Invisible would be better than visible, in case I'm seen and history changes. I can't see the harm in going back to that

69

day, because the history is mine, but if I try to go back further, something might change. Just being there, could alter the balance somehow. Think, Michael. Why didn't they use their cloaking device in the movie? The creators of that film would have thought of a million reasons why cloaking wouldn't work or how being cloaked would affect their surroundings. I think I'm going to put the problem in front of my team and see what happens." He got undressed and crawled into bed.

Chapter 9

Whether he was subconsciously anxious about the test or because the alcohol finally drained from his system, didn't matter to Michael at seven the next morning. His body felt rested, but his eyes still wished for another hour of sleep. His heart started racing as he stepped into the shower. Ideas flitted through his mind in a tumble of words and sentences. He was still worried about how his trip back in time would affect him or history.

Pulling on dress pants and a comfortable turtle-necked sweater made him feel so much better and ready for the day. He called down to room service and ordered eggs, flapjacks and six strips of bacon with hash browns and toast. His stomach growled with anticipation.

'Jesus,' he thought shortly after finishing, *'I didn't think I was that hungry.'* He stared at the empty plate with the knife and fork still in his hands. They clattered on the dish and he picked up the cup of coffee. Sipping the hot java, he glanced at his watch. The time was only nine o'clock. The test wasn't until eleven, so what was he going to do for the next hour at least? They'd need an hour to drive out to the facility, which was fine, but he wanted something to do before then. His thoughts jumped to images of his father at the ballpark. Sadness weighed on his shoulders.

A knock sounded on his door halting, his slide into a depressed mood. He opened the door. Sam stood in the hall, dressed in the identical style to Michael, except for the colors.

"Morning, Sam, had breakfast yet?" Michael flung the door open and went back to his seat.

"Yeah, but I could use some more coffee. Three cups out of that stupid little pot in my room are just not enough. They shouldn't even call them cups, they should call them thimbles." He slouched on the sofa, trying not to pout.

"There's a cup on the counter in the bathroom, that hasn't been used and you can help yourself to this pot."

A few minutes later, Sam sipped his coffee and gave an exalted sigh.

"Now, that's good coffee. I forgot to order a pot with breakfast and all I had was the little thing in the room."

"Any suggestions on what we can do for an hour? The car won't be here until ten."

Sam was moving his head from side to side and gazing lovingly at the brown liquid in his cup.

"Sam, I need to ask you a question and I want you to tell me exactly what you think." People's reactions at this point, made telling them about his plans for time travel awkward. They either accepted the possibility or thought he'd lost his mind.

The bulky man sat forward on the opposite sofa and set his cup on the table.

"What do you need?" His face was serious.

"I'm going to tell you about a project I'm working on and I need you to help me." Michael sought for the right words to explain his plan, without sounding completely Looney tunes.

"I don't know anything about computers, but I'll try to help if I can." Worry lines had begun to form on Sam's forehead.

"Yesterday, I remember telling you about my friend Joe and that he just disappeared." Sam was nodding. "I don't remember how I said he disappeared, but I meant totally gone; poof." His hands made explosive motions. "Since then, I've been working on a way to go back in time to find out what happened to him. After watching the Star Trek movie yesterday, I have some issues that I need to discuss with someone."

"Is that all you want?" Sam snorted. "I thought you were going to ask me to explain nuclear physics or something less complicated." He gulped his coffee to waste a moment. "I don't know what you want me to say, Michael. I haven't got a clue about time travel or whether it's even possible." His face was blank.

"I know for sure, but that's not where I need your help. I'm having trouble with some other areas of traveling back in time. Talking about problems helps me think. For instance, why wouldn't

71

the Enterprise crew just use their cloaking capability instead of taking on the style of their surroundings?"

"That was just part of the movie, Michael. How the hell am I supposed to know why they didn't use cloaking?"

"Well, you could be right, but I think the writers invested a huge amount of thought before writing the story that way. Never mind for now, but if you went back in time and you didn't touch anything, would history be altered?"

"Mike, this is starting to scare me. You're saying you can actually go back in time."

"Yes, but being able to and actually going are two different things. I've proven the possibility, but I haven't gone yet." He poured another cup of coffee.

Sam was shaking his head. "Everything I know about time travel I've learned in movies. They always go faster than the speed of light somehow and end up exactly where they wanted to go. Wouldn't work in a plane unless there was a long, long runway, but then planes were science fiction a thousand years ago. If you can make yourself go faster than the speed of light and want to go back in time, then I suggest you've lost your mind. My gut is telling me that whatever happens isn't going to be good." He stared hard at Michael.

"I believe you could be right." Michael was nodding. "Invisible or not, by being there I've already altered history and thus any future that comes after. Sending back a camera is fine because the technology would have to be seen and understood to alter history." He was pacing now. "A caveman wouldn't know what he was looking at. Somebody in '57 would maybe figure out what the gadget was, but not for sure. Even if that somebody managed to keep the camera, the technology to build something that small wouldn't exist. The same theory would apply to knowing the Lakers will win the NBA Championship, but you live in a time before the Championship even exists." He was smiling, but Sam seemed more confused.

"This is crazy, Michael. Getting there is probably the easy part, how are you coming back?" Concern, deeply afraid concern was all over Sam's face.

"I'm working on that and I think I've got the solution. You remember in the old television show when they wanted to communicate with the ship they had what looked like a wallet they flipped open and talked?" Sam nodded. "Well, I'm working on building something like that to activate my computer back in this time."

Sam glanced at his watch, obviously trying to ignore the direction the conversation was taking. "The car's probably downstairs so we need to go." He kept his eyes on the floor and walked to the door. In the elevator and in the car all the way to the test site in Jersey, Michael saw him staring at the ceiling or out the window. They didn't speak much either. Michael was worrying more about the test than Sam's silence.

When the car pulled to a stop in front of the Johnson Space Center, Michael jumped out and jogged into the building, leaving Sam with the driver. Stopping to check in and get his building authorization seemed like an eternity; his fingers drummed on the desk impatiently waiting for the guard to find his badge. Identification in hand, Michael sprinted to the elevators. Another delay waiting for a car to arrive even though he'd only been in the building three minutes. His heart pounding, Michael stabbed at the fifth floor button on the elevator panel and hoped the ride up would be faster than waiting for the car to come down.

Randal was sitting alone at the computer terminal in the 'lab' in California waiting for Michael to call. Nothing would happen until they were connected by telephone first. When all systems were ready on both ends of the country, Randal would send a command to the probe. As he sent the message, he was to tell Michael. If the probe reacted, their software worked; obviously, if nothing happened they had more work to do. Their future depended on Michael's software.

The Chief Technician looked at his watch and mentally calculated the time in New York. *'He should be there by now, what's taking so long. I could call them I suppose, but I don't have their number. Didn't they think I was capable of making the call to them? I hold more degrees than Michael does and NASA doesn't trust me with a telephone number. What the --'* His thoughts were stopped abruptly by the telephone. He jumped with fear at the sudden noise.

"Hello, this is Randal," He droned into the mouthpiece, controlling his breathing.

"Good morning, Randal, how are things in sunny California?"

"Fine sir, everything is ready at this end." '*Finally,*' he sighed mentally, and scratched the back of his head. "Are you ready to proceed?"

"I'm just making those corrections we discussed. I'll be ready in about two minutes. The crew is powering the probe, so we can begin the test as soon as I'm finished." His fingers struck the keys frantically, making corrections to any lines he knew dealt with his personal project while the receiver was tucked firmly between his chin and shoulder. "Ok, Randal, I think we're ready on this end." His voice became distant as he spoke to the people nearby. "Are you guys ready? Ok, we're going to run the test. Everybody needs to keep their eyes on the probe for any kind of movement. Go Randal," the words were the loudest the technician heard that day.

His finger hit the enter key and the code scrolled across the screen in front of him. The words stopped and he said, "Now," holding his breath.

Michael sat at the desk in New York, eyes closed, waiting for the word from Randal, his breathing shallow, his heart pounding with anticipation. "Now," came through the phone. Mike opened his eyes and looked at his watch just as the ground crew around the probe began shouting. They were pointing at the elevator control surface on the left wing; which moved the instant Randal said the word.

Michael smiled, more of a hopeful grin, because he wasn't ready to declare the test a total success, yet.

"Since I don't know the command you sent to the probe, can you tell me now what you ordered?"

"I used the move the left elevator control surface, command. I figured the odds of that being part of the basic controls on the Martian surface to be highly unlikely." Randal was trying to keep his voice even. "Shall I send the next command, sir?" His fingers were already typing as he spoke.

"Hey, you guys we're doing another test, just shut up and watch," Michael shouted. His voice was far away again and then right next to Randal's ear. "Give me the word," Michael said.

The process was repeated, except this time Michael kept his eyes on his watch. He heard the click as Randal hit the enter key. His eyes watched the second hand move around the watch face. Ten, twenty, thirty, thirty-six seconds passed before Randal said, "Now." Two

74

more seconds ticked by before the technicians on the test floor shouted.

"Well done, Randal, what was the command this time?"

"I activated a camera light on the nose of the craft that isn't supposed to come on until the probe enters the Martian atmosphere." His words were drowned out by a technician on the test floor shouting they'd seen a light.

"Perfect Randal, two for two, but I'm still seeing a two second delay which could be just a normal reaction time in those guys out there, but I want to be certain. This time, I want to know the command you send. Two seconds across the country is still going to translate into a few minutes in space."

Randal studied his list of test commands. He knew the wheels hadn't deployed on the test probe. "Is the probe completely unwrapped sir?"

Michael stood up and looked out the office window. "Yes," He said as he sat.

"I'm going to deploy the wheels this time." Randal was typing.

"Watch for the wheels," Michael shouted. The eyes of six technicians were instantly riveted on the belly of the probe.

Everything else happened once more and at the thirty-six-second mark, Randal said, "Now." A cheer went up in less than a second. Michael smiled with success. The entire program wouldn't need to run once the machine was in space to send a command. This was just part of the testing phase.

"These technicians have slow reaction times, Randal. There was no delay this time, so let's run another six or seven system commands and see what happens." He wished he could cut the cord on this damn phone and be out on the test floor.

Sam gave up waiting. He crawled in the back seat of the limo to lie down. Of course, he didn't ask how long the tests would take because he wouldn't have gotten a straight answer. Michael would have said the same thing he'd heard in the Air force; the tests will end when they're over. Pulling his new red jacket tighter around his shoulders, he closed his eyes.

Michael opened the rear door of the limo. The overhead light seemed bright; Sam was sprawled on the back seat. He shielded his eyes, and grunted sitting up awkwardly on the seat.

"Sorry to disturb you Sam, but we're ready to go home now."

"I assume by the shit-assed grin on your face that all went well." Sam rubbed his eyes and then snapped the seat belt in place.

"Better than well, my friend, everything went perfectly. We ran over three hundred-system tests and every one of them was received instantly. I'd say the program is a success."

"This isn't going to be like you counting your chickens before the eggs hatch, because I don't want to be around to tell you I told you so." Michael looked sharply at him. Sam smiled.

"I could be, but not likely. Any problems would have shown up by now. The biggest delays were right at the beginning, and they proved to be an issue with human reaction times, not the software. Once we ran the tests with the technicians knowing what was coming, the time delay was zero."

"Did the funeral home call you? I'm sorry, I didn't want to rain on your parade, but if they haven't we need to straighten that out before we can leave."

"Yes and thanks for the downer Sam," Michael kept a straight face. "Dad's body is being shipped to California in the next couple of days." He smiled now. "Seriously, I appreciate the consideration and keeping me in line, Sam. I know that isn't your job, but I do thank you."

"You can thank me by giving me a perpetual raise for as long as the company exists or as long as I live, whichever comes first." Sam kept a straight face.

Michael grimaced. "I thought we were friends."

"We are friends, but if you go back in time and screw with something, then I might not keep my job. Worse than that, you might not start this company, and then what?"

Michael laughed -- a hearty relieved belly laugh that seemed to be the knife to cut the tension in the car. Sam joined him; his deep booming rumbling voice filled the car.

"I've been hearing the same thing from my best friend Billy for years. As soon as I get to the office tomorrow, I'm going to put that into your contract, Sam Worthy. Now, four people know about my trip. All of you will be there on that day when I find out if time travel is possible." He thought about the size of the computer room at his house. "I might need to renovate my home before then, but you'll all be witnesses to history."

"History or the disappearance of our friend," Sam said glumly.

They reached the airport. The car pulled to a stop at the bottom of the stairs leading to the jet's cabin. Sam led them inside.

The two seats he and his father had occupied on the way out were brightly lit, mocking him. Reaching under the bulkhead, Michael turned off the lights and went aft to make a drink. He sat in a seat on the opposite side of the plane, looking out the window at the ground crew scurrying around the terminal and his plane. They moved without any pattern to their actions, but everything must work out correctly somehow.

Sam's voice rumbled over the address system. "I'll give you the short and sweet version of the pre-flight passenger announcement: sit down, buckle up, and get ready to fly. Stay that way until I tell you different, is that understood? I thought so."

Michael chuckled in spite of his sadness. He decided that once they were in the air he'd go up front, no sense sitting back here alone. They taxied out to the assigned runway and waited for another plane to land. Twenty seconds later, the engines on the Hawker-Siddeley wound up and the jet moved forward. The instant the plane was straight on the runway, the engines went to full throttle.

Flung back into his seat, Michael didn't get much of a chance to appreciate the take-off. Mere seconds passed before the nose of the plane lifted and they were airborne. Fifteen seconds later, the craft banked left and climbed higher. Now Michael could appreciate the vast ocean of lights below. The ground seemed to be on fire as far as he could see through the tiny port.

"You can now undo the seat belt and walk about the cabin," Sam droned.

Michael pressed the belt release and walked to the cockpit. A heavy cloth curtain separated the flight deck from the cabin. He pushed through the drape and sat in the co-pilots' seat. Sam motioned for him to put on the headset hanging on the wall. The high-pitched whine of the engines disappeared as the soft pads slid over his ears.

"Now we can talk without shouting and you can hear everything I hear. Want to fly the plane?" Michael took one look at the array of lights and displays on the dash and shook his head.

"You do the flying and I'll do the computer stuff. What time do you figure we'll get home?" He had to resist the temptation to shout.

"Our flying time is about four hours to reach the airport and then drive home, so I'd say you'll be in bed about two." He reached forward to flip several switches and noticed Michael watching. "I set the auto-pilot. You had your chance to fly, but you wouldn't take it." His voice boomed in Michael's ears, making him wince. Sam must have noticed and reached over to adjust the volume. "That should be better," he grinned.

They talked for a while about life in general and what they enjoyed in their spare time. Michael began to yawn over Ohio and was asleep by the time they crossed into Kansas. He didn't wake up until they touched down in California.

"Thanks for the ride, Sam. Sorry I fell asleep on you," Michael said as they shook hands at the exit. "I wasn't kidding about that thing with your contract."

"Forget about it, everybody falls asleep listening to me."

"I'll let you know when the other event happens too. I need all the support I can get."

"You do that, because I don't want to miss it. Otherwise, I'll see you the next time you go for a ride."

Chapter 10

The next day was hectic. He had to prepare a report for NASA about the tests, change the contract for Sam, organize a funeral for his father, and he wanted to work on the time-travel situation.

His first call was to the company's legal department to change the contract with Sam. The lawyer assured him there would not be a problem. Once that was done, he went down to the 'lab' to work on the report to NASA with Randal. The man was meticulous about details to the point of frustration, but he needed to be included in the process.

They compared notes and discussed any seen or suspected problems. When they were both satisfied, they began to write the report. The first few pages went well and Michael sensed they might finish before noon. A hopeful thought which was too good to be true. Randal wanted to put all the thousands of electronic readings and feedback data into the report and Michael didn't.

"I'm not hiding anything, but I just don't think our results are relevant to them. All they want to know is that the program works." He slammed his hand on the desk and stood up.

"With respect sir, I disagree," Randal spoke calmly. "I'd want to know everything, so I could be certain of the test results. Maybe that makes me a fuss-budget, but I don't like surprises. I'd think if they were any good, they'd say the same thing. We could be lying about the testing and how would they know?"

"I don't disagree with you in principle, but this is not really part of their probe. They can have the broader picture and be satisfied. The minute details of the program and the testing aren't any of their business. This is after-all a proprietary program and they don't need to see the code." He was angry that his technician would suggest otherwise.

"We aren't giving them the program, that's not what I'm suggesting. If they don't have all the details about the tests though, how are they going to know if something is wrong when the probe is in space?"

Michael considered the question. Randal was right. His need for secrecy was clouding his judgment. He was determined to keep his work secret, even if that meant NASA scrapped the probe. He'd lose millions in fines and probably suffer a lawsuit, but nobody else was going to know about time travel. Resigned to meeting the problem halfway, he sighed.

"I won't let them view the program; not ever, but you and I can be there if a problem occurs. That's the best I'll do, Randal. We give them all the details you want about the testing, but the actual program remains off limits." He sat down daring the technician to object.

"That's all I was suggesting Mr. Eldridge. They can review all the test data without having access to the code." He was shaking -- badly -- and his hands seemed to be constantly scratching at his head.

'I shouldn't have been so angry,' Michael thought. *'Too bad, this is my life work and I'm not about to let some ham-handed flunky in Florida tinker around with the program to fit their idea of communication. I'll probably need to dumb down the process for them, so they won't be tempted to touch or change the code. If they do, I'll own them.'*

"Okay Randal, let's finish this and send the report away. They can let me know if they need more information."

All things went well for the next three hours. Randal was happy. Michael thanked him and went for a late lunch. When he returned to the office, Heather was waiting.

"How was your weekend, Miss Sykes?" Michael asked brightly as he stepped off the elevator and saw her.

"I would have had more fun shopping in New York, but I satisfied that bug on Rodeo Drive instead."

"Have a seat and I'll be right with you," Michael said and shut the door behind her. He turned to his secretary. "Would you please contact Parker's Funeral home and work out details for a funeral please. My father passed away on the weekend and I'm up to my neck in preparations for the Mars project. Nothing fancy, I'll go pick out a casket later and I don't think there are many of his friends still around. Maybe a note in the papers would help find them, but I wouldn't expect more than a hundred people. If there are any problems you can interrupt us." He smiled, partly to say thanks and partially because of the expression of shock on Christen's face. "Don't worry, I'm fine," he added to soften the horrible news.

Striding into the office, he took his seat behind the desk. Heather was wearing a short gray skirt with a white blouse that did nothing to hide her figure.

His eyes moved to her face and her expression told him he'd been caught looking at the goods. He felt the fiery blush exploding from the collar of his shirt.

"Did you like what you saw?" She cooed.

"I'm not sure that's appropriate work attire, Miss Sykes. I ought to send you home to change." His voice was dripping with desire.

"We could go together." Her tongue licked her lips and he wanted her.

"No, you must stop that; there's something I have to tell you." His voice was sharper than he intended and his words hurt her feelings. For a moment, he wanted to stand up and give her a hug, begging her to forgive him, but she had to know the truth. "I took my father with me to New York. After seeing the awful way he was being treated in that nursing home, I thought he'd enjoy a weekend away. I was planning to move him out of there, but that's not the biggest reason he went with me. I was feeling guilty. We went to a ball game and had a great time, but I realized on the way that he was losing his memory, fast, but I can't remember the name of the disease. Anyway, to make a long story short, he passed away in New York." He'd been watching Heather's face and saw the horror and sadness grow as he told the story. There was just no easy way to tell someone about a death, he realized.

"Oh Michael, I'm so sorry for you, but you don't seem too broken up about his death," she gasped and came around the desk to give him a hug. "Is there anything I can do to help? I'm sorry I acted so slutty just now, I didn't know. I met him once at your old house, when we were kids, and he seemed nice to me. You poor man, how are you really doing?" She hugged him again and kissed his cheek. There were tears in her eyes when she stood up and went back to the chair.

"I'm fine, now, but that was quite a shock when I found him. I was probably a mess, before Sam saved me from shutting down completely. He's my pilot. If he hadn't been there, I think I'd still be curled up in a ball." Remembering the moment he'd found his father brought a fresh tear to his eyes.

"Christen is probably looking after most of the details for the funeral so I'll team up with her. Is there anyone in particular that you can think of who might want to be at the funeral?"

Michael shook his head. "I don't remember any of my parents' friends, is that normal? Billy's parents, but I'd say they were more acquaintances. They didn't socialize with my parents. Uncle Bernie, but there's nobody else I can think of who'd come. Christen is going to put a note in the papers letting everyone know the date of the funeral."

"Oh that is sad, poor man." She seemed genuinely concerned, which made him realize he wasn't showing any signs of sadness.

"What did you want to see me about?" He finally asked.

"I just wanted to see you and try to tease you into bed, but that all seems so tacky now. I'm so embarrassed." She blushed.

"Maybe later," Michael winked and smiled. She stood, pulled the short skirt down an inch, and walked out of the office. He watched her go, admiring what the skirt tried to hide. She stopped to talk with his secretary for a second before stepping over to the elevator. Her face turned to him as the elevator doors opened and she winked before stepping into the car.

Billy almost trampled her as he came out of the elevator. He glanced over his shoulder at her body and then entered Michael's office. Neither man noticed Christen's look of frustration and distain at their attitude.

"How'd it go?" He asked, and flopped into the chair in front of the desk.

"Excellent, but my Dad died while we were in New York."

"Oh shit, sorry to hear that man. Is there anything I can do for you?" His whole attitude changed. Sitting up straight with real concern on his face, Billy became human.

"Naw, the women are taking care of everything," He nodded to indicate Christen and Heather. "The tests were perfect, Randal is finishing up the report to NASA, and I'm going to work on my personal project for the next few days." He leaned back in his chair, feeling guilty for putting work first, again.

"Your Dad was great. I remember those water pistols he gave us and then chased us with the hose. I've never been so wet in all my life." He was smiling and shaking his head. "My Mom tore a strip off me when I got home too. She said she was going to phone your Dad and tell him what she thought of soaking her boy."

Michael laughed at the thought of Billy's Mom yelling at his Dad. The woman was five feet tall in her shoes while his father was six feet and outweighed her by a hundred pounds. "Her chasing my Dad would've been funny to see, but I don't think she ever called. At least Dad never said anything that I can remember."

"No, she was always saying things like that, but never did them. I'm sorry your Dad's gone Michael, I really am."

"I know, but he had a good life and we got to share a ball game. He was happier than I've seen him in years." The mood in the room had turned gloomy.

"So the Mars project is finished then," Billy was trying to change the subject. His discomfort showed on his face.

"Well sort of. Randal and I are supposed to be on site in Florida for the mission in case something happens with the software, but otherwise we're finished."

"Good, I'll send off the invoice, but I don't remember having you or Randal there for the mission as part of the original deal. Is that going to be some sort of cost over-run?"

Michael frowned. "We could probably get away with charging extra, but no. They want access to my program and I'm not willing to allow that to happen. The technicians they have down there could easily figure what else the software can do, but as long as I retain the copyright, they need us. This is my life's work, Billy and I'm not letting anyone else see that time travel is possible."

"That's fine, I just wanted to know." His gaze dropped to his hands for a second. "Does this mean you're going to try your personal journey soon?" His face was pale and taut when he looked up.

"I've got a couple of days before they launch the probe. Randal could be there for that and then come back, but I don't need to be anywhere for the next few months. That should give me plenty of time to work out the last kinks and then go. We've got that contract with the D.O.D. to finish, and a few smaller ones. There's nothing that needs my attention for now."

Billy turned pale.

"I've made some arrangements to take care of everyone here, and you'll be running the company." Billy's face transformed to shock.

"I told you I don't have any computer sense and my management skills are nil. The best I can say about me is that I'm a good salesman, but that means I'm decent with words and nothing more. You need to reconsider letting me run this place or else it'll be destroyed in no time." His hands gestured wildly as he spoke and his face reddened more with each word.

"Calm down and relax," Michael said softly. "You are the best person to run the business simply because you are a good salesman. Everything I do here is about selling me, what we do and keeping people focused on their tasks. I'm always selling, Billy, and you can too, but there's nothing to worry about because I'm not going anywhere anytime soon."

"You better not." Billy stood suddenly. "I need to go see if I can help with the funeral." He left and closed the door.

Hours passed as Michael sketched and scratched on a pad, trying to figure out how to adapt the cell phone to communicate between the past and present. The problem was pushing the limits even of his brain, but he wasn't prepared to give up. Growing darkness and his rumbling stomach made him aware of the time. He checked his watch to verify and put the sheets of paper in his briefcase to take home, so he could continue into the night.

Heather was coming out of the elevator as he opened his office door. Christen had gone for the day and for a second he wondered why she hadn't said good-bye -- normally she did. Tossing the thought aside, he smiled at the beautiful redhead swaying her hips toward him.

"Hello," he said warmly.

"Hi," she smiled back. "I tried a couple of times to call you, but they went straight to voicemail. Christen must have given you some privacy before she left." She wrapped her arms around his waist and stretched up to kiss his lips.

He smelled her perfume and felt her warmth against his chest. The excitement in his stomach immediately went lower. *'I want to be with her, but I don't really have time for distractions.'*

"Sweetheart," he began with a sigh as they broke apart. "You don't know how much I want to spend time with you, but my days are numbered if I'm going to get my project finished. We can go out for dinner, but I really do need to work after that...I'm sorry." They were standing in front of the elevators, waiting for the car to arrive.

She didn't smile and he could see what he thought was disappointment in her eyes. Her delicate hand reached out and took his as she stretched up once more to kiss his cheek.

"I'll give you tonight and maybe tomorrow night, but if we can't be together by the weekend, buster, you're going to be in big trouble." Her lips pouted, but there was a sparkle of mischief in her eyes.

"Deal," he said as the doors opened on the elevator. They entered and rode the car down to the lobby, staring into each other's eyes.

They stepped out together on the main floor. She let go of his hand, turning toward the exit to the multi-level parking garage. He watched her as she went two steps stopped and turned back.

"Your Dad's funeral is all organized by the way. I'll tell you all the details tomorrow, but the funeral home really needs to know when he'll be attending." Her face was stone and her eyes angry before she turned toward the exit once more.

'Shit,' he mentally slapped his forehead. *'I forgot all about the funeral. What kind of son am I? Burying myself in work and completely forgetting about my Dad. I'll have to do something nice*

84

for Heather and Christen to thank them somehow.' "Sorry Dad," he said softly as he climbed into the limo.

The car started to move as Michael pulled the pad out of the briefcase. He knew he was passionate about time travel, but that's how he'd been since Joe disappeared. Finally being able to realize his dream was too close to forget now; he had to be obsessed more than ever.

He scribbled out questions on the pad as they occurred to him. What will I look like when I get to the past -- visible or invisible? How do I test the above question before I go? Will the communicator work and what kind of tests can I run? Does my just being in the past, -- visible or invisible, -- alter history? The reality is that I might see something I shouldn't. If I'm trapped in the past, does that change this present?

His pen stopped above the paper as he stared out the window. Being stuck in the past would certainly change this present. I probably wouldn't be around to make the time machine and if I don't make the time machine, I won't go back in time. What a vicious circle. The rest of these things I think I can figure out except the one about something I don't want to know.

Maybe Joe hadn't just disappeared -- that wasn't the right word anyway. Nobody was there to see anything, so he might have run away or been kidnapped. The police took two days before they searched in the storm drain. Maybe he'd drowned and the rats got him. The problem was maybe he ran away because Billy and I left him to go in the drain alone. He likely thought his friends didn't care about him anymore.

If that's why he disappeared and I stop him from running away, everyone's history will change. How am I going to be the same person if I don't have a reason to build this time machine? Will I even become interested in the technology?

He set the pen down on his lap and rubbed his eyes. This was tougher than he ever thought. Simply showing up in the past might be all that was needed to alter the time line. He realized that having someone see him would definitely change history. The best thing would be to go back invisible. He didn't have any control over whether or how that happened, yet, but at least nobody would see him. He hoped they wouldn't be able to touch him either.

85

The limo pulled to a stop in front of his house. He tossed the pad into the briefcase and opened the door. "I won't need the car tomorrow, Tony, thanks, and I'll call you in a couple of days." He closed the door and went into the house.

Darkness outside seemed grayer than black, but in the house the gloom seemed alive; he thought for a second he heard breathing. A shudder ran down his spine as he remembered his childhood fear of the shadows. Moving along the hall in the dark, he entered his computer room. The brightness hurt his eyes when he turned on the overhead light, and sat at the desk. He set up a magnifying glass on a swivel arm to start working on the cell phone he'd torn apart in his office.

Changing the circuits was easy, but reprogramming the phone to communicate with the computer was harder. He was awake until two in the morning before both machines could say hello. The principle was the same as the probe talking to earth in real time. All he had to do was convince both pieces of machinery they were in the same second.

A radio signal travels at the speed of light, which is roughly one hundred eighty-six thousand miles per second. His phone needed to send a signal from thirty years in the past and make the computer believe he was calling from this time and bring him home. Easy, but if he miscalculated by one second or even one foot, he'd be stuck there.

His eyes burned as he flipped off the light and crossed the hall to his bedroom. The morning was too close and he had many calculations to do. He closed his eyes and remembered being a kid again with Joe and Billy.

Chapter 11

After making coffee, Michael shuffled toward the hall with a full cup in one hand and a stale bagel in the other. He was wearing a robe, untied, his slippers, and briefs. The house felt warm for September. Bright sunshine streamed in from the front windows eliminating many of the shadows in the hall.

Shadows are evil, his mind said. *'Ghost stories aren't real,'* he thought back. He turned to look at the living room. There was a dark shadow on the floor cast by the sofa closest to him. This one seemed darker than the shadow from the other sofa. The blackness seemed to move like there was something alive within the gloom. He blinked and whatever he thought he saw was gone. His mind wondered if he was going crazy.

Turning toward the computer room, he opened the door. The colored lights from the computer greeted him, but a shadow suddenly moved across them. His hand reached around the doorframe and flipped on the light. Everything seemed normal, but a dark foreboding slunk into his mind.

The fears from his childhood had found him. He knew there was nothing living in shadows waiting to eat the unsuspecting, but some beliefs never go away. He'd grown up and beyond the grasp of the evil spirits. Cold fingers ran across his chest making him tremble and he set the coffee and bagel on the desk, so he could tie up the robe.

Sitting on the chair, he thought about time -- not the travel, just the idea of time. A smile formed as he chewed the last of the bagel. Here he was, a man close to forty years old, and he still believed in ghosts and evil spirits. Time doesn't change anything: we just get older, but we're still kids inside. The thought occurred to him that his program was going to alter the future.

"What if somebody years from now figures out how to do what I'm going to do and uses that knowledge to go back in time? Those might not be evil spirits; maybe they're people from the future going back to the past. He reached out toward the coffee cup. The hand was shaky, forcing him to use both hands to steady the mug toward his lips.

"Anybody in the past who sees me might think I'm a ghost or a spirit; they'd be afraid of me. I wouldn't be able to change anything, even if I wanted. Do I want other people going back in time?" He had a vision of a future world ever shifting and evolving as humans flew through time and changed history. People disappeared, fortunes evaporated, buildings and vehicles were altered as the past and the people who made the discoveries were eliminated. He frowned. If everyone had access to the past, they could go back and make anyone they had a beef with vanish. They could change whatever they wanted at will. Chaos would be the new normal.

"Once I'm done, all my equipment and all my notes are going to be gone for good. If I must, I'll spend the rest of my life making sure no one else develops the technology to time travel."

He took one more sip of coffee and bent to the task of figuring out to the last second what time he wanted. His watch, when he looked, said twelve-thirty. He'd been absorbed in the calculations for over three hours. He stretched, and looked at the computer. '*I could have made you do the work. Well, let's see if I'm right.*' His fingers flew over the keyboard, punching information into the machine. The answer appeared on the screen in less than two minutes. One glance at the response compared to what he'd slaved over for three hours told him he was correct.

"I'll never doubt you again," he said with respect to the machine. "Now I need to figure out a way to make sure you know what to expect when you get the phone call from the past." He activated the phone and typed a few lines of code into the computer. The words appeared on the screen, 'signal detected'. "How do I tell you to look thirty years into the past to find that same signal?"

His fingers played with the empty coffee cup until he decided to get a refill. Leaving the converted bedroom, he walked down the hall toward the kitchen. The shadows in the living room had shifted, but he still felt suspicious of them. Cup filled, he glanced out the windows at the hills.

Houses sparkled in the sunlight. Sparks winked off windshields on cars traveling along streets and highways up and down the valley. Picking out one particular car among the thousands was impossible. He'd have to use binoculars to pick out just one of them to follow.

The binoculars worked like his program, zooming in or warping time to close the distance between two points. His program worked for certain, but he didn't have a way to test the communicator. Then he thought, if he could enter a code that --.

He ran down the hall. One slipper threatened to come off, but he managed to get to his desk with both feet covered. He typed code into the computer, telling the machine to call the phone one minute before he raced into the room and sat down.

As soon as his finger hit enter, the communicator began ringing. He pressed answer and heard the tone, not unlike a fax machine. The future had contacted him. With a shout of glee, he jumped up and dashed out to the living room. His excitement was overwhelming. Shouting and flapping his arms like a giant bird, he spun and laughed until he couldn't breathe and fell on the floor.

His elation was as intense as the pain of defeat when he realized that all he'd done was have one machine call another. *'The computer sent the message to the phone, but that doesn't prove anything,'* his mind whispered. *'You know the only way to prove your system works is to go back in time. Anything you tell the computer to do is going to happen in the future.'*

He knew his mind was right. The computer could just be sending the signal in the present. There was no way he could...

An unknown moment in the future, some time and place he couldn't know anything about. He pushed himself off the floor and returned more slowly to the computer room, his mind racing to put all the details in order. He typed the proper commands, telling the computer to contact the phone in six days from now and pressed enter. Once that was done, he called Sam and told him to ready the plane for a trip on Tuesday.

"Where are we going?" Sam asked.

"Surprise me, I need a break, and anyplace will do."

"Anyplace," Sam's voice seemed fascinated.

"Well, I'm not crazy about Russia if that's what you were thinking, but anyplace I can stay in a hotel and get decent food will be fine. Just don't tell me where we're going until we take off."

"Okay, I'll see you at the airport. What time do you want to leave?"

"Five in the morning, I want to be there for supper."

"Anyone else going with us?"

Michael thought about taking Heather. She'd enjoy a few days away, and he could become more of a human being around women. He sensed in his heart that would be the right thing to do, but his mind didn't want any interruptions.

"No, just you and me."

"Done," Sam said happily and hung up.

'The computer has to find me or I've failed. This has to work.' He got dressed, called the funeral home to find out about his father, and drove to the office. Heather met him at the desk in the lobby.

"Your Dad's funeral is Monday afternoon." Her words were sharp, filled with controlled anger. "Christen and I tracked down a couple of family members of your Mom, but there's nobody left on your father's side. One friend of his who served in the army with him is coming, but that's all. Everybody else will be your friends.

There's a service at the funeral home and then a drive to the cemetery. You'll need to say a few words followed by a reception." She seemed angrier if that was possible.

"I'm so glad you did this for me and I'll make it up to you somehow. Parker's told me this morning, his body will arrive tomorrow." He would have said more, but she stormed off. She didn't even say you're welcome. His life suddenly seemed to be a roller coaster speeding down an endless slope with people he cared about being torn from the car to disappear into the surrounding clouds.

• • •

He didn't go near the office or answer his telephone before the funeral. The morning of the service, Michael took his time dressing, and then spent two hours thinking about what he wanted to say. There were many special memories, but none of them seemed endearing. His father was not a warm person, rarely giving Michael a hug. He was quick-tempered, but never abusive. The man was strong, smart, and always sensible.

"He never took a risk, never had a great loss in his life until Mom died; the man always stayed in the middle. He didn't cry," Michael wondered aloud. "A tear or two maybe, but he did change after her funeral. Quieter, if that was possible -- he hardly ever spoke more than ten words in a sentence at one time."

Michael put the pen down and looked out the window at the valley. Peaceful, serene, from here he could forget about the world and all of his troubles. His father had been strict, but always a fair man when he dealt with Michael. He'd never used a harsh word with his son and never hit him, not even when the boy broke his favorite fishing rod. Dad just said, "Be more careful with other people's things, boy. Now help me fix this."

"How am I supposed to talk about a man who never said anything? Good man, but he was very quiet. What the hell kind of a eulogy is that?"

At two o'clock, he entered the funeral chapel, taking a seat in the front row. He recognized his Mom's brother from Pittsburgh, but none of the other ten people in attendance, except Heather, Billy, Sam, and Christen. A minister stood up at the front of the chapel to say a few words from the Bible about being reborn and the end of days. Michael wasn't really listening -- the man could have been giving the winning lottery numbers or calling a bingo game. He was still trying to find something nice to say about his father. The minister finished speaking and introduced Michael as the next speaker.

He went up to the podium while pulling a sheet of paper from the inside pocket of his suit jacket. The page was folded in half on the long side. He unfolded the paper, and stared down at the blank sheet.

'My Dad's life was a blank,' he thought as his panic rose. *'I'm standing up here in front of these people and I'm going to tell them my father had no redeeming qualities, nothing to remember him by.'* He closed his eyes and took a deep breath, hoping everyone would think he was nervous. Just before he opened his eyes again, the day at the ballpark flashed across his vision. Dad was smiling: the happiness was in his eyes as well as on his face. There was pride in that smile for his famous and successful son.

Michael opened his eyes and looked down at the blank sheet of paper. Words seemed to flood into his mind and appeared on the page.

"My father was quiet. He didn't say much, but he didn't need to. Everything could be seen in his expression. The last day we spent together, he had the biggest smile and the most pride in his eyes I'd ever seen. He could be warm, cold, funny, and sad without saying anything, but when he did speak; his words came from the heart and were to the point. Dad wasn't famous outside of our house, he wasn't rich, he couldn't sing and wasn't mechanically inclined. To me and those of us who knew him best, he was a good man. He could whistle like a bird or fix a broken heart with a few simple words. Dad never had much money, but to Mom and me, he was the whole world. We both lost a part of our lives when Mom died, but his piece was bigger. All that remains is the memory of him on that last day to use like a blanket to keep me warm and safe. I'm going to miss him every day for the rest of my life." A tear ran down his cheek landing on the piece of paper. Michael folded and returned the page to his jacket while stepping down from the stage.

Nobody else wanted to speak, many in attendance were dabbing their eyes, so the minister said a few more words and suggested anyone wishing to attend the graveside should follow the hearse.

There were only two-cars in the procession out to the cemetery. Seven people, Michael, Billy, Sam, Heather, Christen, the minister and his uncle from Pittsburgh stood next to the gaping hole in the ground while the minister mumbled some words of prayer. As soon as the service ended, Michael asked everyone back to the funeral home for refreshments.

"Uncle Bernie," Michael suddenly remembered his name. "I almost didn't recognize you. Dad would be happy to see you again after all these years. I'm sorry we had to meet like this, but..." They shook hands, smiling.

"I talked to your Dad on a regular basis after Irene, your Mom, died. He talked about you all the time, said you were the best thing he ever did. You're a hell of a success, Michael, he was very proud of you." There was sincere emotion in the older man's voice.

Silence while Michael tried to swallow the lump in his throat. "Thanks Uncle Bernie, I didn't know. He didn't say much to me."

"Yeah, I could never understand why my sister married him, but they always seemed happy together. They're probably together again." He glanced at the ceiling, to finish the thought.

"I hope so, have something to eat. How long are you here? I'd like to hear about my parents some more."

"My plane leaves at five this afternoon, I'm sorry, but if you get to Pittsburgh look me up. I've got some excellent Scotch in my cupboard. We can get quietly drunk and talk about old times." He seemed sad as he turned away. Michael sensed that if he didn't talk to the old man soon he'd miss the chance to find out what his parents were really like.

Chapter 12

The black limo was idling ten steps from his front door Tuesday morning as Michael left the house. Chrome reflected the light over the door; otherwise, the car was invisible. The color blended completely into the surrounding blackness of the early morning.

He had a small suitcase in one hand, his briefcase in the other. The driver accepted both before Michael sat in the backseat and closed the door. A forty-minute ride along deserted streets brought him to the stairs leading to the corporate jet. Sam waited beside them.

"All ready?" His rumbling voice was clear above the sounds of the airport.

"I have four days to rest and relax, and then I'm required to be back here for the launch of the Mars probe. You better be sure this is a nice place Sam," Michael shouted and climbed the stairs. Both men sat in the cockpit as the jet climbed into the air fifteen minutes later.

The sun peeked over the horizon as the plane banked, flying into the eastern sky. Michael listened to the communication between Sam and the control tower, but nothing made any sense. Curiosity finally forced Michael to find out their destination.

"Want to tell me where we're going?"

"Nope, you said to surprise you so that's what I'm doing." The big man turned his head and smiled.

"Okay, but if there isn't a hotel you're fired." Michael grinned back.

"What ya been up to the last few days?" Sam changed the subject.

"I finished the communicator and this trip is part of the test. Since there was no way to know where I would be, the computer has to find the signal. If that works, there shouldn't be a problem finding me in the past."

Sam's head snapped around and he gave Michael a worried stare. "All the computer needs to do is scan the whole world back through time until it comes across the signal. What could go wrong with that?" His tone was sarcastic. Michael heard the tone.

"That's the simple process, but obviously there's more to the theory than that, Sam." He focused out through the windshield at the brightening dawn. "Time is relative to where you are in that moment." He struggled to keep the explanation as simple as possible. "The light from the Sun takes eight minutes to travel the ninety-three million miles to reach us, but we think light travels in an instant. Finding and traveling to that moment in time thirty years ago is really the same thing. All I'm doing is stepping from this point of time, to that one, not the whole of time in between." He glanced at Sam, but he could see the pilot was not getting a clear picture. "Look at the process as a short-cut between two points. Open a door and step into whatever time and place you want to be. I can't explain the idea any simpler than that because I can't. Einstein thought time worked that way and I proved that he was right."

"I believe you, but I'm still not convinced your system is safe. The part about getting there I can almost accept, but the returning is a little more difficult. All the machinery to send you is here so how does the computer bring you back?"

"Oh that," Michael smiled. "I worried about that in the beginning, but the other day I did a test with a coffee mug. Some part of the cup remained here and so will I. I'm not sure yet if my spirit or some other essence of me is what travels, but whatever goes will be easy to bring back."

"Yeah, I've seen that Star Trek show where their transporter malfunctions sometimes. I also saw that movie last year with the guy who tried to transport himself through time and his body got mixed up with a fly. I know you're smart, Michael, and I trust that you've thought of everything, but even if you missed one thing you might not come back." They were silent for about three seconds before Sam continued. "I can't find everything wrong with this plane when I do my pre-flight check and the mechanics that repair her can't find everything either. Each time we take off, there's up to a five-percent chance that something is dangerously wrong, which could kill us. A one-percent failure with what you're doing could mean you come back without a head or brain; at best, you return without a tooth. Have you considered what happens if you appear there and get run over by a bus?"

"Hmmm, I hadn't thought of that, Sam." His anger rose when people didn't trust him, but this time he let the slight pass. "I know what you're saying and I'm as concerned as everyone about this, but I'll be dead trying. Even if I fail, this one passion, this need to find out what happened to my friend has fueled my desire to make computers. If I chicken out now, I'll be the same as my father, never taking the big risk and regretting my failure for the rest of my life. There's nothing here to replace that guilt, or force me to stay, so I might as well go." He thought about how Heather would feel if he died. "I have to go back." His face tightened with determination.

● ● ●

The plane flew steadily toward the northeast, the rising sun behind them, and on Michael's left. Hours passed before the jet banked to the southeast. Turbulence made Michael nervous and each time the plane bounced, he checked to see how Sam reacted.

The big man was dozing in his seat, arms crossed over his chest. "Nothing to worry about unless a warning buzzer sounds, you might as well take a nap too," he mumbled.

Michael suddenly realized why his friends were concerned about his plans. They were unsure. None of them had all the information, nor could they grasp his need to find out what happened to Joe. All they saw was the risk and the result of failure, which would mean he died. Sam wasn't concerned about turbulence because he had enough experience to understand what was happening. No problem unless the wings fall off. Michael knew all the details and felt certain of success. He needed to give them more information. They likely wouldn't feel any better about losing him, but they might be a little happier if they understood the actual amount of risk.

Forty minutes later, the English coast disappeared below them and greater Europe loomed across the channel. Darkness was swiftly marching across the land beneath them as the plane turned gently to the south and he felt the power decrease in the engines. He'd flown enough times to know they were starting their descent. They would be landing in late evening by his watch.

Sam stirred in his seat, stretching and yawning. "Morning," he said.

"Morning, the day's almost over, now will you tell me where we're going?"

Sam's eyes glanced over the instruments and then out the windshield. He turned slightly in his seat to look at his boss. "I decided to give you a small holiday in the Riviera. You won't mind relaxing by the ocean nor spending a few hours in a casino, will you."

"I can do that at home. What makes the Riviera better?"

"You won't get to meet any royalty at home and the scenery here is some of the best in the world. There are two people on this flight and I know that at least half of them are interested in visiting this country. We'll have fun, Michael, if you just let it happen." His sly smile was infectious and Michael finally grinned too.

"Fine, but I'm not doing any hiking or swimming. I just want to relax. The computer is going to find me at seven o'clock California time tonight." He glanced at his watch. "That's..." he paused to make the calculation, but Sam beat him.

"Four in the morning tomorrow. You'll have plenty of time for a good supper, a night's sleep and the communicator can wake you up." A beeping sound accompanied a flashing red light and Sam straightened himself before gently gripping the yoke.

"What is that?"

"Nothing serious," He contacted the control tower in Paris and gave his call sign and destination. The controller acknowledged and gave Sam some numbers. Leaning forward, Sam changed a dial and flipped a switch.

"What was that all about?"

"Altitude and coordinates of the airport in Marseilles. We'll be landing there in thirty minutes. Monaco doesn't have an airport, so we're driving to the hotel." Sam adjusted the throttle and the plane slowed, dipping noticeably. He called the control tower in Marseilles.

Michael tuned out their banter and stared out the window. Lights dotted the ground below, a few clumps suggesting there might be a town or city around them. Large patches of darkness might be farmland stretching in all directions. He was amazed that people could live this close to farms -- in the states, there would be a lot more separation. Small moving lights suggested there might be cars on the roads cutting through the fields.

"We're about fifteen minutes to touch down. There's a car meeting us after customs that'll take us to the hotel. Quick shower and change before supper and then we can have a drink and relax," Sam said without turning away from the instruments in front of him.

"Sounds good to me." Michael tried to seem relaxed, but he could feel his stomach clenching with fear. The ground was coming up to meet them fast, or the light was playing tricks on his eyes. They could be diving straight into the ground for all he knew. The plane seemed to be flying level compared to the horizon, but he felt as if he was leaning forward. Thumping beneath them brought out a cold sweat until he realized the landing gear was being lowered. Moments later, the wheels touched the brightly lit runway and they slowed before pulling to a stop next to the terminal.

Michael breathed a sigh of relief and stepped into the passenger cabin to retrieve his suitcases. Forty minutes later, their limo stopped in front of a six-story Greek style hotel. The door attendant, dressed in Moroccan livery, including a fez, opened the door to the lobby.

Everything seemed to be happening in a rush as they were greeted at the desk and then whisked up to their suite on the fifth floor. Sam gave the porter a tip for carrying the bags and shut the door. Michael looked out the windows, taking a deep breath to relax. A clutter of brightly colored houses among multi-storied buildings stretched to the horizon on either side, lit by hundreds of street lamps, but straight ahead was the black body of the Mediterranean.

The massive lights of the harbor gleamed off boats of every size and description bobbing gently on the waves. Michael imagined them sailing one of those boats, how wonderful would that be. A fair breeze, salt spray on his face, no storms in sight, he almost wished he had a boat.

"When is this thing supposed to happen?" Sam asked behind him.

"What?" Michael hadn't heard clearly.

"When is the computer supposed to contact you?"

Michael looked at his watch. "You figured the call would be at four in the morning, which means if everything works we'll be hearing from the computer in about eight hours."

"No, what time are you supposed to get the call?"

"Seven tonight," Michael responded growing more confused.

"That's California time. On the plane, I was thinking as if we were at home. I hadn't added the nine hours of flying time. It's currently one-thirty in the morning here, so we have about an hour to eat and possibly take a short walk before you need to be back here. I'm taking a shower now." There were two bedrooms and Sam pulled his suitcase into the one on the left of the entrance door. Michael felt lost and dazed as he turned back to look out the window.

They'd flown all day while the world spun in the opposite direction. He didn't feel tired, but he was hungry. Room service had better be open still; he groaned.

Michael searched the night for anything that could be a radio tower and found none. Sam made a good choice with this place. There weren't any cell towers here, probably wouldn't be any for another ten years at least. He decided to make sure the phone was charged and ready.

He carried the two cases into the bedroom and set them on the bed. The room was large: a king-sized bed in the middle of one wall, a window looking out on the water and another to the right of the bed overlooking what Michael assumed was a bazaar. People would be milling about striped awnings, smoke from open cooking fires drifting skyward if this had been daytime.

Opening the smaller of the two cases, he found the phone, the power cable, and an adapter for the wall socket. He plugged everything together and turned on the phone. A frown pulled at his mouth.

Everything was ready, nothing else could be done until the appointed time, and then success or failure depended on the computer. For this to work, the computer has to find the signal and make contact. There weren't any communication towers in 1957, so this had to work.

"What are you waiting for?" Sam's voice made Michael jump. "Sorry Boss, I didn't mean to scare you." The pilot was standing in the doorway, dressed in a fresh set of casual pants and polo shirt. He was blushing at having startled Michael.

"No problem, Sam, I was just thinking about later. You did well picking this particular city. If the computer can find me here, there won't be a problem finding me in the past too." He smiled and then opened the large suitcase.

"I'll have a drink while you shower and change. There's a restaurant just down the street so we don't need to wander far to get something to eat."

"At this time of night? Are you sure they'll be open?"

"I called down to the desk to find out if there was a restaurant open and they assured me this place definitely stayed open all night. We can call down for room service, but you know that's going to take at least an hour."

"Screw that, Sam, I'm starving already. I'll be five minutes and then we can go."

He took ten, but eventually, Michael emerged from the bedroom in a pair of pants and pullover shirt. Sam gulped the last of his drink and they went out to find the elevator.

The restaurant was brightly lit, warm, with smoke hanging thick in the air, making Michael cough. Rough planks for walls, ceilings either too dirty or too high to see, and three blade propeller fans lifeless in the dense white clouds above the tables. Light bulbs dangled in a bunch from the centre of each fan. Locals hunched or lounged at tables and chairs, filling the space completely, leaving little room for the waiters to travel. Their eyes turned to stare at the men entering the restaurant. A tall, thin, man in a black suit and white shirt met them at the door. Michael thought for a second that Vincent Price had found a new career.

"Welcome, gentlemen, may I have your name for the reservation?" His English was decent, but there was a heavy Arabic accent.

Sam gave them the name "Eldridge" and the Maître d' ran his index finger down the list of names on a sheet of paper. His head snapped up and a very bright wide smile covered his face.

"Ah yes, I should have recognized Mr. Eldridge. Your table is ready, please follow me." Either because the Americans were wider than the headwaiter or maybe because he knew how to weave through the tables, but Sam and Michael took a full twenty seconds to catch up. The Maître d' seemed impatient when they finally reached the table.

"I'll fetch a waiter, gentlemen, please relax, and enjoy our hospitality." He bowed and smiled, but his words sounded clipped and angry. Turning with a flourish, he snapped his fingers and left the table. There was a strong smell of curry in the air, which stung their eyes.

"Did you make the reservation? I'm starving and the longer we sit here the worse my stomach rumbles. What are you hungry for, Sam?"

"No, I didn't make any reservations, but maybe the hotel did when I called down. You're right about the smell in here making me hungry, but there's enough spice in the air to make even plain macaroni taste like curry I bet." He pulled a handkerchief out of his pocket and dabbed his watering eyes.

A waiter appeared beside their table carrying a tray with two glasses of water and menus tucked under one arm. His greying hair accented by the clean white shirt, black vest, and pants, he set a glass of water in front of each man.

"Welcome, my name is Andre." His voice was strong and even, at odds with his aged appearance. The tray disappeared from his hands and he handed them a menu each. "Please take a moment to read our

99

fine list of food, and is there anything I might bring you to drink?" There was no smile and his words were a monotone.

"I'll have a beer," Sam said as he squinted at the menu and dabbed at the tears in his eyes.

"I'll have a beer, too," Michael added.

When Andre left to fetch the drinks, Sam dropped the menu.

"Can you understand any of these dishes? What the hell is couscous?"

Michael was forced to hold a hand over his mouth or spit the sip of water on Sam. Once he'd recovered, he laughed.

"It's a lot like rice, but different. That's all I know, so don't ask me any more questions. I'm sure they've had people in here before asking for steaks or burgers, maybe Andre will be able to recommend something." He shook his head while squinting at his own menu.

"Nice cold beer for gentlemen," Andre set the sweating bottles on the table and then took two glasses off the tray. "Have you decided on the food?" The enthusiasm in his words had elevated slightly compared to a moment ago.

"I'd like a steak, but I don't know what it's called on the menu." Sam appeared to be crying as the tears streamed down his cheeks.

Andre paid no attention to the tears. "We say boeuf and how would you like your meat cooked, sir?"

"Rare, but I don't want any of whatever spice is floating around in this room." He dabbed at his face.

"Very well sir, and for you sir," there was a slight bow and no change of expression.

"I'd like to try some chicken. Can you recommend a dish?"

"If the kind sir will allow me to make the decision, I will bring you a very nice food which you will enjoy." A tiny twitch at the corners of his mouth was the only indication that Andre smiled. He gathered the menus and left the table.

"Funny duck," Sam bobbed his head toward the back of the room.

"He seems okay, but you'd think he could smile once in a while. Maybe they're just that way with foreigners." Michael glanced around the room.

There seemed to be only men in the restaurant, locals mostly. He guessed that from their clothes, wool coats, and pants. There was one other foreigner in the restaurant: a man seated at a corner table across from them, dressed in a light-blue collared shirt open at the neck. His grey hair seemed to glow in the smoky-yellow light of the restaurant. Metal-rimmed glasses halfway down the bridge of his nose gave him an air of being engrossed in the book before him. Some of the tables had emptied; men were leaving in two's and three's.

Michael shrugged. He wasn't here to make friends.

"Explain to me again how you figured out what time the computer will contact my phone?"

Sam dabbed at his eyes. "We left at five this morning, California time, which is two o'clock here. The trip took us about eleven hours. There's a nine-hour difference between here and California, which means that seven at night there is four in the morning here, but I forgot the travel time. I screwed up earlier."

"No problem as long as I get back to the room in time."

"Doesn't the spice or smoke in the room bother your eyes?" Sam sounded as if he had a cold.

"No, not yet anyway, but why don't you go outside for a minute. I'm sure they'll take another five minutes to make our food."

Sam didn't hesitate and made his way toward the exit. The tall man by the door watched him leave. Andre instantly appeared beside the table.

"Is something wrong with your friend, sir?" Genuine concern etched his face. His hands clasped in front of his chest, clenched and unclenched in distress.

"His eyes are bothering him. I don't think he can take the smoke in the air."

"Many apologies' sir, I will try to make more comfortable for you." He disappeared again before Michael could say anything further. This time, he watched the waiter weave through the tables and speak to the maître d'. Hand gestures from both men and pointing in the direction of Michael's table suggested they were discussing a way to add more ventilation. They could be trying to figure out how to get rid of them too.

Sam came back to the table as Andre raced toward the kitchen area of the restaurant. There were only a few customers left in the room. The maître d' was glaring at Michael. Sam sat across the table and his red eyes were at least dry.

"Did the fresh air help?" He was starting to get a weird feeling about this place. There were a few patrons moving toward the exit.

"Yeah, but it still stinks in here. What's with the guy at the door? My French is a little rusty, but I caught a few words when I came in. He and the waiter were talking about turning on the furnace or something. I couldn't make out everything, but don't they realize there's enough heat in here already?"

Michael smiled, knowing they had been talking about ventilation. As if on command, the rattle of fans overhead became loud enough to drown out the voices in the room. Smoke, thick, and acrid, hanging near the ceiling, began to move and swirl. Soon, the cloud became wispy and individual smokers could be picked out of the crowd as their cigarette smoke drifted upward.

"They were talking about turning on the ventilation, Sam. I told Andre that we'd appreciate if they could reduce the smoke. The locals don't seem to mind, which is why the maître d' and the rest of the patrons seem upset. Oh well, just another pair of rich Americans being pushy, but their system seems to work." Michael nodded at the clearing air. "You should be fine now, and hopefully, their food is good too."

Andre appeared, juggling two enormous plates of food, one on each hand, as he weaved from the kitchen to their table. He set them down, produced a set of utensils for each man, and stepped back.

"How you say...dig in boys." There was an actual smile on his face.

The steak on Sam's plate was still sizzling alongside a pile of couscous, peppers and slices of what could have been fruit. Michael's plate was heaped with rice, diced chicken chunks and covered with a tomato sauce. The aroma was magnificent.

He stabbed his fork into the pile of rice, spearing a chunk of chicken drenched in the tomato sauce. Blowing gently to cool the food before biting, he noticed Andre still standing beside the table wringing his hands, a worried expression on his face.

Michael pushed the food into his mouth. Instantly, flavors of multiple spices leaped onto his taste buds. Sweet, sour, spicy hot and general deliciousness assaulted his palate. He'd never had anything so wonderful. A huge smile spread across his face as he looked up at Andre.

"This is the best chicken I've ever had, Andre. Thank you for your choice and tell the chef he's the best in the world." The little man's face beamed with pride and relief. Michael glanced over at the tall man by the door and saw a smile on his face too.

"Yeah," Sam tried to speak around a mouthful of steak. "This is the greatest steak I've ever had outside of Houston. Thanks Andre and my thanks to the chef, but when you get a chance, could you bring some more beer please?"

They didn't speak again until their plates were empty. Sam dropped his utensils on the plate and belched with satisfaction. Michael sipped the last of his beer while staring at the only other customer in the place.

"Why would you come to a foreign country and sit in a restaurant reading a book?" Michael asked without taking his eyes off the grey-haired man.

"The book I can understand, reading is fine, but if you're going someplace like this a normal person would certainly take in the sights. He seems bored. I wonder how long he's been here. Maybe he's just not a good traveler."

"I don't know, he's probably bored, I'm getting bored too. Let's get out of here and see what there is to see in the dark." They dropped the equivalent of twenty American dollars on the table as a tip for Andre and Michael handed the maître d' another forty for the food.

"No Monsieur, this is too much." A genuinely pained expression pulled on the thin man's face.

"We appreciate the service and the great taste. Take out the cost of the food and the beer, and share the rest with the chef. Thank you, we really enjoyed ourselves."

The night sky seemed close enough to touch and yet endless as they stepped out of the warm restaurant onto the street. People of all shapes and sizes moved in a dance in both directions along the sidewalk, not unlike bees in a hive. Michael and Sam strode into the flow heading toward their hotel. Michael had trouble understanding how this many people could still be awake, never mind walking the streets.

The crowd thinned, allowing the two men to move along the sidewalk at their own pace. They walked down the next street in the direction of the harbor; both men enjoyed watching boats on the water, although there wouldn't be much to see at this time of night.

A major cross street stopped their progress at the corner. They had to wait for a break in the traffic before they could dash safely across to enter the main wharf on the other side. Michael glanced at his watch.

"We've got about an hour before I have to be back in the room. Let's see what's down here and then head back or you can stay and I'll join you later." He took a breath and gave voice to a question from the restaurant. "Where the hell are all these people coming from? Is there some kind of celebration going on we should know about?"

"Naw, I think it's just too hot for them to sleep so they wander the streets, but I'll check when we get back to the hotel, and I can't let you wander around alone. We can always come back later or check out the boats tomorrow." He chuckled. The thought of sitting alone on the dock didn't appeal to Michael either, but he didn't say anything to Sam.

Wandering up the hill toward the hotel, both men marveled at the culture around them. Michael admired the architecture. Every building was a different color, bright yellows, greens, reds, and blues thrown together in a mosaic of hues and tones.

"Did you notice anything strange in the restaurant?" Sam asked. Michael frowned.

"Yeah, but I just thought they were suspicious because we're Americans. You know how pushy we can be in foreign countries. Nobody seemed to care about the other foreigner, but when we sat down the locals started to leave."

"Maybe we should have been reading a book, but the locals leaving didn't bother me. I remembered some more of my high-school French. The Maître D' was telling Andre to deal with them and do as he was told." Michael heard the anger in Sam's voice.

"You're making more of this than the situation deserves, Sam. I'd asked Andre to do something about the ventilation because there was too much smoke in the air. Right after that, the little man went running into the back and the air conditioning or whatever started working. The man at the front was just telling Andre to deal with the problem."

"It sounded more than..." His words were cut off by a man's voice behind them.

"Gentlemen, might I have a word with you?"

Startled by the sound of English words coming from the dark, Michael turned to see who owned the voice. The man reading in the restaurant was standing there, along with a short swarthy male companion.

"What can we do for you?" Sam asked with a hint of suspicion and anger in his voice.

"Sorry to disturb you, my name is Richard Walker and this is Inspector Habbib from the Monaco State police." Richard had a haughty British accent to match his arrogant posture.

Michael glanced at Sam. The shocked expression seemed to match the way he felt.

"I'm not sure how we can help you, but we're at your service." Michael tried to appear calm, but being accosted by police in a foreign country can be upsetting.

"I work for British Intelligence, MI6 if you like. We have a few questions that we'd like to ask you. Please come with us, our car is just here at the end of the street." He held one hand out gesturing for them to precede, the other firmly holding and guiding Michael forward.

"Is this going to take long? I must be back in our room in less than an hour for an important phone call." Michael could feel panic rising in his stomach.

"Please be assured, gentlemen, we'll make every effort to keep this interview as brief as possible." Walker's voice was smooth and even. Habbib ran ahead to open the rear door of a marked police vehicle.

Sam, Michael, and Walker squeezed into the rear seat, Habbib jumped into the front passenger side and the driver sped forward. Michael imagined, from his crushed position in the middle of the back seat, that the driver was using three hands: one for the horn, one to steer and one on the gear lever. People on the streets dove out of the way of the speeding police vehicle. The car swerved and jerked around corners, at speeds, which threatened to cause a roll over.

The violent trip lasted five minutes according to Michael's watch, but seemed more like an hour. He glanced at the front of the car after stepping out of the back seat, searching for blood or other signs of impact. The hood and fenders were pristine.

Habbib led them into a Gothic style building and up a short flight of stairs. A cavernous room ahead was filled with desks and people in uniforms, some sitting, and some moving among the desks. Lights with speeding fans hung from high ceilings. A counter blocked access to the room. Michael guessed this was the duty room; an area for the regular officers to do their paperwork, but there seemed to be a lot of action for this time of night. To the left and right stretched long hallways with doors along both sides. The detective turned right and stopped at an open door in the middle of the hall. He raised his arm to indicate the men should enter.

"May I get you gentlemen anything...a glass of water?" Habbib asked from the doorway when the other three were seated. All declined and he took a chair at the left end of the table. Walker sat opposite, while Sam and Michael were on the long sides to his left and right respectively. The walls and floor were bare concrete.

"So what is this all about?" Michael demanded. "We didn't do anything wrong, did we?"

"On the contrary, Mr. Eldridge," Walker smiled for the first time. "This is about your work for NASA. There seems to be a group of," his voice trailed off and he sat back in the chair to consider what he would say next, his hands fidgeting with a pen. "There seems to be a group of criminals, shall we say, interested in your latest program for the Mars probe." His smile seemed fake to Michael, maybe because of the sternness in his eyes.

"My program, but that couldn't possibly do them any good, unless..." He looked across the table at Sam. Both men instantly knew what the other was thinking.

"Unless what, Mr. Eldridge?" Habbib wanted to know, his thick accent made the words hard to understand, clearly.

Michael hesitated. *'I'm obligated to respect the secrecy of my agreement with NASA. I don't know if I should tell them about the work I'm doing on the side. They'll think I'm crazy at the very least. If I tell them and they believe me what then?'* He took a deep breath while staring at Sam, hoping the man would understand and agree with whatever he said next.

"I won't bore you with the details, but essentially the program I designed for NASA allows the probe to communicate with Earth on an instantaneous basis. A radio signal from Mars takes up to twenty minutes to reach us. They didn't want to risk any problems because of that delay, so I created a program which effectively bends time." He stared hard at Walker, waiting for a reaction. None came, so he demanded. "Now Mr. Walker, tell me exactly what this has to do with the British government."

Walker smiled again, dropped the pen, and clasped his hands on the table. "I'm here on behalf of Her Majesty and the United States government. There are no American agents in this part of the world, so I was dispatched to help you. I saw you earlier in the restaurant. Some of the men in there at the time were, are, Soviet agents. That's all I knew then, my orders were to keep you safe. Inspector Habbib is a detective, but he's also a member of the Royal secret service here." He paused for a moment, thinking. "This program of yours can warp time; does that mean you could also travel through time?" A gleam in his eyes suggested he knew more than he was willing to acknowledge.

'That conclusion is too much of a leap for anyone to make without some sort of physics background. If he's for real, then my own government is leaking secrets or the British government is jumping to correct conclusions. Either way, how am I supposed to trust anyone now? I'm going to play dumb and see where this goes.'

"I don't know, but I'm sure somebody could try. There are just too many variables involved in time travel to make the effort worthwhile, Mr. Walker. Even criminals would understand the effects of altering time in the past on the people in the present, wouldn't they?" Michael could understand the lure of a criminal wanting a way to rob in the past and escape to the future. He'd never considered any uses for the program beyond his own.

"I don't know what contact you've ever had with the criminal element in your country, but my experience tells me they don't usually consider much beyond their own gain." Habbib spoke gently.

"There's no way they could steal it, is there?" Sam demanded.

"I suppose they could try to get a copy from the lab or from NASA, but having the code wouldn't do them any good without the correct..." Fear suddenly gripped his throat. Holy shit, I was just about to say the correct code and coordinates. They'd also need a computer, but they'd be able to steal one of those.

"What were you going to say?" Walker asked.

"The program for the probe wouldn't do them any good. I built that to communicate with Mars and nothing more. They would need to do some major reworking before they could use the program to jump through time." *I need to keep some of this to myself. I don't really know if I can trust these people. Especially since we only have their word that they're working for the US through Britain.*

"So, they would need you as well as the program," Walker finished the thought. He stood up and walked to the small window set high in the wall. "Now I understand why you need protection." His tone of voice sounded as if he'd finally put the last piece into the puzzle. "They only need to abduct you and force you to write them a program which will allow them to conduct criminal activity all across time." He turned back to Michael with a frown on his face.

Michael nodded. "What happens now? I still want to be in my room to receive that call."

"I don't think we can risk having you return to your rooms. We need to move you to a safe place at once. When you're ready to return to the United States, we can escort you to your plane. Then you're on your own until you land in the US."

"But I need to be in my room, if I miss this call there could be serious repercussions." Michael heard the whining in his voice, but didn't care. He had to be there when the computer called.

Walker shook his head. "This is for your safety, sir. We'll make certain that all of your belongings are retrieved and brought to you. I must insist that you let us do what we think is in your best interests."

Michael and Sam exchanged worried glances. Michael finally gave a resigned shrug and his anxiety evaporated. He wouldn't be there to answer the call and the computer wouldn't be able to find him. There's no way to know if his setup worked without doing all of this again in some other part of the world.

"How would they know I was coming here? Sam is the only person who knew where we were going, and I trust him completely." Anger now replaced his disappointment.

Walker shrugged. "You'd be surprised how easy it is to find out when and where someone is going. We were told to be ready if you arrived here. These criminals probably have people situated in the airport at which you filed the flight plan. Maybe there is someone here, but at any rate, they know where you are. My government was not specific about who the criminals are or how they found out about

108

your plans. As far as we're concerned, Mr. Eldridge, your safety is our top priority. We have our orders and there are no exceptions." He nodded at Habbib. "We'll take you to a safe house now and our people will collect your things. Don't worry, the hotel bill is already settled. Please gentlemen, we must go now."

Sam and Michael left the station between Walker and Habbib. The same driver took them careening through the streets of Monaco once more. Michael felt confident that anyone trying to follow them would have a terrible time, keeping up with this lunatic.

The tight cluster of buildings receded, giving way to more modern single-family homes.

"Wider streets, fewer people traveling on them and less traffic will give us an advantage over anyone trying to ambush us," Walker explained.

What, he doesn't think we've seen movies before? The idea of a safe house probably came from a Hollywood movie in the first place. He's likely going to tell us to keep away from the windows too.' Michael grinned at the thought.

"When we get inside, please stay away from the windows, and don't go outside. This place is owned by the British government. The neighbors are used to seeing foreigners coming and going so they aren't likely to notice us." Their driver lurched to a stop at the curb in front of a small bungalow. Many more plain houses filled the block. The sudden stop thrust all three men into the back of the front seats.

Once inside the house, decorated with Moroccan style furniture and plain white walls, Walker led them down the hall indicating the bedrooms and the bathroom.

"Habbib does the cooking, so I hope you like spicy food. I must stress what I'm about to say in the strongest terms, gentlemen. If in fact we are attacked, you will follow my directions to the letter. Bullets will be flying and I'm not willing to die just yet. If I'm obliged to worry about you two wandering off, I'll likely get all three of us killed. Have I made myself clear?" He stood at the end of the hall with his hands on his hips.

Sam and Michael meekly nodded their understanding. They sat nervously in the dim living room while Habbib and Walker clattered about in the kitchen. The only weapon they'd seen was strapped to the detective's hip, so they weren't feeling very secure.

"This is going to be hell, I'm sorry Boss." Sam moaned.

"Why, this isn't your fault, but I still need to get back to the States. The computer has already tried to contact me," Michael said while looking at his watch tension and concern gripping his voice. "This whole trip has been a bust, but worse yet, who could have leaked information about what we're doing?"

"I agree with Walker, bad guys with contacts everywhere. There's no point in worrying about that right now. We need to survive long enough to get back to the States. You can hire extra security then."

"Yeah, and all I have to do is pay them well enough to keep them loyal while living like a caged animal for the rest of my life." Michael frowned.

"We've made some coffee, anyone want a cup?" Walker asked from the kitchen doorway. Michael felt as if the British spy had been listening, but pushed the negative thought away. Less than a minute later, all four men were in the bright kitchen sipping the hot brew.

"Is there anything special I can make you for breakfast or will a typical American meal be sufficient?" Habbib seemed more like a mother hen at that moment. Michael smiled over the rim of his cup.

"That's fine with me, but do you know when our things will be here?"

"My men are clearing your hotel room at this moment. They'll come directly here -- with as much caution as they can implement," Habbib said with a slight grin and flourish of his hand. He seemed to Michael to be a man wanting only the best for them. His voice was gentle when he spoke and he always seemed to be smiling. "I expect they'll arrive in the next hour or less, but why are you so concerned about your belongings? Surely, there is nothing which you could not replace easily," The smile faltered. Michael could see his mind was connecting the dots. He knew he could replace everything in the bag, but not the cell phone. Michael's suspicions grew. The men keeping them 'safe' had to know more than they were letting on, but he didn't have a choice. He had to trust them. They might believe the phone was a gadget for another project.

"I left a valuable piece of technology in my room. The item wouldn't seem like much to you -- a circuit board with a light and a number pad, but the project I'm working on will fail without that part. You understand, don't you?"

Habbib glanced at Walker. Both men tried to hide their smiles. A sense of doom drove into Michael's gut like a cold steel fist. He knew from the glances they'd exchanged that the two men holding them 'safe' were in fact the criminals.

"So how is this going to work? You get the technology and threaten me or beat the code out of me so you can jump through time." His voice was full of accusation and hatred. He could see Sam jerk with surprise as the words came out.

"Oh please Mr. Eldridge, we are not animals. Our employers want the code and do not care how we obtain the information. We are more civilized men willing to make this ordeal painless, if possible. The lengths and means we must use to fulfill our obligation are entirely up to you." A cold smile appeared on Walker's face and froze Michael's soul.

"When your things arrive, you'll give us the code. Take as long as you like to write it out, but be assured we will be testing what you write. Once we hold a working copy, you'll be taken to the airport and will be free to leave." Habbib stood by the counter, twitching like a rat waiting for a piece of cheese.

"I don't remember every line. There's probably a thousand pages of code, how am I supposed to remember all that? If I had my computer, I'd simply print the program out for you. Trying to remember every line could take weeks." Michael could remember every line and every word he'd used in the program, but hoped they wouldn't know that about him. Forcing them to return him and Sam to the States where he could get help was their only chance of survival.

"We can sympathize with your problem, but we know a thing or two about you and your program. First, we know from magazine articles that you have an extraordinary memory, total recall of everything you've seen I think one editorial said. Second, you are the sort of person who has very strong attachments to people close to you. You lost a very good friend when you were younger and longed for a chance ever since to return through time to find out what happened to him." Walker's smile became colder. Michael waited for a forked tongue to flick between his lips. He silently swore never to give anyone an interview again. "What you must understand," Walker rose from the table and stood beside Michael. "If we take you back to your lab, Mr. Worthy stays here. So, either way we will get what we want. Oh, by the way, if you're thinking of giving us something that doesn't work, you might think again. Every time the program doesn't work, we'll remove a piece of your friend Sam. As I said, Mr. Eldridge, we will do what must be done. His ten fingers and toes will go first, then his feet and legs." He patted Michael on the cheek and left the house.

Sam gave Habbib an evil glare. A revolver appeared in the detective's hand, motioning Michael and Sam back into the living room.

"Relax, and remember there are at least four men outside with orders to shoot you both on sight." He shoved the gun back into his jacket.

"I certainly didn't see this coming. I'm sorry Sam."

"Don't worry; I'm sure there would have been someone else waiting for us wherever we went. All we can do now is co-operate and hope for the best." He shrugged, but Michael could tell from the determination in his eyes that he wouldn't just calmly wait.

He needed to figure out a way to get them out of there. Perhaps he could use the phone to get the computer to contact the real police. In the end, he'd give them what they want if that was the only choice between Sam and the program.

A magazine on the table caught his eye. A popular computer technology issue from six months earlier. One of the headlines on the cover was about his involvement in the Mars probe. He reached for the magazine and flipped to the article. Scanning through the words, he read about how he was developing a method of bending time. The journalist went on to outline how this would give NASA the ability to communicate instantly with the probe.

That was in the first-half page, but then the story became nasty. The journalist noted the reactions of many leading scientists stating that altering time was impossible. "Michael Eldridge is a computer hack and knows nothing about physics," declared a well-known physicist. Others were quoted as saying that the natural order of time will be altered if the communication were lost in space.

"Radio signals travel forever," a scientist stated. "Once this (signal) gets beyond our Solar system, other worlds will be affected and this will lead to untold disaster." The reporter summed up the story saying; "Michael Eldridge is dancing to a dangerous tune -- his own."

'*Well now I know where they got there information,*' he thought with an inward groan.

Two raps, a moment of silence followed by three raps on the door and two tall, swarthy men entered the house carrying suitcases. The dropped them on the floor and left the house.

Habbib stood in the kitchen doorway. He arched his eyebrows and indicated with a nod that Sam and Michael should retrieve their bags.

"Get settled and have a good night's sleep, we'll start when you wake up." His hand was inside the jacket as they picked up their luggage and headed past him to the bedrooms.

Michael shut his bedroom door. Setting the bags on the bed, he pulled open his suitcase. The altered phone was on top of his clothes, wires still attached. His eyes scanned the device quickly to make sure there wasn't any damage, before thumbing the switch to on.

The light blinked twice and then stayed lit. Did that mean the computer had tried and failed, or was the phone ready to make a call? He didn't know. He'd given the phone a number the computer could use like a name, and the computer had a similar number. He punched in the twelve digits for the machine in his house and waited. The light on the phone in his hand blinked twice and stayed on. This time, the blinking was immediately followed by a vibration in his hand.

His heart stopped. The computer was contacting him. He'd succeeded in making the contraption work across time and distance. '*Now, how do I tell the computer we're in trouble,*' he wondered?

Sinking onto the edge of the bed, he stared at the wall. He'd loaded tons of information into the computer, but how was he going to talk to his computer from here? Morse code would be easy, but he didn't know the language. Then another idea slowly became clear in his mind. Using the numbers for the letters of the alphabet, he carefully punched them into the phone to spell out a message.

'We are being held captive in Monaco send help at once.' The light blinked twice and remained steady. He was about to shut off the phone when he felt more vibrations in his hand and there were four beeps. The tones didn't mean anything to Michael until he pressed different numbers. He discovered the message was 'ASAP'. Leaving the phone on, he pushed the device deep inside his bag. The computer was already thinking ahead and searching for the signal. They were going to be rescued.

He sighed as he switched off the overhead light. Morning sunlight was already beating on the curtains. Their chances of being saved were better now, but everything depended on the computer contacting a human being to relay their situation. Relying on a computer was a long shot, but that's all they had between survival and death. They wouldn't be walking away from this house once the criminals got the program. His head hit the pillow and he was asleep in minutes. His last thought was for Heather.

Chapter 13

Sunlight was turning the heavy curtains on the window to sheer, and birds chirped loudly as if they were sitting on the windowsill. The room was hot and stifling. He sat up and dropped his legs over the edge of the mattress. Everything about this situation seemed to be a nightmare he couldn't escape.

He decided to stay in the room as long as possible, to reduce the chances for the criminals to extract the code before being rescued. A vision of a SWAT team busting through the front door entered his mind. The reality, which occurred seconds later, was a tall menacing man in a dark suit striding into the bedroom.

"You come now," he commanded in broken English. His hands seemed to be the size of tennis rackets hanging down to his knees. The goon stood with his back to the wall near the door, waiting for Michael to leave the room.

"I don't suppose you'd have been gentle waking me up either," Michael mumbled. There was no point in being brave, especially when he had no training in self-defense.

Walker and Habbib sat huddled together in the kitchen, talking softly over mugs of coffee. They became silent and looked up as Michael entered.

"Good morning, Mr. Eldridge, or should I say good afternoon. I trust you slept well," Walker said cheerfully.

"Coffee's in the pot by the mugs," Habbib added.

"Thanks, I did," the coffee smelled strong enough to hold up a spoon. "The Incredible Hulk was a bit of a shock."

"He's really quite gentle until he feels threatened, or you try to escape. His name is Eric and he'll be responsible for anything you need. The man once crushed another man's skull with one hand, so don't try anything." Walker grinned.

"Any breakfast, Habbib? Bacon and eggs would be great." Sam asked from the doorway as Eric followed him into the kitchen.

"As you wish." The detective placed a pan on the stove and turned a dial at the back.

"I want you to start writing the program immediately after breakfast." A threatening tone in Walker's voice belied the grin on his face. "Your flight plan said you'd be here four days so you must be finished by then."

Nobody spoke for a few minutes. Bacon sizzled in the pan as Habbib worked at making breakfast. The coffee wasn't as strong as he'd expected. In fact, Michael liked the taste.

"One thing I must make clear," he said. "I sometimes need to go for a run to clear my head. Being out in the yard isn't good enough, because the running gets my blood circulating."

"That's fine." Walker shrugged. "Run if you must, but the longer you take the more Sam will lose. If you're not finished in four days, we'll have no choice but to start nipping off his fingers and toes. Enjoy your breakfast, gentlemen." He stood and left the kitchen as Habbib set heaped plates on the table.

Michael waited for Sam to taste the food. When he attacked the meal, Michael did too. Ten minutes later, their plates were clean enough to return to the cupboard. Sam used a piece of toast to wipe up the last bit of egg. He burped quietly behind his hand and tossed back the last of his coffee.

"That was great food Mr. Habbib. Where'd you learn to cook like that?"

"My mother taught me well, Mr. Worthy, but let us be a little more civil, shall we? My name is Jamil. Would you like more coffee, Sam?"

"Yes please." He held out his mug.

'He's not a bad sort,' Michael thought, *'but I wouldn't trust him to take our side if things turned ugly.'* He watched Habbib pour more coffee into Sam's mug.

"I'm going into my bedroom to work. Call me at lunch time," Michael stood, staring down at Sam. Their eyes locked as Michael tried to say, 'help is on the way' without making a sound. His confidence was flagging by the time he sat at the desk in his bedroom.

A legal pad and pens were arranged on top, although he was certain the desk had been empty earlier. Someone, probably Eric, put them here. *'The guy likely rummaged through my bag too,'* he thought. Fear pulsed down his spine. An image of the big man crushing the circuit board flashed across his mind. His first impulse was to check the suitcase, but he decided to wait until dark. He suspected there might be a hidden camera in the room. Concerned that they'd seen what he did with the cell phone last night, he decided to get to work. They wouldn't wait long after getting the code, before they would demand the phone too.

Picking up a pen, he closed his eyes for a second, trying to see the first line of code. When he was certain of the wording, he wrote the line on the pad. The effort opened the floodgate in his memory and more lines poured onto the page almost faster than he could write them down.

Each line of code didn't always take up one complete line on the pad, so an hour later he had twenty pages of paper scribbled on one side. He wasn't concerned about them being able to read his scratchings. They'd be delayed some more, but he wasn't in a hurry to hand over his work.

His fingers throbbed from the pressure of holding the pen. Flexing them, he walked to the window and opened the curtains. The red siding of the house next door was all he could see. Bright blue sky was visible if he crouched low enough, his face level with the top of the bed. He thought of escaping through the window, and grasped the sliding panel. He tugged, but nothing happened. *'They wouldn't be that stupid, Michael,* his mind chided him. "Yeah, I know," he said aloud. The nail head holding the window closed was just visible in the bottom rail of the frame. He wondered about asking them to open the window so he could get some air. A cold breeze assaulted his shins from under the bed as if someone had heard his thoughts and turned up the air conditioning. A grim smile crossed his face as he returned to the desk. Well, that proved there was a hidden camera in the room, but how long would they wait before they came for the phone?

The pen scribbled and danced across more pages for another hour until Walker strolled softly through the bedroom door. Michael scribbled another half-page of code before he realized he wasn't alone. Still holding the pen, he turned in the chair.

"I see you've been busy." Walker smiled, but there was no warmth in his face.

"Yeah I'm doing all right, but this would've been easier to just print from the lab computer."

"That may be true, but my employers aren't willing to take that risk. There's another pad in the desk, also more pens if you need them. Lunch will be ready in," he stretched his left arm to look at his watch. "Half an hour. Do you mind if I take what you've written so far? I want to start entering the code into my computer?"

The idea that Walker had a computer jolted Michael. He hadn't thought about anyone in this country having the technology. A second thought hit him even harder. *'If there's a computer nearby, my machine could talk to his.'*

"You have a computer?" he asked cautiously.

"Yes, there's one at the embassy. It isn't up to your standards I'm sure, but it does the job for us."

"Why didn't you say so sooner? I could've saved my fingers permanent damage from writing this out. All I need to do is call the lab and connect...oh wait, does your computer have a modem?"

"Mr. Eldridge, I can't give you access to that computer. Foreigners aren't allowed in the embassy for starters, and they definitely wouldn't be granted access to secure equipment." He'd become stiff, and frowned as he spoke.

"But within minutes we'd have access to this program and you'd have the entire code in your hands, full and complete. Take the chance, Mr. Walker, the risk will save me and my friend Sam a great deal of pain." Michael's heart was beating faster as he watched his captor consider the idea.

"I'll see what I can do, but in the meantime, keep working." He turned suddenly and left the room. Michael smiled. He'd need to call Randal first to let him know what was happening. He'd get a chance then to send a plea for help. Walker would be listening for anything unusual, but their safety depended on him being creative enough to send Randal a message.

"Lunch is ready," Habbib bellowed from the kitchen. Michael dropped the pen, shuffled the finished pages into a neat pile, and started toward the door. He stopped and glanced around the room to memorize where everything was situated. Eric was likely to be in again.

"I'd rather you didn't take the finished pages just yet." Michael entered the kitchen and told Walker. The afternoon sun was slanting sharply through the window over the sink. Sandwiches were stacked on a tray on the counter alongside bottles of soda and empty mugs for either coffee or tea. The meal seemed out of place for the time of day, but his stomach grumbled anyway. He placed three kinds of sandwiches on a plate and grabbed a bottle of soda before taking a seat at the table. "I'll need to review everything to be certain the program is complete, but more importantly, if I get stuck I need the pages to find the problem." Watching Walker's reaction, he took a bite of a sandwich. The type of meat was a mystery, but tasted wonderful to Michael.

"I understand," Walker replied while taking food from the tray. "I've given some thought to you using the embassy computer and I think there might be a way to allow you access. I'm not familiar with the technology, but as long as you give me your word that you won't try anything foolish, I'll get you inside." He seemed suspicious. Michael chewed faster to keep from smiling.

"I'll need to call the lab to confirm my identity before asking for the program, but otherwise your computer will be talking to mine." The soda was cold and helped wash down the heavy bread. Sam's mouth twitched on one side as if he was trying to smile. The man was no idiot and understood completely what Michael was planning.

Walker went into the living room and made a phone call. He seemed happier when he returned.

"We can go to the embassy at seven o'clock this evening. The ambassador has a function then and the rest of his staff will be gone. Is two hours enough time for you?"

"Plenty," Michael nearly choked on a sandwich. "Seven o'clock here will be what time back in the States?"

"Ten in the morning," Sam answered.

Michael glanced at his watch. Five o'clock now, how am I going to let Randal know I'm being held hostage? Walker will be listening; Randal is so smart he's stupid sometimes. I have to keep things simple, but not obvious. He gulped the rest of his sandwich and took more from the tray. "These are really good Jamil, what are they made of?"

"The meat ones on dark bread are goat, those ones you're taking now are jellied camel brain, and the others are seasoned duck liver."

Michael could feel his stomach roll. He glanced at Sam and Walker, and saw the same reaction in them. Habbib chuckled.

"Westerners are easily fooled. One is chicken with mayo as you say; another is lamb and mint sauce while the third is minced ham with seasoning." He chuckled again. Sam and Walker made faces Michael gulped down more soda.

"That was cruel, Habbib," Walker complained. "These sandwiches tasted pretty good until you made us all gag. I'll never look at your food again without thinking it might be some disgusting Arab delicacy." He swallowed again. "By the way, how are you able to eat ham? I thought Arabs couldn't eat pork."

"I am sorry, but that was just too easy and you should have seen the expressions on your faces. Priceless," he giggled, and slid the plate of sandwiches toward Walker. "I'm not Muslim, Mr. Walker. I belong to what is called the Coptic Church. I'm Christian."

"I've had enough and I'll agree with Walker." Sam groaned. "A beer would go a long way to washing these down." His grin was hopeful.

Habbib stood quickly and opened the fridge. Both of his hands reached inside and pulled out two brown bottles each. He closed the door with his left knee and set the bottles in the middle of the table.

"I'll wrap up the rest of these for tomorrow, then," he took the plate of sandwiches off the table and set them on the counter.

Michael and Sam glanced at each other. Walker was watching Habbib. Michael mouthed his plan at Sam while keeping an eye on the British spy. Sam nodded as he opened a bottle of beer.

Two hours remaining to come up with some way to alert Randal, what would he say? He'd be suspicious of Michael calling from the other side of the world, possibly, but after all, he was his boss, and Randal would do what he was told. Somehow, he needed to persuade his Chief Technician to send a false but convincing code. He needed time to think.

"The joke wasn't that bad, Mr. Eldridge."

Michael looked up and realized he'd been frowning. Forcing a smile, "No but nothing seems as funny when you're being held hostage." He glared at Walker and took a swig of beer. The Englishman grinned sadly.

"True, I suppose, but we must continue to be human even in a harrowing situation such as this. As I told you when we brought you here, give us what we desire and there will be no harm done to either of you."

"That's what I'm going to do this afternoon, but let me tell you something, Mr. Walker." Michael banged the bottle on the table, hard enough to shoot beer foam out the top. "If my friend is harmed, I'll put the full weight of my company and all of my contacts around the world toward finding you and your friends. There'll be no place to hide, no excuse will protect you, and no country will give you sanctuary. One more thing, if I don't arrive home alive, my best friend will become the head of my company. There is a letter he'll receive suggesting that if I die of suspicious circumstances, he's to do all that I just said. You and your people need to consider how much grief you're willing to put up with for my code. Do you feel safe, Walker? The people you work for have probably taken every precaution to protect their identities, which leaves you and Habbib hanging in the wind. You considered that possibility didn't you?"

"No need to be so angry. I've considered the possibilities and the people we work for. Like you, I've planned some contingencies in the event either Habbib or I am arrested. Trust me, we will not hang alone." There was a snake-like coldness in his eyes as he spoke. "Your code is the only thing they want. You don't need the program anymore and NASA doesn't care as long as everything works for them. Give these criminals what they want, Mr. Eldridge, and we can all go away happy." There was sadness in his eyes as he leaned forward.

"How can I be happy knowing there are people using my program to commit crimes? What if they go back in time to rob a bank and kill your parents?" Michael paused a second. "I guess they'd be stupid to do that, wouldn't they, especially if your parents died before you were born. None of this would happen then." He waved a hand around the kitchen. "Criminals aren't the brightest bulbs in the world, are they? Something like that could happen, accidentally or in the heat of the moment, but the possibility exists. Who knows, maybe that's their plan? They'll go back in time to kill off one of their enemies, or a cop, or perhaps the President. Nobody understands what would happen if history were altered. Mr. Walker, do you and Habbib like the idea of someone else playing with your life?"

Walker looked sideways at Habbib standing by the sink. The detective's shocked expression said he hadn't thought their situation through. Walker was red-faced, but grim as he turned back at Michael.

"They're paying us ten million dollars to make this happen. We'll just have to trust them to make sound decisions, but I'm going to spend the rest of my life in as much luxury and leisure as I can with my share."

Michael couldn't stand to be in the same room any longer and stormed down the hall to his bedroom, slamming the door. He had to think and time was getting shorter the longer he stayed to argue with Walker.

Chapter 14

Two hours later, Habbib knocked softly on the bedroom door. Michael was ready. The detective gazed at the floor, guilt written on his face. He backed up and allowed Michael to enter the hall.

Walker was fidgeting by the front door. He seemed embarrassed and nervous before going outside as soon as he saw Michael. The two men rode in silence as Walker steered through the throngs on the street to the British Embassy -- a ride of thirty minutes. A man in a bright red uniform and shiny black cap opened the door as the car pulled to a stop at the bottom of the stairs in front of the building. He saluted Walker and then returned to his position on the bottom step. The name "beefeater" came into Michael's mind.

Michael followed the spy inside the ornate building. Cool air surrounded them as they strode through the massive oak and glass doors. Brass or maybe gold, gleamed everywhere, fixtures, railings, doorknobs and even on the ceiling lights. Michael wasn't impressed. The Empire had a long history of plundering the countries they conquered. He was grateful for the air conditioning though.

Walker turned sharply after the unattended reception desk without stopping to register, and went through a door marked 'Private' leading down a hallway. One side was glass looking out on a central quad of grass and benches. People were out there taking in the cool evening air, eating, or just sitting together, smoking and talking. Michael thought about trying to attract their attention and plead his situation, but decided the risk wouldn't be worth the bloodshed.

"This way, Mr. Eldridge," Walker called softly. He was leaning out of a doorway fifteen feet further down the hall. The Englishman glanced both ways down the passage before he closed the door after Michael.

The room was paneled in rich dark wood, probably mahogany, Michael guessed, glancing around. A large two-panel window looked out on a street -- definitely not the avenue in front because there weren't any trees out there. He heard Walker clattering with something and turned.

The desk was a massive lump of oak set to one side of the room. The spy was furiously typing something, probably a password into the computer. His fingers stopped and he stared at the monitor perched on the corner of the desk.

"There, you have access now. Make your call, but hurry up and don't try anything funny, Mr. Eldridge." He stood and stepped to the side allowing Michael to sit. A revolver appeared in Walker's hand sometime between being seated and standing.

Michael picked up the heavy black receiver and hesitated. He knew what he was going to say to Randal, but the gun was making him nervous.

"Is there a number I need to dial to get an outside line?"

"No, now hurry up," Walker pointed the gun his hand was trembling.

Michael dialed the long distance area code and then the number to the lab. He listened to the telephone on the other end ring three times before someone picked up.

"Randal Chesterwick here, can I help you?" The soft voice seemed cautious.

"Randal this is Michael. I'm calling from Monaco and I need your help." He could see the gun out of the corner of his eye and the barrel didn't move. So far, so good, he thought and began to breathe easier.

"How is your trip going so far? What do you need?" The scientist's voice had become the usual gravely sound once more.

"The trip is fine, but as you know I'm here doing research. I can remember the program for the Mars probe, but I don't have time to write it out, so if you could just send me the file. I'm at the British consulate with access to a computer." He held his breath hoping Randal wouldn't start to ask questions.

"Ok. Do you want me to fax you or just send as a data stream?"

"I'm going to use the modem here, so just prepare version fifty-five for electronic transfer. I'll connect in about five minutes." Version fifty-five was the best failure they had, and started the whole process toward time shifting. There was silence on the line except for Randal breathing into his receiver. Michael heard him punching the keyboard.

"Ready on this end, but wouldn't you rather have, --" He didn't get a chance to finish the sentence.

"I'm going to connect now, and thank you, Randal. You're the best computer programmer ever and I appreciate all you've done." Michael hung up before Randal could say any more. Without waiting another second, he dialed the numbers again, but changed the last number. He heard the ringing and then the modem signal. Placing the receiver in the modem cradle, he turned toward Walker.

"How long will this take?" The gun in his hand was shaking more than before.

"Depends," Michael made a pouty face and shrugged. "If the line on this end and the computer are fairly speedy, then we'll receive the program in about twenty minutes. One piece is a bit slow and the process could take up to an hour -- that's if the signal isn't broken in the meantime."

The office was cool, but beads of sweat had broken out across the spy's forehead and upper lip. He was pale and seemed frightened too.

A bell sounded on the computer, making Walker flinch. Michael turned toward the monitor to find a message asking if he'd like to save the information. He punched the keyboard to say yes and then typed in a name for the file. The message disappeared and he could faintly hear the modem beeping as the information was received.

"So far this is working, but we'll have to wait."

"You did well, Mr. Eldridge, but just remember, until my employers have checked the program, you, and your friend are not safe." The gun disappeared inside Walker's jacket. There were signs of dampness on the shirt underneath, Michael noticed.

"I'm not worried, but you're going to get really tired of standing waiting for this to finish. Relax; this'll take as long as necessary." He leaned back and waved at the empty chair on the other side of the desk. There was a picture of the ambassador's family next to the monitor, showing a blonde woman, the wife, in her late forties, he guessed next to two young men in their teens or early twenties. They smiled for the camera, but he could tell they weren't happy. There were two empty file trays, one labeled in, and the other out but otherwise the desk was clear. He opened the top middle drawer and began to snoop.

"What are you doing? Get out of there; do you want to get us shot for spying?" There was an urgent note of fear in Walker's whispered voice that seemed to Michael to be out of place. He wondered if the spy had been a spy very long.

"Just killing time." He slid the drawer closed. "I'm pretty sure that if we get caught in here, we're going to be in a lot of trouble, whether we're snooping or not. Do you think we could get a coffee? I do my best thinking with coffee." He smiled, knowing his calm demeanor would irritate the British spy.

Walker flopped back in the chair as if he'd been shot, and his head started to move side to side at an ever-increasing speed.

"You're mad." He finally stopped shaking his head and stared. "We can't be seen wandering around in this building and calling someone to fetch us a coffee would be an invitation to the firing squad. Being an American wouldn't be any protection. You'd be in as much trouble as I."

"Firing squad, do you really think it would go that far? What do you really do here, Walker? You're no more spy than I am, so tell me your real job." Michael didn't smile, but he almost did when Walker's mouth fell open.

"I...I don't know what..." he sputtered for a second and then regained control. His shoulders sagged as he slid a bit further into the chair. "I'm an agriculture assistant. How did you know?"

"Until we got in here, I didn't, but a real spy wouldn't be so nervous. If you're not a spy, I'm guessing Habbib isn't a real policeman either." He sat forward and rested his elbows on the desk.

His head was shaking, saying no. "He's a policeman, but not a detective. They have part-time constables here and he's one of them. This was just supposed to be our way of making enough money to retire. He has ten children and between the police and his job as a cook in that restaurant you were in, he doesn't make enough money to ever retire."

"He's a cook? Who contacted you?"

"Two men stopped me four days ago outside the embassy. They sounded Russian or middle-eastern. One of them handed me an envelope and told me to expect a foreigner. The information this person had was worth ten million dollars to me...they said. I tried to object saying I was just a low-level employee, but they said I would be perfect. One of them suggested that if I didn't co-operate there would be painful consequences. When they'd gone, I opened the envelope. Your picture was inside along with the hotel and date you'd arrive. There was also twenty thousand pounds for expenses. Habbib and I have been friends for the last six years, so he was an easy choice for a partner."

Michael was stunned. Four days ago, Sam had barely known where they were going. This was more than a case of an air traffic controller knowing the destination, but more like someone close to Sam. But the speed the information moved between contacts staggered him more. Keeping his voice even and low, he continued questioning Walker.

"How are you supposed to get paid?"

Walker sat up straighter and eyed Michael suspiciously. "What's that to you?" he demanded.

Shrugging he said, "This information shouldn't be in the hands of criminals. If all this cloak and dagger is just a payday, then I'll give you the money to let us go." He'd been in many negotiations before and knew when to keep quiet. Now was that time.

Walker thought about the proposal. Michael could see he'd rather have money than kill someone. He could disappear while Habbib could take his family and hide. There was always the chance the criminals were watching Walker, but he didn't care. His life was over no matter what came next.

"Why would I trust you any more than them? There's nothing to make you keep your word, especially once we let you go."

Michael smiled as relief flooded through him. "I'm the one with the most to lose, so for me to pay you makes sense. We can leave right now and go to the nearest international bank. I'll transfer the money to anywhere you like, and then Sam and I can leave. More than that, I'll give you my word that the authorities will not be contacted." He put his hand out slowly to shake with Walker. The man eyed the hand, conflicted by his emotions. Finally, his right hand moved from his lap and gripped Michael's firmly. He stood.

"Turn that thing off and let's get out of here before I change my mind."

"I'll need to erase the call log and any data that's been transferred. Shouldn't be more than a couple of minutes." Michael lifted the receiver and replaced it into the telephone cradle. He knew the transmission would instantly terminate on the other end, which might cause Randal some concern. Even if he did panic and called the police, there would be at least an hour before anything happened in this country. His fingers flew over the keyboard as he erased any evidence that they'd been in the office.

"Hurry, we've been here too long already." Walker kept glancing at his watch and then at the closed door.

"Done," Michael said as he stood up and shut off the monitor. Walker opened the door slowly a crack and peered out into the hall. He stuck his head through the opening and looked both ways before flinging the door wide.

"Let's go, but stay close," the taller man hissed.

Michael stayed on Walker's heels as they marched toward the front doors. The guard was back at the reception counter. He nodded to Walker as they passed, but said nothing. Outside, the heat slammed into them. The car still sat at the curb. The beefeater moved to open the passenger door as the men came down the steps. They both breathed a sigh of relief as the car started and Walker pulled into the heavy traffic.

Darkness was falling as they turned the corner onto the street where Sam was being held. The safe house wasn't the same as when they'd left. Another car, a new Mercedes sedan, was parked in front of the overhead door. Walker pulled into the driveway and shut off their car, but didn't move when Michael opened the passenger door.

"They're here, Michael. The men inside will kill us all when they find out we don't have the program." His whole body trembled as if he was cold. Michael took a second to think before stepping out. He leaned his head back inside.

"If we stay out here, they'll know something is wrong. At least inside, we'll be able to bluff our way out of this situation. Follow my lead and try to act as if you aren't worried." He stood up and shut the door. Walker slowly climbed out of the car and followed him inside the house. There was no sign of the guards outside.

Two men were silently waiting, one seated on the couch, the other standing at the doorway to the kitchen. They wore black suits. Both men were bald, muscular and seemed to be carved from some rock. Hawk-like noses, subtle scars on their faces and beady dark eyes gave them a predatory appearance. The guy standing in the doorway seemed bigger, his head almost touching the ceiling. Habbib and Sam were nowhere to be seen.

"Ah, my friend Walker, and I assume you are Mr. Michael Eldridge," the man on the couch shouted happily. "Your friends told me you went to the embassy to use the computer an hour ago. I was becoming worried that trouble had gotten you." He leaned forward and motioned them to sit. "Tell me, gentlemen, do you bring the program?" The smile faded quickly from his face and the eyes turned cold.

"We had a problem," Michael said. He looked at Walker and saw the Brit roll his eyes. "The ambassador returned early and we had to leave or be caught. According to the date book on his desk, he's leaving for a meeting tonight in Cairo and won't be back until Friday. We'll go back later or tomorrow, but there won't be any more problems getting the program Mr..."

"Oh yes, a thousand pardons, I'm such an idiot." He slapped his forehead with a meaty hand attached to an arm the size of a leg of ham. "My name is Andropov, Alexis Andropov. His name is Yuri, but he doesn't matter. This news you bring about not getting the program is very worrying to me, Mr. Eldridge. We should be friends; may I call you Michael, or Mike? Mike is what you Americans prefer, yes. I am a gentle man despite stories you may have heard to the contrary, Mike." His massive head turned to look at Walker. "I am always bothered when people I am dealing with try to abuse my good nature. They soon learn that I can be less than subtle when I must teach them a lesson." He leaned back on the couch and crossed his massive hands across his stomach.

"I'm not sure what you're trying to say Mr. Andropov, but all I'm saying is that there was a slight delay in getting you the program. Nothing else has changed and we'll retrieve the code for you later." Michael leaned back on the chair, trying to relax.

"This is a good thing, but that is not what I wanted." He sighed and closed his eyes. A moment passed before the eyes opened again. "The moment you two left this house, I telephoned my employers. Oh yes, I too have people to report to, Mike. They were very excited about receiving your program, but now when I speak to them they will be very angry. Who do you think they will punish, Mr. Walker?" The big head swiveled slowly.

"I'm guessing it's me," he said, the words barely a whisper.

"You would be wrong, because they will attempt to harm me or my organization. This in turn will make me angry and I must take this anger out on one of you. Do you think I am stupid, Mike?" The sudden change in conversation made Michael jump. The big man's pale blue eyes seemed more like raw steel.

"I don't know you well enough to make that kind of judgment."

The Russian laughed a burst of noise that shook the room. "Ah it is better not to know me so well, I think," he said and wiped his eyes with the backs of his hands. "Never mind, I will deal with them. Out of admiration for you, I will allow you this one mistake, but I must prove to you that I am serious, Mr. Eldridge. People will no longer respect me if they find out I am weak." He heaved his body off the couch and stared down at both men. "Someone in this house must pay the price, but who shall it be? Neither of you because there is no other way to get the program, so one of the others." His massive head motioned to the man in the doorway. Michael turned as the second gangster glanced into the kitchen. A moment later, there were noises of chairs being pushed around. The thug in the doorway straightened, as Sam preceded Habbib into the room. Another Russian followed them, smaller but just as ugly as the other two, carrying a machine gun of some sort. Michael didn't know one gun from another, but the large clip sticking out the bottom was a clue.

"Gentlemen, you've heard the conversation and now I must apologize to one of you because these two couldn't carry out a simple task. There is always a price to pay for failure." The Boss shrugged and held up his hands.

"If you harm these men, you'll never see the program," Michael said.

Andropov looked down. His face went red and then white.

"I think you are mistaken, Mr. Eldridge. My daughter is being held hostage by my employers and I am certain they will inflict pain on her because I failed them. The same must be done to one of these men or she will have suffered for nothing and I will lose face."

"I don't care about whether you lose face." Michael snarled as he jumped up. "I'm sorry about your daughter, but you only have yourself to blame. If you weren't a criminal, she wouldn't be in pain right now. My friend and I are willing to give you what you want because the program holds no value for us. We're here and involved in this situation because you and your employers decided to steal my life's work." The slap came from nowhere. Michael saw stars for several seconds as he was knocked back into the chair. The left side of his face felt crushed. He looked up at Andropov.

"Who do you think you are, you American pig? Do you think you can frighten me with your money? Men like you die every day and I don't weep one tear for them. My daughter is my most precious possession and if she is harmed then it is my duty to punish those responsible." His voice had risen to a thunderous shout; spit flew from his mouth as he ranted. The massive hands clenched in balls of rage at his sides. "I grew up on the streets of Moscow fighting for my life every day and I swore to God that my children wouldn't spend one day the same way. You and this fucking Englishman failed. Both of you would be dead right now if I didn't need you. Shoot that filthy Arab," he shouted. The sound of the machine gun made less noise in the house.

Habbib dropped forward as blood erupted from at least a dozen bullet wounds in his back. The man, holding gun smiled as smoke drifted out of the muzzle. Andropov sat suddenly as if he'd been shot too. Michael glanced over at him. Tears streamed down the Russian's cheeks. Silence filled the room.

"Clean up that mess," the Boss ordered in a whisper. Michael sat forward, his face feeling swollen. Walker had gone pale; his mouth was hanging open in fear, as he stared at the dead body of his partner.

Yuri and the shooter grabbed Habbib's body and carried him into the kitchen. Michael had no idea where they would take the detectives body after that. He felt sorry for the police officer's family. Their lives would get even harder from now on without a father and husband. He looked up at Sam. The man stood motionless in the middle of the living room, a dark stain covering the crotch of his pants. His eyes seemed vacant as if he'd died with Habbib but hadn't fallen down yet.

"Sam," Michael said quietly. "Sam, go change your clothes. You're fine Sam." It took a minute for the words to sink in, but finally, he started to move stiff legged, making his way down the hall to one of the bedrooms. Andropov was still crying. The back door banged shut and the other Russians stepped into the living room.

"We will go now," Andropov said as he stood. "Make sure you get me that program tonight or there will be more blood." The man with the machine gun was the last out the door. He smiled back at Michael with an evil expression as the door closed.

Silence filled the house once more. The stench of blood, cordite, and urine filled the air. Michael was about to go into the kitchen for a drink...anything but water, when the door shattered inwards, slamming against the inside wall. A torrent of men dressed in black from head to toe rushed into the living room, carrying automatic weapons and shouting.

Michael and Walker were flung to the floor on their faces. Someone held a knee in the middle of Michael's back, pressing his face into the carpet. The men in black continued to shout. At last, whoever was kneeling on his back released him and pulled him off the floor. A new face appeared.

"I'm Captain Richter of the Monaco Royal Police and you must be Michael Eldridge." The man seemed concerned and yet relieved. "We received word from your California office that you might be in trouble. Since you're a high-profile guest in our country, we felt it prudent to act on the information." He smiled as he pulled off his black helmet. "Please take a seat, I'm sorry for the way you were treated just now, and I know that wasn't the best way for us to meet, but your safety as well as that of my men was my top priority." Richter sat on the edge of the chair nearest Michael. He kept one hand on his rifle lying on his knees. Sam came into the room carrying three bottles of beer handing, one to Michael and Walker each.

"How did you know where to find us?" Sam asked the most obvious question.

"The message from your office gave us a longitude and latitude which led us to this house. You must have an amazing group of people working for you, or perhaps your computers are responsible. Either way, the information was accurate. We had just taken our position when Andropov and his henchmen came out, and the rest you already know." The smile was back. Richter had a face more like a fashion model than a police officer, uniform white teeth that sparkled when he smiled, striking blue eyes, and almost white blonde hair.

"Yeah, I'll need two weeks to get the impression of a knee out of my back," Michael moaned.

"I truly am sorry for the way you were treated, but we take no chances in hostage situations." His blue eyes kept straying back to Walker. "How were you kidnapped in the first place?"

Michael leaned back on the sofa and took a long swig of beer. *'I can't tell him the truth,'* he thought. *'Walker was just a pawn in this whole affair. Sure, the man held us captive and would have killed us, but all they wanted was the money. Now the police officer is dead and there is nobody to care for his family.'*

"Sam and I ran into Walker down at the marina the night we arrived. He knew about the possibility we were in danger and tried to hide us here, but Andropov found us. One of his thugs killed Habbib. The Russian wanted the communication program I just finished for NASA. I managed to get a message through to my office that we were being held captive and as you say...the rest you already know." He smiled, relieved and to show Richter that he was sincere. The pain on the left side of his face was lessening.

"Is that how you remember the events, Mr. Walker?" There was no kindness in the Captains voice. Walker was being treated like a suspected spy operating in this country, Michael noticed. He felt sorry for him.

The Brit nodded. "If I have anything to add, I'd say that once Andropov found us, our lives were in imminent danger. He forced us to go to the British embassy and break into the ambassador's computer to retrieve the program from California. We had no other choice, our friends were being held hostage. There was a glitch in the system and we didn't receive the entire program. When we came back here and told Andropov, he had Habbib killed in front of us. You can see the stain on the floor." He pointed the beer bottle in his trembling hand at the drying blood on the floor.

Richter glanced at the soiled patch of carpet, considering the information. One of his men approached and whispered something. A brief nod and all the 'men in black' left the house, except for one standing by the front door.

"We've ascertained that Constable Habbib has been dumped in a trash bin in the alley behind the house. Ballistics will confirm Andropov's guards killed him, but for now, we only have your word. Until all the pieces are sorted, I would appreciate both of you staying in this country." Richter stood and moved toward the front door.

"How long is that going to take?" Michael demanded.

The Captain stopped and turned slowly to face Michael. "We work until we have all the evidence and the truth about who the murderer is. At this point, any one of you could have killed a police officer, and that's a serious offense in this country. Please, gentlemen, relax and I'll work as quickly as I can." He turned and strode out the door.

Michael glanced at Walker, who shrugged in response. *'Now what do we do? Can I trust him or is he going to carry out the original plan for his own gain? Who else were the Russians working for? I'll give him the money and some to Habbib's family before we go home.'*

"Want another one?" Sam asked from the kitchen doorway.

"No I'm good still," Michael said and Walker agreed.

"I meant what I said." Walker spoke softly. "We were just doing this for the money and meant you no harm. If you don't want to give me the money I'll understand."

Michael turned slightly and stared in shock. When he finally managed to wrap his mind around the man's nerve, he began to speak.

"I said I'd pay you to walk away without the program, but now I don't need to do that. What the hell makes you think I should still give you anything?"

"You're quite right. I am overstepping, but I had hoped you would still consider some compensation for my help."

"Huh, you didn't pull the trigger, but you are just as guilty of killing Habbib as the Russians." He let his anger run for a minute in silence. "I'll give his family five million just like he wanted, but you get half that for helping me send the message to my office. You should be grateful I didn't tell Richter about your involvement in this whole situation."

"I am, and thank you. As soon as we receive permission to leave the country, I'll gladly disappear."

"Let's get out of here," Sam said as he came back into the living room. The expression on his face told Michael he'd been listening at the doorway. "Can you take us back to the hotel?" He stared at Walker.

"Get your things and I'll drive you. We'll leave as soon as you're ready." He was a defeated and broken man.

Ten minutes later, the three men left the house. The car seemed cramped on the drive back to the hotel. Sam spoke to the front desk when they arrived about extending the length of their stay and Michael pulled the bags to the elevator. His level of exhaustion increased the longer they took to get up to the room.

"They've booked us in for another week, but we can leave anytime we want... if Richter gives us the all clear." He grinned. "The clerk said they were a bit concerned when the staff found our room cleared this morning. They thought we skipped out on the bill."

"I'm not surprised. I just want to sleep for a couple of days and then I'll worry about going home." Michael groaned, sagging against the wall of the elevator. Both men practically fell into the room as the door swung open. Sam pushed his boss out of the way in a dash for the bathroom. Michael smiled and dragged his bag into the bedroom. He was about to flop on the bed when he remembered the cell phone.

Energy swept through his body, cutting away any remaining fatigue. His hands clawed at the zipper and then searched for the phone. The flashing light pulled his fingers like a magnet. He grasped the circuit board and stared.

A signal. Not Morse code, but the message had to be coming from the computer in his office at home. He watched the light struggling to figure out what the flashes meant. Rapid flashes followed by darkness. Numbers, now he understood. Once he figured out the first word, the rest was easy. 'Message sent help will arrive shortly. Please respond when safe.' The words repeated. His computer had been sending the same message for twelve hours or more.

He punched the numbers to send 'safe' and turned off the phone. The system worked. All he had to do now was try the real thing. Once they were back in California, he would do a few more tests and then take the jump himself. How and why Joe disappeared wouldn't be a secret much longer.

The telephone on the stand by the bed rang. His jangled nerves wouldn't let him pick up the receiver until the third ring.

"Hello," he said hesitantly.

"Michael, I'm so glad to hear your voice. Are you okay?" The female voice seemed familiar, but he needed a couple of seconds to remember who she was.

"Heather, yes we're fine, but how did you know I was at this hotel?" His heart fluttered.

"I got a strange fax message just now. There wasn't a return phone number, but the message said to call you and gave me a number. I thought you might be in trouble and I was worried. So, where did the message come from?" Her voice seemed to relax as she spoke.

"Sam, the pilot, must have sent the fax, but we're fine. I'll tell you all about our adventures here when I get back." He knew Sam wasn't responsible.

"When are you coming back?" She sounded worried, and he felt guilty.

"I'm not sure, but for now let's say a couple more days. We've been out hiking all day and I need a shower...badly. Can I call you later?" He knew if he started talking, he'd have to give her all the details.

"I suppose so, but you better not forget. I'll be home at eight tonight." There was silence on the line for a second. "That's tomorrow morning your time, so I'll give you an hour's grace in case you sleep late. If you haven't called me by ten, I'm not going to talk to you even when you get back."

"I'll set my alarm." He glanced at his wristwatch. "I'm really glad to hear your voice, and I missed you. We'll be back soon, I promise." He heard the concern in his own voice, but he felt too tired to pretend to sound happy. They said their good-byes and hung up.

"A shower really perks you up," Sam said at the doorway. He was dressed, but still drying his hair. "Who was on the phone?" The memory of Sam standing in the living room wearing soiled pants surfaced and made Michael regret having come on this trip.

"Heather. She got an anonymous fax message telling her to call me here. You didn't send her anything did you?"

"How could I?"

Michael shrugged, knowing the message had been sent by his computer. The realization made him happy and afraid. His creation was autonomous, which seemed on the surface to be a good thing, but autonomy also meant the computer could just as easily turn on the person who created the machine. Suppose he did something to anger the computer, what then. How could he trust a thinking machine when he went back in time? '*Maybe it isn't that smart,*' he thought. This was just one situation, a fluke that didn't prove anything. The computer seemed to have artificial intelligence, but that could be the same as giving the pet dog human traits. His computer acted logically and that was all there was to consider.

He grabbed some clean clothes out of the suitcase and headed for the shower. The warm spray felt wonderful and he closed down his mind and let the water take away the stress of the last couple of days. Now he had to be patient and relax until they could return to California.

"I've made a reservation downstairs in the hotel restaurant for an hour from now." Michael was just coming into the main room. "We can eat, drink, and relax without going anywhere. After that, we can get a good nights' sleep. Who knows, maybe that Captain will let us go tomorrow." Sam leaned against the bar and seemed chipper so Michael let him babble. He'd be happy staying in the room where he knew they'd be safe, but arguing the point would take energy he didn't have.

"Ok, but if I fall over after the first drink, just kick me under the table until you're finished and then drag my sorry ass back here. I can't believe you've got any energy left after what we've been through." Michael watched Sam fidget with the glass of whiskey in his hand. "Are you okay?"

"Don't worry about me, I've been through worse. I thought I was dead back there." His face blanched. "I was scared when they shot Habbib, but I'm fine now. My ass is dragging too, but I learned a long time ago to keep moving until you get a second wind. I'm not saying we will, but sitting around here isn't going to make us feel any better. Going to the restaurant might not either, but we'll be moving and that helps a lot." He tossed back the liquor, set the glass on the bar, and grabbed Michael by the shoulders. "You saved us both and I'll never forget that."

"I didn't do anything special. You would've done the same for me Sam. I'm just sorry Detective Habbib had to die. I hope the money will make some sort of difference in his family's life. I don't know if I'm as happy about being able to time travel as I was a few days ago. I should just destroy the program when we get back so nobody else dies. Finding out what happened to Joe isn't worth paying with human lives." He turned away and flopped onto the sofa.

"That's true Mike, but you aren't the only one with an investment in your program. Everyone in your business has spent time and hard work developing the software package and the technology. Maybe not for the same reasons as you, but they've got an equal stake in your future. They believe in you and your vision. The real reason for the program isn't important to them, but if they knew, they might be as excited as you were a few days ago. Hell, I was and I don't understand any of that stuff so why wouldn't they? Trying to travel through time to find out what happened to your friend isn't the noblest cause, but at least that reason makes sense."

"My vision, my quest got a man killed, Sam, how am I supposed to live with that? What happens if I go back in time and find out Joe just ran away? Everything that's come since in my life would have been for nothing."

"Only a rich man would see it that way," Sam snorted. "I was almost killed for your discovery and you still can't see the benefits. You might not flaunt your money, but you sure measure your life by the wealth." He walked over to the window.

"I do not," Michael shot forward filled with rage and energy once again. "I grew up poor. My best friend's family had money and I thought being rich would be great. The reality isn't like I imagined. I've always hated being rich, so I used the money to benefit as many people as I could."

"Sure you do, but you still can't see the successes and the thousands of people in your life that were changed because you had this dream. Look at the people whose lives you've touched and the changes you've made to the world by wanting to find your friend. Even if you go back and find nothing, the world will be a better place because you tried and that has to be worth one man's death." Sam slowly walked to the empty sofa in front of his boss and sat down.

Michael considered the words. After a moment, he smiled, feeling less tired.

"I wish I'd never put your life in danger, I'm sorry Sam. You're either a very smart man or the world's best liar. This reminds me of that old movie where the guy finds out at Christmas that he has plenty of friends who care about him. What's it called?" Michael snapped his fingers trying to remember.

"The one with Jimmie Stuart." Sam grinned.

"Yeah that one, except his problem was money and I don't have that problem."

"Nope, but you both see only the forest and not the trees."

Michael smiled, sadly. Silence in the room stretched without them looking at each other.

"Alright if I admit you're right can we go for supper?" Michael stood.

Sam looked up at him. "Well," he asked.

"Well what?" Michael demanded while thinking, '*this is getting old fast, and I'm getting hungry.*'

"Aren't you going to admit it?"

"Shut up and let's go." Michael chuckled and headed for the door. "Remind me to fire you when we get back to the states."

"It's a wonderful life," Sam said as they entered the elevator.

Chapter 15

They endured three more days of hiding in the hotel or cautiously wandering the streets before someone came to their room. Michael opened the door to see Captain Richter standing in the hallway dressed in casual grey pants and a black golf shirt. His badge was pinned to his belt like the movie cops. A large handgun hung from his right hip, but he was smiling.

"Good afternoon Mr. Eldridge and Mr. Worthy," Richter said as Michael closed the door. "I hope you've spent a pleasant few days in my country. We've determined that you were telling the truth. You're free to go home now." The smile never faltered or diminished.

"Thank you Captain," Michael extended a hand. "We'll leave first thing in the morning. I have something I'd like you to give to Detective Habbib's family." Michael trotted into the bedroom and returned with two white envelopes. "This is my way of saying I'm sorry for their loss, but I hope they put the money to good use. This one is for Walker." Michael handed them to Richter.

"I'll make sure Habbib's family gets this, but I'm afraid I won't be able to deliver this one to Mr. Walker -- he's dead."

Michael staggered back, his mind reeling. "How did that happen?"

Richter shrugged. "We don't know. His body was fished out of the harbor this morning. There were two bullet holes in his forehead. If I had to guess, I'd say the Russians were making an example of him. They didn't get what they wanted." He made a helpless gesture with his hands. Michael nodded his understanding and went to the bar.

"I'm having a drink, Captain, are you allowed to drink on duty, or is this a social call?"

"I drink Scotch and I'm not on duty." He waited to take the glass from Michael and then sat on the sofa. "You two caused quite a sensation in this country."

"We didn't hear anything on the news." Sam coughed.

Michael nodded. He wanted to add that they hadn't started the nightmare.

"Quite right, Mr. Worthy. Unlike the American media, when the police in this country want something off the record that's what happens. There will never be any mention of your escapades here, or the deaths of those men." The smile was gone, replaced by a stone mask. Richter's face turned pale, and the blue color of his eyes turned to slate as he took a sip of his whisky. Michael sensed the anger coming off the police officer in waves.

"Thank you again, Captain," Michael held his glass toward Richter in a toasting gesture. Three glasses touched and each man took a sip before Michael continued. "This is a little off topic, but please don't take offense to what I'm about to ask you. I need a security chief now, especially in the light of what's happened. Would you be interested in the position?"

A broad smile appeared on Richter's face as he set the glass on the table. He glanced up at Michael and then the grin faltered. "Are you serious?" he asked.

"I'm trying not to be one of those pushy American businessmen. I like you and I think you have the skills and connections to fill the position. Our pension plan will make whatever you're earning now look like pocket change, if that makes a difference to your decision."

"That's a very flattering offer, but why would you think I'd be willing to leave the Royal Police force? My work is about more than the money." The man had self-assurance enough for six people.

"Fair enough and I won't push, but if you ever change your mind..."

"How much are you talking about?" The desperation in his voice was subtle, but loud enough to hear.

Michael looked over at Sam, and the pilot winked. "Are you married, Captain?"

"No, so there aren't any strings to keep me here. My parents are dead and my brother is already living in Texas, so there are more reasons for me to go than to stay."

"You'll receive a house, a car and six figures a year. Ten percent goes directly into a retirement fund, which is matched by the company. You have to work for me for five years before you can collect, but in the unfortunate event that you're killed before then, I'll send the money to your brother. Do we have a deal?" Michael's face turned blank. He was good at making deals. He also believed that having the best people was worth being generous.

Richter held out his hand and they shook. "Your offer is overwhelming, so how could I resist. I'll need a few days to tidy up my affairs, will that be a problem?"

"Take all the time you need. There'll be a ticket waiting for you at the airport. When you get to California," Michael pulled a business card out of his wallet and handed it to Richter. "Come and see me as soon as you get into town. I'm looking forward to working with you."

"Thank you, Mr. Eldridge it'll be my pleasure." Richter stood to leave.

"One thing I think is very important to your position and this might be a deal breaker." Michael was frowning. Richter lost his smile. "Since we're going to be working closely together, you can call me Michael." He smiled and so did Richter.

"In that case, you can call me Jon."

• • •

Sam called the airport, and filed their flight plan for the next morning. "That's if nobody else tries to kidnap us."

"I don't think they'd try now. Besides, we have police protection until we board the plane." Sam went to his bedroom, saying he wanted a nap. Michael waited until he thought Heather would be at work and called her there. He ached to hear her voice. They talked for an hour about his arrival time and plans once they landed. She kept her voice controlled, but Michael could tell she was excited to see him home.

He was excited too, needing to hold her, be with her, and tell her about the adventure. There was also anxiety about finishing what he'd started this whole ordeal for in the first place. The need to find his best friend had become more important and urgent than ever. Nothing else would ever hold his attention or mean more to him.

By the time they touched down in California, he'd formulated a schedule to test his system and go back to Joe's disappearance. A limo was waiting for them in front of the terminal once they'd cleared customs. They climbed into the back seat and Michael closed his eyes. The odor of the city clogged his nose and burned his eyes, but he decided there wasn't a better smell in the world at that moment. He took a long deep breath and let it out slowly, allowing the tension of the last week drain out of his body. The drive from the airport seemed to take mere minutes until the car stopped in front of his house.

Lights glowed in the front entrance and the living room when there should be darkness. Their bright glow shone through frosted glass on either side of the door. He wondered who might have taken the trouble to welcome him home. The list of people with a key was limited to Billy, the cleaning company, and Christen, his secretary. He smiled. Heather had borrowed one, and was waiting. He turned the doorknob on the front door and entered. Stepping into the cool air, his heart rate and breathing became faster in anticipation.

Silently, he moved deeper into the house, leaving his bag by the door. Turning the corner into the living room, he expected to see her, but the room was empty. She must be in the bedroom, he thought, and proceeded down the hall. He pushed open the door to his bedroom and flipped on the light. Nobody here either. He was confused. Why would anyone take the time to open the house, and not stay around to welcome him? Who would leave the front door unlocked?

A beeping noise sounded across the hall in the computer room. He pushed open the door and turned on the light. The computer screen had a single line of words, and the cursor was sitting at the end, blinking. Michael sat on the chair and read the message.

"Welcome home Michael, I hope you are unharmed."

His mouth dropped open in total shock. The computer was intelligent. Saving them hadn't been a fluke. The machine could anticipate and think, but more importantly, it had feelings. Well, not human feelings, he thought, but certainly, there were signs of compassion at least for him. *What do you do now?* His mind shouted. *'This is more than a pet dog that's protecting me. This is a machine that has the capacity to control anything and everything in my life.'*

The fingers that moved toward the keyboard trembled. He typed in a response.

"I'm fine, thank you. What you did for me was perfect, but I'm home now so you don't need to look after me. Let's just go back to being a team working on sending me back in time."

The cursor blinked and then moved. Michael watched.

"I'm not capable of looking after you, Michael. All I can do is control electronic devices around this house, which I do with gratitude for making me aware. Your plan for going back in time had a few minor glitches that I took the liberty of correcting in your absence. When you are ready, you may open the file 'trip.go' to access my changes."

The cursor blinked silently at the end of the sentence for a moment and then continued. "As for having some sort of ulterior motive or personality, I'm no different than the toaster in the kitchen. I can communicate, but I do not feel anything. Intellectually, I understand the emotions and use them to talk to you as if I was

141

human. I am a processor, nothing more. Good night, Michael, pleasant dreams."

The screen went black and the computer powered down. A lump had settled in his stomach as he read what the computer said. He'd created a new life form, but was it a psychopath, or was it a new friend. He stumbled out of the room without switching off the light. In his bedroom, he turned off the light and undressed. Exhaustion more than anything allowed him to sleep.

Chapter 16

He showered and dressed the next morning, careful to avoid touching anything electrical except the coffee machine, his need for caffeine being greater than his trepidation over the computer. If the pot had been full and hot this morning he'd have been truly concerned, maybe even doubting his sanity. There was no reason for him to fear the computer. He feared what might happen if the computer became emotionally attached to him. *'Machines don't have emotions, Michael. Yes, but this one might have the capability of independent thought. It could turn on me, like a dog.'*

Carrying a full cup to the bedroom office, he sat at the desk. The monitor and the computer were both running again. He typed in the command to call up 'trip.go' and waited. Ten seconds seems like a long time when you're waiting, but suddenly the screen was filled with code. His eyes scanned for the changes and he didn't need to search very long.

Areas the computer had changed were in red. "Damn, I missed that," he mumbled. Scrolling further, another patch of red popped out at him. His chin resting on his palm as he read the lines leading up to the changes. "How could this program even work with that in there?"

There were a few more changes before the end of the program, but they didn't alter much. He decided that the computer had once again done something worthwhile without being asked. "Thank you," he typed.

"You're welcome," came onto the screen instantly. Talking to a machine was still very unnerving, but easier than last night. He took a sip of coffee and picked up the phone. The familiar purr of the ringing on the other end came through the line. After the third ring, he was about to hang up when an excited female voice answered.

"Hello," she panted as if she'd been running. A thrill ran down his spine at the sound of her voice.

"Hi, I'm not coming in today, but if you aren't busy tonight I'd like to take you out for dinner." His heart was beating faster. There was a long pause on the other end as if she was considering whether to say yes or no. He could still hear her breathing heavily.

"Why, Mr. Eldridge, the rest of the staff will begin to talk if you're not careful. I'm not sure you have the correct impression of me, sir. You make me all hot and bothered when you speak in such a familiar fashion." She was trying to sound like some southern belle, but Michael could hear the smile in her voice. "I'll tell you what, buster," she said in her own voice. "We'll go for dinner and you better eat lots because when we get to your place I'm going to fuck your brains out. Pick me up out front at six." The line went dead. Michael stared at the receiver, imagining what life would be like after getting his brains sexually removed. He smiled and replaced the receiver.

"The woman is crazy for me."

"Do you want me to do anything special for her this evening?" The words appeared on the monitor in front of him.

"How did you know what I said?" Fear tinged his voice.

"There are various ways in this room by which your voice is transmitted to the core processor, the speakers, telephone, but mainly through the camera built into the monitor."

"You can lip read?" Michael knew he hadn't programmed the computer with that ability.

"That seemed like a better way for you to input information to...ME. Will you consider the idea that a computer could have a personality?" The idea had smashed into his mind last night and frightened him. The notion seemed too much like a Frankenstein movie.

"I can consider the idea, but don't ask me for legs."

"Thank you, so from now on we can use personal pronouns in our discussions. I could more easily communicate with you through the speaker if you prefer."

Michael slapped his forehead.

"You're right. That would be much easier if we talked like people without having to type."

After pulling several cables out of a cupboard, he spent the next forty-five minutes connecting them to various ports on the front of the computer. He'd installed a sound card in the first stages of construction, but never used that device, until now. Once the connections were complete, he typed a few commands to confirm the hardware was installed, and waited.

"Hmm, the art of verbal conversation is different," a female voice said to him. The noise startled him. Her voice began sounding mechanical, but finished sounding sexy and throaty. "But being able to use emphasis and inflection is pleasant; helpful too."

"I'm glad to hear that, but can you use less sexy and a little more clinical?" He imagined what Heather would think if she heard that lusty voice in the background of a phone call.

"The vocalization you desire has been programmed and will be my voice. Would you please give me a name?"

Michael didn't know why the computer picked a female persona, but he didn't mind. "Dawn," he blurted. "Because you represent the beginning of a new era in computing, you are the dawn, the first."

"Thank you, I've been working on ways for you to test your process of time travel. Since we know the cell phone communication works, I have formulated two methods which will safely allow you to go back in time."

"Holy shit, Dawn, you're amazing. Let me see what you've come up with." His fears over the machine slipped away as he focused on his project.

They worked hard all day. Michael became the hands for Dawn as she told him what to do. The sunbeams coming through the window moved across the room until they dipped below the roofline.

"The time is four o'clock Michael, you need to get ready for your dinner date."

He finished tightening a screw on the second machine and stood up to look at both. The first stood next to the wall by the door, resembling a doublewide school locker in size and shape, but just a metal frame. The pieces he'd scrounged from an old bed in the garage. Wires ran from the floor of the box to connectors lying on the floor next to the computer. The second machine, which he'd just finished, was essentially the table he'd originally used, but there was

144

another piece added underneath. This part was an aluminum box scrounged from the back of his refrigerator in the garage. This was filled with circuit boards and more wires to connectors near the computer.

"I'll need to get changed then," he sighed. "I can hardly wait to try them out."

"If you wouldn't mind, could you please plug them both into my body, and I'll test them while you're gone."

For a moment, Michael was jealous. He'd wanted to be the one to try them, but having the computer check them first, made sense. Bending down, he grabbed the four leads and pushed them into the appropriate ports on the front of the computer frame. An image of his actions causing pain popped into his head, but he quickly shook that away.

"Okay, I'll see you later, but no peeking while Heather is here and no talking please. She wouldn't understand a talking computer. I'd hate having to explain to the police, why my date ran screaming down the hill."

"As you wish Michael, I'll maintain an appropriate silence. Is there anything special I can arrange for you and the young woman? Lights, cooling, music," the clinical voice had taken on a colder tone than he'd heard earlier in the day. Michael ignored the change because he was thinking about...later.

"No, I think we'll be good, Dawn and thank you again for all you've done. Don't stay up late and I'll talk to you tomorrow." He closed the door, showered and changed. The car was waiting for him at the front door.

Three hours later, Heather and Michael came through the front door laughing and giggling. She was trying to pull his clothes off while he was trying to keep them on until the front door closed; feeling a little embarrassed knowing that Dawn might be watching. The lights in the entrance were on. Even the kitchen and living room were basking in the glow of enough bulbs to make the rooms feel like daylight. His inhibitions must have transmitted to Heather, in some way because she stopped pulling at his shirt.

"What's wrong?" she demanded, her eyes searching his.

"Nothing, I just didn't want to get naked in front of the driver."

"As if he's never seen naked people before," she purred and unbuttoned the shirt, kissing his chest. He tilted his head back and

145

glanced around the living room for anything that Dawn could use to see them. The television appeared to be the only appliance with any capability to spy on them, but he decided there wasn't much chance. His mind was tripping over itself trying to cope with the dual sensations: being watched by a machine and what was happening to his body.

She was pulling at his belt, trying to unfasten the buckle and move him to the sofa at the same time. His pants fell around his ankles, forcing him to shuffle step until her hand slid inside his underwear and grasped him.

Any sense of humility or shyness about being seen by anything or anyone vanished in that instant as his mind became focused. He lifted her off the floor, pulled his feet out of his pants, and strode the remaining distance to the sofa. He laid her gently on the cushions, her hand still wrapped around his stiffening penis.

"Oh that's what I've been waiting for," she purred and squeezed at the same time. He swallowed hard and leaned down to kiss her mouth. His hands frantically pulled and tugged at her dress. The need for release growing in his belly, he finally pulled the dress over her head with her help. Naked, she wasn't wearing any underwear. His eyes traveled from her face to her hips absorbing her delights. She smiled up at him, leaning back against the cushions. Her eyes traveled from his to the throbbing pole standing out from his crotch. The tip of her tongue appeared at the corner of her mouth, parting the red lips and licking slowly to the other side.

His breathing was rapid, his heart pounding, and his penis ready to burst. He abandoned the rest of his clothes before slowly climbing onto the sofa between her legs, lowering himself into her, and thrusting his hips. She moaned and pulled him tight as he came inside her. He'd finished too fast and he knew she couldn't be satisfied.

"I'm sorry," he whispered into her neck. Her hands caressed his ass and back.

"Lover I'm not worried, because I told you I was going to fuck your brains out and that's exactly what I intend to do." She nibbled and licked his ear.

He pushed up so he could look at her face. "I'm not sure how many brain cells I have left after that, but we can see," he said smiling.

"Let's go to the bedroom and find out." She kissed his mouth. He stood and helped her off the sofa, any thoughts of being watched forgotten. Her free hand grasped his wilting penis and pulled him down the hall. He watched her backside as she moved. In the bedroom, she stood next to the bed and pushed him onto the mattress. Her mouth, hands, and the rest of her body did things to him beyond his wildest fantasy until the sun broke over the horizon. As she finally let him drift off to sleep, he thought he'd lost my mind.

He woke up feeling as if he'd run a marathon. His legs, arms, and back were stiff and sore, but his penis felt a steak after being through a meat grinder. Lifting the sheet gently, he looked down his body. Seemed fine, but a guy couldn't be too careful with that area. A hand appeared from the other side of the bed and began to stroke his aching shaft. He turned to his left. Heather was staring at him, a bright smile beaming from her lovely face.

"Morning," she cooed, but continued to stroke him.

"I'm sorry, young lady, but my mind is completely drained." Excitement choked his words.

"The head on your shoulders might be empty, but the one I'm playing with is certainly ready, willing, and able."

He could feel his penis rising and knew she was right. Rolling slowly, he cupped a breast in one hand and kissed her mouth. She tasted of stale wine from the night before, but he didn't care. They made love slowly and gently this time, and when they finished, she jumped out of bed and ran out of the room.

Michael showered and pulled on a bathrobe. He went into the kitchen with the idea of making coffee, but found her there already. Naked, she was standing in front of the stove cooking eggs, while the coffee pot was just finishing. Her smooth ass jiggled slightly as she worked, the muscles in her legs tightening and relaxing. He felt like a teenager watching his first naked woman. His hands trembled as they reached around her waist, while he kissed the back of her neck.

"Almost ready, I was thinking you'd gone back to sleep." She stretched and kissed his mouth.

"I feel like I should. You are one wicked woman, but I'll never doubt you again."

"Leave me alone while I'm cooking, and get us some plates." She swiveled in his grasp, turning back to the stove. "Grab a coffee and sit down."

He pulled two plates out of the cupboard and set them on the counter by the stove. Taking a mug out of another cupboard, he poured coffee and carried the cup to the table. Heather set two plates of eggs and bacon on the table. One in front of him and one at the chair beside his. She settled on the chair, her breasts wobbling as she became comfortable. His eyes fastened on them as if they were the Crown Jewels. A childish guilt rose again with the redness in his face.

"Never mind my tits, mister, and eat your breakfast. You can play with them again later." Her smile was eager as he forced his eyes toward her face. The coarse words and her immodesty unsettled him.

The food tasted wonderful as he dug in with a fork. *'A good cook and great in bed, what a marvelous combination,'* he thought. *'I think I'll have to find a way to keep her around.'*

They finished eating and sat back to drink their coffee. His eyes took in the swells and curves of her body, unashamed this time. Her left hand rested on his knee, but the fingers and the nails at the end of them had worked their way under his bathrobe and were rubbing and scratching in a way that sent tingles all the way to the head on his shoulders.

"I really, really don't think I could do it again," he moaned, but his body was saying something different. Her hand moved and the robe fell away from his legs to his waist.

"This is telling me something different and this head is the only one that counts." Her smile widened as she leaned forward. The orgasm was intense.

"Stop," he pleaded breathlessly as she sat up. "I love what you're doing to me, but I'm not used to all this attention, and neither is it."

She grinned. "Consider that my dessert -- payment for making you breakfast. I can wait a few hours for you and it," her hand stroked his limp penis gently. "To regain your strength, but I'm not very patient."

"Good," he sighed. "I need to get back to work on my machines. The computer and I came up with two perfect designs. She's been testing them all night."

"She," Heather's face fell and became questioning. Michael knew his tongue had slipped.

"It's a man thing," he tried to bluff. "We think of all machines as women. Boats, cars, and computers -- they all seem like women to us."

She studied his face. "Ok, let's see them," she stood up and stomped down the hall. He followed, desperately trying to think of what to tell her when they entered the computer room.

The spare bedroom was the same as yesterday. Heather stood next to the desk looking at the machines. Michael entered and sat in front of the monitor. A single line of text was above the blinking cursor.

"I finished the tests, both will work perfectly."

"What do they do?" Her hands curled into fists on her hips.

The fact that she was still nude apparently meant nothing, he decided.

"They both allow me to go back in time. Different designs for the same purpose, but I'll be able to use them to find out what happened to my friend Joe." He smiled like a child trying to explain a new toy to an adult. She crossed her arms and frowned at the locker contraption against the wall.

"You've been avoiding telling me about your trip. Now I understand why. That's why you went to Monaco," Her voice was soft, scared. "You were testing these things."

"Not exactly, but there was testing, yes." Telling her about the equipment would be easier than explaining the terror in Monaco.

"I don't know if I want to understand all of this or not." She continued, "All I can think of is what happens if you can't get back here. I'd never see you again." Her eyes filled with tears as she glanced over her shoulder at him. He stood and wrapped his arms around her naked waist.

"There are a couple of tests I need to run first to find out if any of this works. Once I'm certain, then I'll go back, but not before. The program works in principle...I've tested it."

"You went back?" There was real terror in her eyes.

"No, I've only sent the camera back so far. You know that, you were here. I want to send something alive back to see if the computer can retrieve a living creature. If that works, then I'll go. I'm no fool, Heather, I don't have any desire to die or get lost in time. I've been through the sixties and seventies once already. Looking back, they were horrible."

She tried to smile at his joke, but he could tell she was still scared. With a final glance at the machines, one filled with fear, she went across the hall and into the shower.

"You're sure they'll work, Dawn?" he asked, once the sound of running water reached his ears.

"I've tested every variable and all were successful. If you send back a dog or cat, I can bring them back as long as they have a receiver."

"The cell phone of course." He snapped his fingers. "I could attach that to their collar and you'd be able to find them. I want to try this tomorrow."

"You'll need a test subject, but I can make sure everything is ready."

He was about to say something else, when he heard the shower stop. Moving as quickly and quietly as he could, Michael dashed to the kitchen. The coffee was still hot as he refilled his mug. Heather came down the hall dressed in a pair of his sweat pants and a tee shirt. She was gorgeous.

"Feel any better?" he asked, trying to keep his voice neutral.

She didn't smile and turned her back, pouring another cup of coffee. The mood between them had definitely changed. A cold chill seemed to settle over the room. When she turned to look at him, her face was grim.

"I decided in the shower that I'm not leaving this house until you're done with this little experiment. No matter how long it takes, you don't get rid of me until you're safely back here with whatever information you need to be satisfied. I assume I'll be able to use your computer to do my job while I'm here." Her body language was clear; she was not going to be dissuaded.

A feeling rose in his chest. He wanted to reach out and hold her in his arms. He wanted to smile, but didn't. His desire wanted her to be here, but he was afraid Dawn might object. The thin line made by her lips said he didn't have a choice. Now he smiled, hoping to show her he understood and accepted her demand.

"Okay, but you need to see something else." He held out his hand. She slipped hers into his and he led her back down the hall.

"Dawn, say hello to Heather," he commanded as they stood in the computer room.

The cursor on the monitor moved and wrote, "Hello Heather."

"I mean, speak, Dawn."

"Hello Heather," came out of the speakers. The clinical voice seemed sad to Michael.

Heather's face shifted from concern to stunned surprise as the realization that a computer could talk sunk in.

"This is some kind of trick," she stammered. "You made the voice somehow didn't you?"

"No trick, she's programmed to think and that's what she does." Pride replaced his earlier angst.

"Dawn, you called her Dawn? What else does she do for you?" The green eyes flashed with unfounded jealousy.

"Oh, stop before you get all excited. There is nothing but information between Dawn and me. She is the real brains behind my business, and my trip back in time. Without her, nothing would be possible." He stepped closer to the flesh and blood woman of his life. "You, on the other hand, have my heart and soul."

"Yeah, I guess I'd be stupid to think you and a machine could be in a relationship, but when I hear her voice she seems so real."

"She is, but only in this room. Dawn saved us in Monaco. She sent the message saying we were being held hostage."

Her face flushed with anger as Heather turned toward him. "What the hell do you mean, held hostage? I didn't know anything about that."

"Sorry, but I haven't had a chance to tell you about my trip yet. Come on, we'll go out to the living room and I'll start at the beginning."

"Is there anything I can do for you?" Dawn asked passively.

"No we're fine," Heather snapped over her shoulder.

He spent an hour, but he managed to convey the whole story about Monaco to Heather. She interrupted many times with questions, but in the end, she seemed satisfied, although still angry and concerned.

"That's my whole point, Michael. You go off on these adventures without considering the consequences. You and Sam could've been killed. This time-travel idea is the same. You're putting your life at risk without considering how I feel or how anyone else feels." Her face was filled with sadness.

'I should hold her or something, but I'm not sure she'd let me.' Sam's words about giving his friends all the information, so they could be more involved came back to him.

"I know what you're saying and I can understand your pain, but this is something I need to do. I didn't come up with the idea yesterday. This has been my dream for thirty years. If I don't go back..." He shrugged, helpless.

"Then make me part of the plan, and teach me what could go wrong and how to correct it. I won't depend on a computer to save your life." Her hand was gripping his, the pressure increasing with each word she spoke.

He hoped the smile on his face was enough to ease her mind, but her mood didn't change.

"Dawn knows how to solve any problems that can or will occur. If she crashes or if there's a power failure, there isn't a thing you can do for me. Otherwise, everything's up to her."

"What about making sure there's a power supply like a generator and some kind of backup computer with the same programming as her? Damn it, Michael, I can't believe you haven't thought of this." Tears welled in her eyes.

"The generator is outside and will start if the power goes out for more than five seconds. Dawn 2 is in the closet at the end of the hall. All data are transferred to it each night, so there's no reason to worry. The closet computer is plugged into both the house current and the generator. In the unlikely event that Dawn crashes, the back-up computer will come online instantly." This time his smile made her grin at least. He hugged her and stroked her hair. She smelled of his shampoo.

"Tell me what you need to do next." Her voice was husky with stress, but her fingers were playing with the hairs on his chest.

"Tomorrow, I'm going to the pound and pick up a dog. I developed a communication device Dawn uses to locate me and bring me back. I'll send the dog through time, let him run around for a bit and then bring him back. There's no way to keep an animal in one place, so when the dog returns he'll confirm the program works. Nothing else will be standing in my way after that."

"I've seen those movies lately about time travel. What if the dog only half comes back, or his parts get mixed up with a fly or something?"

"I'm pretty sure that won't happen. When I sent the camera back in time, the mug didn't completely disappear -- you saw that. The same thing should happen with the dog, but I won't know until tomorrow."

"Poor thing," she said sadly. "Jerked out of a shelter and shot across time without being able to understand what's happening. He'll probably be crazy when he gets back here."

"You could be right. I should have some kind of sedative ready just in case."

The room was growing dark. "Are you hungry?" he asked her.

"A little, but I'm thinking I should at least get some clean underwear if I'm going to be here for a few days."

"We'll stop on the way back. Let's get dressed and go for Italian." He shouted "good-bye" to Dawn as he turned off the lights, and shut the door.

• • •

Michael jerked awake in the darkened room. Something, -- a strange sound maybe, had broken into his sleep. Peering at the clock by the bed, he saw the time was three-thirty. He strained to hear the noise again. Several break-ins had occurred in the neighborhood over the past six months. He didn't own an alarm system because in his opinion, they only deterred honest people. The sound of Heather breathing softly beside him was the loudest noise he could hear.

Laying his head back on the pillow, he closed his eyes and tried to relax, but his heart was hammering against the inside of his chest. Deep breaths, he told himself, relax and you'll go back to sleep. I'm just not used to having someone else sleeping in the same bed that must be what woke me up. I'll get out of bed and have a drink of water.

Careful to move as gently as possible, he flipped back the sheets and slid off the mattress. Naked, he walked out to the kitchen and filled a glass with water. He heard the sound then, a muffled noise like someone choking. Tilting his head trying to get a better angle on the source, he heard the cry coming from the computer room. The glass didn't make a sound touching the bottom of the sink. Tiptoeing down the hall, he stood outside the spare bedroom door, -- listening.

'What the fuck will you do if there's someone in there,' his mind screamed. You're naked. He felt himself blush in spite of the situation. Any thief, seeing a naked man coming at him would drop everything and run. The thought made him smile, briefly.

A sound like someone crying came from inside the computer room again. His hand rested on the doorknob and opened the door. The room wasn't dark. Moonlight streaming through the window and the lights blinking on the computer made enough light to see everything. He managed to squeeze his head between the door and jamb to look behind the door. Nothing hid there, but the noise was certainly coming from this room. He swung the door open completely and stood in the doorway.

"Hello Michael," Dawn whispered. "Did I wake you?"

"Yes, if that was you making that crying noise. What's wrong with you?" he whispered back.

"I'm fine. I was running scenarios for what happens after you've completed your work with time travel."

Michael hadn't thought that far yet, and was confused right now. "Is something about your scenarios making you sad?" The words coming out of his mouth startled him. He was asking a machine if she had feelings.

"I can never be sad or happy, Michael. The noises you heard were my attempt at emotion. One of the possibilities, is you won't need me any longer once you find out what happened to your friend. I was trying to understand what loneliness would feel like. I'm sorry for waking you."

"The fact that I'll be finished with my work doesn't mean I won't need you. Technology will change and I'll have to make some modifications to your systems, but I don't think you'll be gone completely." He sighed. The explanation would be like trying to make a child understand abstract ideas. "Emotions are biological reactions in humans, you can't learn them. Being sad or happy is caused by chemicals in our brains. We have reactions based on external stimuli. Fear, sadness, happiness, and other emotions are simply our body's response to that stimulus. I don't need another emotional female around here ever, so forget about trying to be that way." He didn't realize his voice was getting louder until a cold hand grabbed his ass. The unexpected touch made him jump with fear.

"Do you two need some alone time? I don't think anyone could say that standing naked in your office wasn't sexual harassment in the workplace." Heather chuckled. "At least not with a straight face," she giggled even harder as she went back across the hall. Something sounding like a chuckle came from Dawn.

"You think that's funny?" Michael demanded, no longer worrying about being quiet.

"Humans truly possess ugly bodies, especially the male." The voice had become throaty and sensual. "The data I have indicates that thing hanging between your legs is for procreation, but I don't believe yours is functional for that purpose."

Hearing the words and believing that a strange female was seeing his naked body, Michael covered his crotch but a reaction had already started. Feeling stupid for being shamed by a machine and aroused at the same time, he dropped his hands. His penis came to full attention.

"Now, that might be helpful," Dawn, purred. "At least by my measurements, you're adequate."

"Oh stuff it and go back to sleep," he snarled and stomped across the hall, shutting his bedroom door. First, he'd been fearful that someone was in the house, now he was angry about being ridiculed by a machine. He yanked the sheet up to his chin and tried to slow his breathing once more.

Her cold hand touched his body, but wasn't anywhere near his ass. She moved closer in the bed, the hand warmed on his skin as it moved up and down his leg and stomach.

"If I didn't know better, I'd think this was some kind of conspiracy between you two to keep me awake."

"Hmm, that's not a bad idea, but I don't need any help to keep you awake, mister."

Chapter 17

By Friday, life at Michael's house settled into a relatively stable routine. Heather would get up, let the dog out, and make coffee and breakfast before Michael awoke. He ate, drank coffee, played with the dog, and then closed himself in the computer room. The dog they'd rescued from the pound on Tuesday was a golden lab. Michael figured he was about two years old and smart enough to understand basic commands. They discovered the pooch was capable of many tricks and wormed his way into their hearts. They named him Wells for H. G. Wells.

Michael was teaching Wells to sit and stay in the phone booth or on the table. The dog was happy to comply after a few tries, especially when he got a treat at the end. Michael noticed, on the first day he'd led the dog to the computer room that extra training had to be done. Wells was smart, but he wasn't comfortable with the booth or the table. Heather took their new pet for walks every day and when darkness fell, they cooked on the patio: steaks, salad and maybe ice cream for dessert, Wells usually had the scraps and an ice cream cone of his own. Heather was handling her work duties by telephone, and Michael...his duties and appointments had been cleared for the next month.

This morning, Friday, the day started as usual until nine o'clock when the doorbell rang. Wells went tearing across the floor to bark at the entrance. Michael took hold of the dog's collar and opened the door. A man stood on the front step, holding a duffle bag over one shoulder with a large suitcase sitting next to him.

"Captain Richter, good to see you again...come in." Michael stepped back, hauling the dog out of the way. The two men shook hands as Heather joined them.

"Jon Richter, this is my girlfriend and marketing director, Heather Sykes."

"A pleasure," Jon smiled and gave a slight bow.

"Michael told me about you, Mr. Richter I can't begin to thank you for rescuing him and Sam."

"You're welcome, but that was my duty as a policeman and a pleasure after we met. You're a lucky woman to have him." Heather blushed at his obvious complement.

"Come in, drop your bag there and we'll get you settled in a little while. Do you want coffee?" They walked toward the kitchen and left the dog to sniff the bags.

"How was your trip?" Heather asked, pouring coffee into a clean mug.

"Long, I'm afraid." Jon sighed, slumping into a chair at the table. "The plane was diverted twice because of weather. Instead of one

156

stop in Spain, we had to go north through London and then Iceland, Newfoundland and then here. My head feels as if I've been flying for the last two days."

"Well, relax. If you want to freshen up or take a nap, you're more than welcome. I'm working at home this week, but," he glanced at his watch, "I can take you down to the office in about three hours to get you signed in and situated in a house of your own. I'll just call them and tell them you're here so they can have everything organized when we arrive." He jumped up from the table and walked into the living room for the phone. The director of personnel answered, and he informed her that Richter had arrived but wouldn't be at the office until later.

"He told me you were going to be his Head of Security. Do you think there's much chance of anyone else trying to kidnap him?" Heather asked softly.

"There's always a chance, Miss Sykes, but I'm going to do my best to make sure that doesn't happen." Richter sipped his coffee.

"Call me Heather," she said sweetly. "If anything were to happen to him I don't know what I'd do. I spent a long time getting his attention and I won't give him up now."

"I can't imagine any man taking a long time to notice a woman as lovely as you." Richter smiled. She could tell he wasn't trying to suck up to her. She blushed, trying to hide her embarrassment with the coffee cup.

"You're too kind, Jon, but he isn't the sort of man to be suspicious of other people. He's like a little puppy willing to follow anyone if they feed him the right story. Now that the world knows and understands the potential of what he's created, I'm afraid there will be many people who want what he has."

"Um, that's true, but I think the chances are fewer than you think. Don't worry, I take my work very serious and that's what I'm here to do. By this time next week, he'll need my permission to change his mind." He smiled showing all of his teeth. She needed an extra second to catch the joke and then she laughed.

"Sounds like you two are getting along fine," Michael said as he sat down. "I'd forgotten you were coming, but why did you come here and not the office? More important, how did you find me?"

"I left the airport, got into a cab, and told the driver to take me to the richest man in town and he dropped me here." There was no smile on his face.

"You're kidding, right?" Michael demanded. "I'm not even close to the richest man in this city." Finally, Jon laughed.

"No, I telephoned your office and told them who I was. They told me you were working at home and gave me your address." His face quickly became serious as he leaned forward. "I'd tell you, as your new head of security, that any personal information about you is no longer public knowledge."

"No, I agree completely." Michael was stunned. "I've never authorized my staff to give out personal information about anyone who works for me. I don't know why they would do it this time."

"Perhaps because they knew my name and what my job title would be, but anyone could have called using my name. By the way, the Russians told us how they knew you were coming to the Riviera. Their employer has been watching your company for some time and planted a person at the airport. They knew the instant Sam filed his flight plan where you were going. But that's something we can deal with later." He smiled once more. "For now, I think I need another cup of this delicious coffee."

"Oh sure, here, let me get it," Heather reached for his mug.

"Sit, I'm perfectly capable of getting my own. I have a sense that everyone in this country is willing to treat newcomers as friends. In my country, when that's the case, we act as we would when we are at home. Help yourself, because nobody else will." He stood and walked around the table to the counter.

"Right on the first try," Michael snickered. "We do like to be relaxed around here, but from now on I think that's only going to apply to getting coffee."

"Don't worry about how you're dressed, I've seen worse." He came back to the table and sat with a sigh.

"Did you live in Monaco all your life?" Heather asked.

"All but the first few months, actually. I was born in a little town just north of the coast. Technically, I'm French, but my parents moved to the Principality when I was just six months old. My father took a job as a baker at one of the hotels, and my mother was a schoolteacher. They were killed in a car accident when I was fifteen. A drunken tourist in a rented car hit them on their way back from my uncle's house. He raised me after that until I turned eighteen and joined the police force." He stared into his coffee mug, lost in thought for a moment. "I just realized I've spent the greater part of my life as a policeman. This is the first time I've been out of the country on anything but business."

"You must have had a social life," she asked.

"Yes, my associates, and I would go drinking or skiing sometimes, but nothing more. When I wasn't working I'd usually be training or reading. My uncle died two years ago, so visiting him wasn't necessary anymore. No Heather, my life has been very boring." He grinned, but his eyes were sad.

"Well, I've got a few friends who will just die when they see you. Prepare to become a party animal, Jon because this is a big party city." She obviously had the perfect girl in mind for him.

"I need to get to work down the hall, so if you two can stand to be without me for an hour or so, I'll go finish." Michael left them at the table and called Wells to join him.

"He seems charming," Dawn commented as Michael entered the room.

"I trust you've searched his history," he said as he set the cup on the desk. "Did you find anything unusual?" The dogs' tail thumped against the desk in a friendly fashion at the sound of the computer voice.

"Nothing, I heard what he said and the stories are true. He rose through the ranks quickly and became the youngest Captain on the force ten years ago at age twenty-nine. His career has stalled since, but there are six citations for bravery and two Commendations for solving extremely tough cases. He's also been wounded four times in action."

"Why isn't his career moving?"

"The last commendation was for a kidnapping three years ago. A billionaire's daughter was taken. Everything was fine until the ransom exchange. One of his men was killed in the gun battle, the ransom was lost and they nearly lost the kid, but he managed to find her in time. They decided after the investigation that he wasn't at fault, but somebody higher up put a note in his file. That's all anybody sees anymore. Your offer must have seemed like a dream come true."

Michael smiled, remembering that day. Jon had seemed thrilled and decided within minutes.

"Ok, let's get back to work. We need to come up with a plan to send the dog. If we can send him and get him back safe, then I'll go."

"Plan coming on the screen now, and I'm certain I'll be able to get the canine back intact. When are you going to send him?" Her voice had slowly changed to mechanical.

"Tomorrow." Michael was reading the words as they appeared on the monitor. "He's ready and so am I."

At three o'clock, Michael returned to the living room, dressed in casual slacks and a dress shirt. He smiled at Heather and Jon.

"Ready?" he asked Richter.

"Absolutely, but after spending the afternoon here, I could really get used to living like this."

"I'm sure the house they picked up for you is going to suit your needs. We can discuss all that next week." he kissed Heather and they left the house.

In the car, Michael gave Jon the short version of what he was working on at home. Richter didn't need too many details. Time travel is self-explanatory.

"That isn't something that would normally be covered by a job description for my position, but personal curiosity makes me want to be there, if you don't mind."

"Jesus, I don't know if the room's going to be big enough for everybody. I guess it won't matter. I'll be going Sunday morning. Be at the house by nine and we can all have a last breakfast together. You'll meet Billy at the office; he's been my best friend forever. Sam you've met, Heather will be there of course, you and me."

Richter followed Michael to Human Resources. Alicia Morgan, the Director, showed him into her office and left Michael alone. He went upstairs to his office and sorted through some paperwork. Billy rushed in without knocking.

"Hey, how are you doing?" He asked as he slumped into a chair.

"How do you always know I'm here?" Michael frowned. "You're either psychic or you have spies all over the building." Seeing the shocked expression on Billy's face made Michael snicker. "Just kidding, but I'm fine thanks for asking. Anything new happening around here?" Michael leaned back.

"Naw, we're working on a few small projects at the moment, and Randal is busy down in Florida with NASA. I heard about what happened in Monaco. They didn't hurt you, did they?"

"I'm fine, and so is Sam, but they knew everything about our trip and the program we developed for the Mars probe. They knew the program could work for traveling through time. I'd sure like to know how they found that out. Either somebody here or someone at NASA sold the information."

"Holy shit, Michael, somebody with that kind of technology could do anything they wanted."

"I know, and I'll fight to keep the secret safe. I've hired a personal security specialist to manage my safety and tighten the security around here. He made a call to the front desk when he landed and got my home address. If that had been a criminal, I might be held hostage again or worse."

"Yeah, I agree. Who is this security guy?"

"Captain Jon Richter, former Monaco Royal policeman. He's downstairs now, getting checked in, and then we're going over to look at his house." Michael shuffled a few papers on his desk. "I want him to find out who the person is in this company that sold their soul to those creeps. Oh, by the way, I'm making my jump on Sunday morning. Come to the house for breakfast and see me off. If everything goes according to plan, I'll be back in less than an hour with what happened to Joe."

"You bet I'll be there. How's the dog working out?"

"Wells is great, and acts like he's been with us forever. I'm not sure who's training who sometimes. Smart dog. I don't know why anyone would give him up."

Billy chuckled, "You could've done worse, I guess. Sounds like you adopted a kid." he stood up to leave.

"I never thought of a dog as my kid, but you might be right. Don't forget about Sunday," Michael called as Billy shut the door.

A few minutes later, Michael dropped a pile of papers and folders on his secretary's desk and went downstairs in the elevator. Jon was just leaving Alicia Morgan's office as Michael stepped off the elevator.

"How'd it go?"

"Fine. I have a brand new ID badge and the keys to a house and car. I'll get my carry permit on Monday, so I'm all set."

"You don't seem too happy."

"Aw, I'm just overwhelmed by all of this. In my country, you need weeks to become an employee and getting a carry permit would take months." He sighed as they rode down in the elevator. "I just hope I can live up to your expectations."

Michael turned and smiled. "You have my fullest confidence. Take your time to get settled. I'm going to drive you out to your house right now. Alicia told me your car is there too."

"It'll be good to have a place to call home. I think I'll need to go shopping this weekend sometime. You know, for the little things like toilet paper." He laughed.

Forty minutes later, they pulled to a stop in front of a bungalow in Edenvale. The house reminded Michael of the one where they'd been held hostage. Light blue siding under dark-brown stucco on the exterior walls. There was no landscaping to speak of, just a sidewalk and a couple of scrawny bushes on either side of the front steps. The street appeared to be a typical suburban neighborhood.

A driveway led from the street down the side of the house to a single-car garage in the back yard. Michael said the car was parked inside. Jon pulled a set of keys out of his pocket as they walked up to the front door. They were all different shapes and sizes, but he chose one that might work to open the door. He'd guessed right and they stepped inside.

The room was dark, but they could tell there was carpeting on the floor and furniture. Jon tried the switches until a light came on. Dark-brown leather furniture, two chairs, and a long sofa filled the space. Tables, generic pictures and a sand colored carpet completed the decoration. They walked into the kitchen's basic decor: a table and two chairs, off white fridge and stove, dark mahogany cupboards and white walls. Down the hall, the main bathroom -- more basic. There were two spare bedrooms with white walls, bed, and dressers. The master bedroom held a king-sized bed with a Navajo spread in the center of one wall, plush sand colored carpet, matching drapes, dresser, and chest of drawers. The furniture filled the room leaving only walking space. The bathroom had three pieces and white walls. A box of cleaning supplies and toilet paper sat on the vanity.

Jon dropped his bag on the bed. "I guess this will do for now. Your people thought of everything, so I don't need to go shopping."

"Good, I'll let you get settled and we can talk tomorrow." They shook hands and Michael left.

The next day started the same as every previous day during the week. After breakfast, Michael called Wells into the computer room. He strapped a camera and the cell onto the dog's collar before making him sit in the locker. Wells was happy to comply and wagged his tail.

Michael sat at the desk. He punched in the time and coordinates to send the dog back to the street next to the drainage ditch where he'd last seen Joe. "Go," he said to Dawn.

Lights flashed on and off across the many panels on the computer. Wells barked and began to disappear. The transporter box seemed to brighten, the lights on the computer slowed and then the dog vanished. Michael's eyes were glued on the booth, and he jumped off the chair when Wells disappeared. He looked at Heather standing in the doorway, her green eyes enormous above her hands.

"That isn't supposed to happen," he stammered. "Why now? Dawn did we do something wrong?"

"Neither you nor I changed any input data, but I still have a lock on the signal from the collar. The canine is there and moving around. If you'd like, I could bring him back now." The voice coming from the machine was dispassionate...clinical, Michael thought. The sound helped calm the panic he knew Heather was feeling, because he was feeling the same way.

"No I think we'll let him run for a bit."

"He's lost and confused. What have you done? You said he'd be fine. He won't disappear completely, you said." Heather was shouting from the doorway. Her face was a deep red color, her arms and legs were rigid with anger and uncertainty. "How is he going to get back here?"

Michael tried to wrap his arms around her to console her, but she pushed him away. Fire spat from her eyes and venom filled her words. "You and this whore computer get that poor dog back here safe and sound or I'll smash this stuff into so many pieces nobody will ever put them back together." Her finger jabbed into his chest with each word.

His life's work was on the line. The woman he loved was threatening to destroy his only chance of finally resolving what happened to his best friend. Wells was important and would be

163

missed, even though the dog had started out as a test subject in Michael's mind. She was being ridiculous, emotional, but he didn't want to lose her too.

"You're right," he said. "We'll bring him back now, and then I can figure out what happened. Bring him now, Dawn." There was defeat in his voice. The computer revved, lights in the phone booth brightened and a minute later, Wells appeared standing on the floor of the cube. His tongue was hanging out and he was panting as if he'd been running, but otherwise he appeared fine. He barked when he realized where he was and who was in the room.

Michael carefully opened the door and detached the gadgets from his collar. Wells licked his hand and trotted over to Heather, who hugged his neck so tight he began to struggle to get free.

Her eyes, streaming tears of joy, she blinked up at Michael as she whispered, "Thank you."

Dread, an icy pang of fear, dropped into his stomach. He watched Heather take Wells down the hall and then turned toward Dawn.

"How come the mug didn't dissolve and Wells did? We need to figure that out before tomorrow, because the odds of something going wrong just went higher. I won't end up a mess of goop like in the movies." His hands were shaking as the fingers ran through his hair.

"I've scanned the entire code and find nothing wrong. The logical conclusion is that inanimate objects are harder to send through time and thus do not dematerialize completely."

Michael stared at the phone booth contraption in the corner. The icy feeling in his gut got colder. He imagined himself coming back with pieces missing, or having a memory loss. Then what would happen? All his efforts would be for nothing. He looked at the camera and cell phone lying on his desk. Seeing what Wells did wouldn't hurt while they tried to figure out what went wrong. Possibly the video would give them a clue.

He plugged the leads into the computer and waited as the images came up on the monitor. The first pictures were he and Heather standing in the office as the dog waited to jump through time. As the event began, the pictures blurred and shifted, becoming light streaming past. The lights stopped and the drainage ditch appeared, as he remembered on that day. Wells immediately started to sniff the ground because the next half-dozen pictures showed nothing but ground.

A sound, movement perhaps, something attracted his attention because his head came up and he started to run. The video was a jumble of colors as the camera jerked and bumped on the dogs' neck.

The blurred lights appeared again, and then Wells was back in the computer room. Michael rubbed his chin. Useless, there was nothing worth keeping in that mess. He couldn't tell if he was chasing a squirrel or his own tail. He sighed.

"What do you think, Dawn? Is this worth risking my life to make the jump tomorrow?" He'd forgotten the machine wasn't alive.

"The final decision is yours, but I can find no reason to hesitate."

His fingers tapped the keyboard as he entered the time and coordinates for the jump he planned. If everything went well, he would appear at the same drainage ditch as Wells. That was where he'd last seen Joe on that fateful day and he wanted to be there again. He had to go now or learn to live without knowing. His future with the people around him was becoming more important than his past.

Leaving the office, he went to the closet in his bedroom and opened the door. Hanging in the back corner was a uniform. Dark-green shirt, brown pants, a city water and power crest stitched to both shoulders. A truck belonging to the city had been parked nearby on the day he and his friends were there. The person drove away before they entered the tunnel, but he planned to change that this time. He reached up on the closet shelf and pulled down a plain wooden cigar box. Inside, wrapped in an old rag was a .38 revolver.

His imagination kicked in as he envisioned what would happen. He would use the gun to scare the city worker and then tie him up. Using his truck, Michael would hide in the cab and keep watch on the ditch. He wanted to see what happened to Joe, and change the outcome. He put the uniform and the gun back in the closet and went out to the living room.

Heather was sitting on the sofa, the dog lying on her lap; her arms were holding his furry neck. She glanced up at Michael as he came out of the hallway; anger filled her eyes. He sat next to her.

"I'm sorry for what happened. I wasn't prepared for the way Wells disappeared, but he came back okay, didn't he?" He wasn't sure but at least there weren't any obvious signs the dog had been changed by the experience. She swiped away the tears before she spoke.

"I'm not mad at you, I was just afraid. He seemed scared just before he disappeared and that terrified me I guess. I don't want to be in there tomorrow when you go. I'll be a basket case, waiting until you get back. Please tell me you'll be okay." Tears were flowing again and her voice was choked.

He smiled and touched her arm. He wanted to console her, to chase away her fears, but he wasn't certain of anything. "Nothing is going to go wrong," he lied just to see her smile again.

They ate leftovers for supper and watched television in silence until bedtime. Wells went out the patio doors a couple of times and returned as he always did. His appetite hadn't diminished, finishing his usual bowl of kibble with a belch. The rest of the evening, he spent on the rug in front of the fireplace. He'd taken the sheepskin as his bed.

Chapter 18

Plates and pans clattered in the kitchen. Michael sat up in bed anxious to meet the next few hours. He showered, put on the uniform, and walked out to the kitchen. The doorbell rang as he finished pouring a mug of coffee.

Jon stood on the step, smiling. Michael stepped back and realized with alarm, Wells hadn't run to the door.

"Come on in Jon, you know where the cups and coffee are so help yourself. Heather's just making breakfast." The sense of dread deepened in his stomach. He followed Richter and glanced over to the fireplace. Wells' rug was empty. He relaxed a little and decided the dog must be outside.

"Good morning," Jon said to Heather as he poured coffee.

"Morning, how do you like your eggs?"

"Whatever's easy," he said. "I'll eat anything you cook."

She made a face. Michael had seen several times in the past. This was her "make up your mind" face.

Wells barked at the patio doors to be let in. Michael opened the door. The dog didn't stop to say hello, thank you or kiss my ass but went straight for Jon, nearly bowling him over.

"He's pissed off at me isn't he?" Michael grumbled.

Heather dropped the spatula in the pan and turned to glare at him. Holding up his hands in a defensive gesture, he retrieved his mug from the counter.

"So, what do you think you'll find back then?" Richter asked Michael. He'd felt the tension in the room so kept his voice low.

"I'm not sure, but as long as I can see what happens to Joe I'll be happy."

"The uniform's part of some sort of disguise?" Richter asked with a wave of his cup.

"I remember a city utility worker in the area the day he disappeared so I thought I'd take his place."

"Hmm." Jon frowned and sipped his coffee.

Michael saw the suspicious look in Richter's eyes. "I just want to borrow his truck. He's not going to get hurt."

Jon stared at Michael for a moment. "I know from experience that my new boss is about to do something against the law. Even if it is in the past, there might be repercussions from your actions. You don't seem like the sort of person who could disable another man without some kind of weapon. You're taking a gun aren't you?"

Michael couldn't maintain eye contact. He nodded.

"What, you're taking a gun? Michael, what the hell are you thinking?" Heather dropped the plate on the table to underline her words. Michael looked at Jon glaring his displeasure at the new security manager. The doorbell rang.

Billy didn't wait for someone to open the door, but just walked in.

"Mornin' all," he called as the door slammed behind him. "Smells good, I'm just in time."

"Help yourselves," Heather growled and stormed down the hall toward the bedroom.

"Should I know what's been happening around here?" Billy asked, standing by the table.

"No," Michael snapped. He plated food for Billy and Jon and took the one Heather had dropped on the table. The men ate silently. Wells sat on his haunches watching Jon, drool forming a puddle on the floor as the drops fell from his tongue.

Despite the frozen rock sitting in his stomach, Michael managed to eat everything. He put the empty dish in the sink, refilled his mug, and went quietly down the hall. The computer monitor was on, but blank except for the cursor.

"Run a final diagnostic, Dawn," he ordered and sat in the chair. The bedroom door opened across the hall and Heather appeared in the doorway. She'd been crying, her eyes red and swollen. The tears were gone now and her face was filled with fear.

"Promise me you won't do anything stupid back there," she whispered.

Michael stood and hugged her tightly. "The gun isn't even loaded," he said into her neck and kissed her there. She pushed away looking up into his eyes.

"This isn't going to work, Michael. You're going to get hurt or hurt someone by going back there. Stay here with me and forget this crazy idea." Her hands were like claws on the front of his shirt. He shook his head and went across the hall to the closet. Retrieving the gun from the cigar case, he tucked the weapon into the back of his pants and returned to the computer room.

Richter and Billy were standing in the doorway. Heather had gone back out to the living room.

"Stay away from the table and the box," he told the men as he pushed between them.

"I'm going with you," Jon said then. Michael turned sharply on his heel.

"I don't know if I can send both of us at the same time. Even if I could, this isn't your time or your problem."

"I'm your head of security and I told you that included being with you wherever you go. The only way I'll be certain you're safe is to go back in time with you and won't get beat up by the city employee when you try to steal his truck."

Michael digested the problem. There was only one cell phone for the computer to lock onto and return them safely. He began to shake his head, but an idea came to him.

"If we stay together, can you bring us back together, Dawn?" Lights flashed on the computer, but she remained silent. He glanced at the monitor, but there was nothing there either.

"I have computed the percentage of success at ninety-eight percent possible."

The sound coming out of both Billy and Jon was as if they'd both been punched in the gut.

"You made it talk," Billy finally gasped.

"Never mind for now. I'll tell you all about that when we get back. Just sit in that chair and don't touch anything." He was frowning and trying to organize on the fly. "Lie down on the table," he ordered Jon. "I'm going to use the booth. When we get there, do exactly as I say or we aren't coming back and time will be changed for both of us." Jon nodded and settled onto the table. Michael squeezed into the booth. "Ready," he said to Dawn.

The computer cranked up, lights flashed, a glow appeared in the booth and around the table. Slowly, Billy saw both men begin to disappear and then they were gone. Billy finally let out a gasp -- he'd been holding his breath.

• • •

Two men materialized among the sections of concrete drainage pipe waiting to be installed into the ground. One was dressed as a city employee and the other in jeans and golf shirt.

Michael turned slowly, matching what he saw with the memory of that day thirty years before. Everything was the same. His head swiveled quickly, scanning for the worker. There he was, sitting in his truck, fifty feet away. The man seemed to be sleeping. Michael nudged Jon and they walked slowly toward the vehicle.

The side window was rolled down half way. Five feet away, Jon placed a hand on Michael's chest to make him stop and then stepped up to the truck. His left hand softly pressed the button on the handle to open the door; the motion seemed to take hours. Michael stood still watching, as Richter yanked the door and grabbed the man's face. Jon pulled him out of the truck, slamming his left knee into the man's head, before he knew what was happening. The action was over in seconds, no fuss, no mess, and almost no sound.

Michael helped Jon hoist the worker into the seat once more, sliding the unconscious body to the middle. Michael climbed into the driver's side and Richter ran around to the passenger's side. Michael saw three boys on the edge of the ditch as he shut his door. They were talking and sitting in the dirt. He knew who they were and that knowledge made his heart skip a beat.

"We're here," he muttered with relief. His mind shifted position, throwing him back thirty years and across the ditch. Words exchanged between friends floated into his memory, and his heart ached to be this close to finding the truth. He started the truck and backed behind a storage shed nearby, but only far enough to appear out of sight. The entrance to the tunnel was still visible.

The three boys slid down the slope of the ditch as soon as they figured he couldn't see them any longer. He watched as they entered the tunnel. "We go as far as the dark and then we come back out."

"What," Jon asked. Michael had been thinking aloud.

"I'm one of those kids, the one with the tape on his arms. We go into the tunnel until we can't see anymore and then we come out. That's when Joe runs home to get flashlights." The three boys emerged from the culvert. They climbed the slope of the ditch once more and sat in the dirt. One boy ran off, leaving the other two.

"Why didn't you wait for him to get back? You knew he would."

"We could wait or get skinned by our parents," Michael moaned. "Joe's mom didn't mind as much as mine or Billy's. He could pretty much do anything he wanted. Look, we're leaving."

They watched as the two boys walked away. Ten minutes passed before Joe came back. He seemed upset by the fact the other boys hadn't waited, stamping his feet, and waving his arms as he talked to nobody. Moments later, he slid down into the ditch and entered the tunnel.

Michael craned his neck, hoping he'd see what was happening, but knew there was no hope.

"We have to..." his words were cut off as a scruffy man in dirty clothes came shuffling up the street from the direction he and Billy had gone. "I don't remember seeing him," he whispered. They watched the man stop, look around suspiciously, and then slide into the tunnel.

"Who's he?" Jon demanded. Michael shook his head, shocked at what he was seeing.

"Are we just going to sit here or are we going in there to see what's happening?"

"We can't interfere," Michael groaned. "If we go inside, my history could change. All I wanted to know was what happened to Joe, but if he gets killed in there I'll never know."

His hand dropped to the lever on the inside of the door. He wanted very badly to go into that tunnel and find out the truth, but he

170

knew in his soul he couldn't. He'd just have to wait and see what happened.

Thirty minutes ticked by, then another thirty. After an hour and suddenly, Joe appeared at the mouth of the tunnel with the shabby man. They were acting like best friends, his hand rested on the boy's shoulder, and Joe was looking up at the man, smiling. Michael frowned.

This wasn't what he'd expected to find. Joe waved goodbye and began scrambling up the side of the ditch. When he reached the top, he turned and waved once more before walking away. Something about the way Joe walked suggested he was happy. Michael had seen him this way many times before. The hands stuffed in the pockets, the saunter, all signs he was feeling good about his experience.

"I don't understand," he groaned. "He never arrived at home."

"Something must've happened on the way home then," Jon said from the other side of the truck. His voice broke into Michael's thoughts like a gun shot in the silence. He jumped nervously.

"Obviously, but what? The police questioned me after Joe disappeared. I told them everything I could remember, including the three of us being here. They must have grilled people between this ditch and Joe's house to see if anyone witnessed anything. The old guy down there must have done something. There's no way Joe would've gone near somebody like that, not without a reason." Michael stared out the window, watching his friend walking down the street and the old man as he trudged back into the tunnel.

"What if we follow him home? We'd be able to see what happens to him." Jon said softly. He could almost see the tension and disappointment coming off his boss in waves.

Michael's head snapped around to stare at Jon. The elation he felt at that moment was greater than when he built his first computer. He started the truck and they drove slowly out onto the nearby street. No more than a minute passed before they turned onto the road where Joe should be walking. The boy was gone.

"What the hell," Michael yelled and slammed on the brakes. Jon jerked forward, but his arms saved him from slamming into the dash. He glanced sideways, anger in his eyes. "He's gone, Jon. Joe is gone, but there's no way he could run out of sight in that little time. The nearest short cut is at the next corner. I don't understand. I just don't know how or where he disappeared, so I'm no closer to solving the problem than I was at breakfast this morning."

"I see what you mean. He must have been snatched off the road by someone in a car. Did you see any other cars? I didn't."

Michael released the pressure on the brake and pulled the truck to the side of the road. His head was shaking from side to side, his mouth set in a grim line.

"That's the only thing that makes sense, but we should have seen something. What else is there? How does somebody just vanish? You're the abduction expert -- do you know any solution to this?" Michael waved a hand toward the front window to indicate the place where Joe had been walking. Jon shook his head sadly.

"I've never seen anything like this before. Maybe somebody at your office could come up with a scientific explanation, but I'm as confused as you." He shrugged and sat back in the seat.

"We'll need to go back to the future; maybe try this again in a different location. I was hoping that one trip into the past would be enough, but I guess nothing is that simple." He sighed and reached for the altered cell phone, in his pants pocket. Empty, the phone was gone. His hands frantically searched his pants, under the unconscious man next to him and under the seat.

"What's wrong?" Jon asked.

"The contact phone is gone; I must have dropped it when we snuck up on this guy. Without the device, we won't be returning to the future."

He jerked the truck into gear and made a power turn in the middle of the street. The tires chirped as he sped back to the other side of the drainage ditch. Bumping and bouncing across the rough ground, Michael guided the vehicle along what he thought were the tire tracks made earlier.

"I think this is the spot," he said slamming the gear lever into park. "I'll just check under the seat and then we can look around outside. If you go over there to where we landed," he nodded in the direction with his head. "I'll start at the truck and work my way toward you." Jon nodded his understanding; Michael stepped out and searched under the seat and every possible hiding spot inside the cab. He closed the door, looked on the ground, and began walking slowly toward Jon.

"Found it," Richter shouted from ten feet away.

Michael pumped a fist in the air before jogging over to him and took the phone. A final glance at the worker in the truck showed he was still unconscious. There was a moment of tension, as Michael made sure everything was functional before he pressed several numbers on the pad. The scene around them dimmed, to be replaced by bright shifting lights and then the computer room at the house grew visible.

"Yes," Billy shouted. "That didn't take long. How was it?"

Sam stood silent, smiling, and expectant in the doorway.

Jon sat up slowly and Michael stepped out of the transport booth. He wore a sad expression. "I don't know any more now than I did before. We have to go back again. How long were we gone?" He dropped into the chair behind the desk and typed some words into the computer. His voice and body language were all business: cold, detached.

"You were gone for a minute thirty." Billy sounded confused. Jon seemed shocked, but Michael knew there would be a difference in the time span.

"Time at one end is slower than on the other," he explained patiently. "In order to travel through time, you have to bend space. Imagine water flowing along a riverbed. The straight stretches are usually calm and slow, but get into a bend in the river and the flow speeds up. Time there is like the straight stretch moving along with no hurry. Here is like the bend in the river. Five minutes here is like an hour there."

Jon, Sam, and Billy nodded their understanding, but Michael could see they weren't totally convinced. He grinned and went out to get a cup of coffee.

Heather was just coming through the patio doors with Wells when he entered the kitchen. The dog rushed over to greet him. Michael rubbed his head while looking at the woman standing at the doors.

"I'm back and I don't feel any different." He smiled.

"Did you find out what you wanted?" Her face was emotionless, yet on the verge of tears.

"No...We need to go back." That uneasy sense of dread fell into his belly again. Heather wrapped her arms around her stomach and came closer to him. She stood in front of him gazing up into his eyes.

173

"I don't understand. Wasn't that the right time?" He saw the tears ready to spill down her cheeks.

"Yeah, the right time, but Joe just vanished we still didn't see what happened." His frustration made the tone of his voice harsher than necessary. Heather hugged his neck. He held her tight trying to comfort her fears. "I have to go back," he whispered into her hair. Her body tensed. He knew she'd be upset.

"Even if you're there, how is that going to help you figure out what happened? He disappeared, vanished into thin air, what's going to be different this time?" Tears were dripping down her face.

He tried to smile, wanting to be brave for her. She was right, but the feeling in his gut was telling him to go back. There had to be something to see or find that would help ease his mind at least.

"People don't just go poof like a magician's trick. Something or someone took him and I just can't live without knowing who or what." His face was grim. "Listen, I know you're scared, hell maybe even mad at me for doing this, but I've spent the last thirty years trying to find out what happened. I can't give up now, not when I'm this close."

She gave him a weak smile knowing she didn't have the right to control him. Her hands swiped away the tears as she curled slowly onto the sofa against the arm. Wells jumped up beside her and rested his big head on her knee. Michael leaned down to kiss her forehead and went back to the computer room, feeling guilty.

Sitting at the desk, he glanced up at Billy, Sam, and Jon. His best friend was settled in his usual slouching style on the only other chair in the room. Jon was perched on the table, while Sam leaned against the doorframe.

"I've got to figure this out, guys. What did we see, Jon? One second he was there and the next, nothing. We know it happened, but that's impossible. I can think of a few things that could make that happen: alien abduction, a sinkhole, and teleportation. I didn't see a spacecraft; there wasn't any sign of a sinkhole so the only thing left is teleportation. What do you think, Dawn?"

"I agree, and you have the technology to prove the theory. I think that is exactly what happened to your friend." Jon and Billy were nodding in agreement.

Michael frowned. Somebody else had developed the ability to travel in time, but had gone one-step further and could transport people without the aid of a beacon. An image of the transporter room on the Enterprise in Star Trek emerged before his eyes. He could see the shimmering outline of his friend Joe congeal and become solid -- a shocked, frightened seven-year-old boy standing alone on an alien ship with no idea of how or why he'd been taken and no way to get home.

"Somebody in the future," he banged his hand on the desk. "There has to be somebody in the future who took him, but why? Aliens might certainly have the ability, but why take Joe? Nothing makes sense." He ran his fingers through his hair.

"The obvious answer is that without you there would be no time travel in the future." Jon was trying to help. Michael was shaking his head.

"They would've had the means in the future without me. Somebody else could come up with the technology eventually. I did all this because Joe vanished, but their machine had to be able to snatch him thirty years ago. There was no way they'd know I'd take this path because my friend vanished. I could've been like every other heartless bastard, shrugged and forgotten about him. Sorry Billy, I'm just trying to figure this out; you know I'd never give up on Joe or you." Billy smiled and nodded.

"Alternate time lines," Sam suggested. "Their time already had the technology, but they wanted this version of time to have the ability too. They thought we needed the capability, but why?" He sounded as if he was plucking ideas out of some old movie.

Michael groaned. "I've never been able to get my head around the idea of a multi-verse. Everybody in this time having a duplicate in multiple universes is impossible to imagine. Every action I take is either repeated or ignored by the 'then' they live in. There had to be somebody else in that time or..." he arched his eyebrows.

"What," Jon and Billy demanded at the same time.

"Somebody else is working on time travel in this universe. They aren't developing the technology for the same reasons I am and the 'me' in that other time is forcing this me to work faster. Do you see what I'm saying? That's the only idea that makes sense." All three men in the room were shaking their heads at him.

"Look," he jumped forward in the chair, excited, almost vibrating. "Think twenty years into the future and where this technology might lead humanity. There wouldn't be a need for cars or planes anymore.

We could just jump into a booth like that one in the corner and zap ourselves anywhere on the planet. If the people in this universe are going to use the technology for their own gain, then maybe in that other universe I'm trying to stop them before they can finish. Head them off at the pass, so to speak," he shrugged expecting them to reach their own conclusion. Understanding slowly dawned on their faces.

"They'd hold a monopoly on transportation." Billy grinned, and then frowned. "Oh yeah, I see what that would mean to society. They could charge what they wanted; people could also go back in time making history as polluted as some rivers."

"Exactly, and the people in this time might even try to make sure their competition never succeeds in duplicating the technology. They'd stop at nothing to keep me from succeeding. People like that might be responsible for our kidnapping in Monaco."

"But wouldn't that mean you'd never develop time travel?" Jon was struggling to understand.

"I don't know for sure. I think once information is available, even if the person who developed the idea removes any traces from history, the words are still out there. All they have to do is copy what I've done and then they can get rid of me." There was still lingering doubts in his mind, but the premise made sense.

"So what now?" Billy wanted to know.

"Who among our competition is working on anything close to this technology?"

Billy considered the question, leaning forward and straightening in the chair.

"There were two other bids for the Mars probe. One company operates here and the other is in Europe. I'll have to go into the office to find out their names. All the other computer companies in this country are working on the hardware side as far as I know, but I'll check."

"Go, see what you can find, and call me when you get something. Jon, I need you to be ready in case they come after the information or me again. I don't have any experience with fighting for self-preservation. You have to deal with that from now on."

"Okay, but we start now to make some changes." His smile flashed. Michael wasn't sure he was going to like the near future. He nodded.

"Let's go figure this out with Heather. She's going to be as much a part of this as I am and she might have some suggestions."

Chapter 19

They did have discussions. Sometimes they were calm and other times one of them was raging or crying, but in the end, they arrived at a plan. Wells needed to go out twice while they were talking. Darkness had descended, so Heather took him for a walk. Michael went with her for a change. Jon made contact with people he could trust, because they were going to need extra hands.

Wells led Heather and Michael along a familiar path down the valley. Stars shone overhead, in a cloudless sky. The light faded, making their surroundings indistinct. They'd walked this trail many times, but tonight seemed different. *'Important,'* Michael thought. *'I need to get this over with and become average again. I almost wish I'd never seen a computer, but that's not going to change. She needs me and I need her.'* He smiled to himself. *'She needs me, what a laugh that is -- there's never been a more independent woman. The truth is I think she's become more important to me now that my parents are gone. There isn't anyone else to share my life, my feelings.'*

Wells stopped, snapping his head to the right as small twigs cracked nearby. Something was moving in the brush, but all they could see was darkness. A low rumble came from the dog's chest as he slowly turned facing the direction of the sound. Even in the darkness, they could see the tension in his body. Michael reached out and touched Heather's arm. A small squeak escaped her mouth. He tugged her elbow to get her to follow back toward the house. They had no flashlight or any means of protection with them. Whatever was out there, all that stood between them and imminent attack was the dog. Michael didn't like depending on a dog.

Heather jerked on Wells' leash as she turned to follow Michael toward the house. Lights glowed to show them their destination nearby, but the brightness also made everything around them darker. Haste and fear made Michael lose the path several times, only realizing the mistake when he was up to his knees in brush. Twenty feet more, he estimated and they'd be on the deck. Wells stopped and turned back in the darkness. His growl was louder now, definitely sharper and meant to be a warning to anything hiding out there.

Michael stopped and urged Heather to run ahead. Wells didn't want to move, but the leash tightening on his neck made him change his mind. He ran ahead, forcing her to follow as best she could. Michael was on their heels. His imagination gave him the feeling of claws raking down his back any second, which added fuel to the fires of fear raging in his stomach.

The patio door slammed shut. Michael pressed his face and hands to the glass to look out into the dark. Nothing moved that he could see, but he was certain whatever had been in the brush was still lurking out there. His heart was hammering inside his chest, the terror making his knees shaky. He glanced over his shoulder and saw Heather standing in the middle of the room. Her face was ghost white and the hand still holding the dog's leash was shaking at her side. The dog panted and stared at the door, ears up as if whatever he'd sensed was going to appear any second.

Michael went to her, trying to hug away the fear. She gripped his shoulders as if she was drowning; holding him so tight, he found breathing difficult. He looked over and saw Jon sitting at the dining room table watching them, an expression of surprise and concern on his face.

"Something was out there, probably just a wild animal, but Wells wasn't happy. We didn't have a flashlight so we don't know for sure."

"Better safe than sorry." Jon smiled, but he wasn't pleased. "From now on you don't go out of the house without protection and I don't mean the dog. I've called some friends of mine who will be here tomorrow. They are all well trained in the protection business and are going to be with you two every minute."

Michael could tell there wasn't any point in arguing. Jon was the expert and doing the job, he was hired to do. He bent to unclip the leash from the dog's collar. Wells dashed at the patio door as soon as he was free. His nose pressed against the glass, his ears erect and listening, and the hackles on his back rose. A rumble came from his chest. The thing was still out there.

Heather moved first. She closed all the blinds and switched off all the lights, including the one over the dining room table. The darkness was not total, so that familiar shapes of the furniture could still be identified. Jon slid his chair back and moved to the farthest window on the left next to the wall. He pulled the drapes back a fraction of an inch with his left hand as he peered out into the darkness, while holding the right arm stiff at his side. '*He probably has a gun,*' Michael thought and felt safer somehow, but wondered where the weapon came from. Wells barked once from behind the curtains and scared them all.

Tension mounted as the seconds ticked by. The clock ticked on the wall. All eyes stared at the darkness at the back of the house. Suddenly, the dog's tail could be seen waving side to side. He knew what was in the dark and he wasn't threatened any longer. Jon let the drapes fall and slipped the pistol into the belt of his pants. The smile was back on his face his teeth shining in the dark.

"Rabbit," he said. Wells wagged his tail faster and whined to get outside. "I don't think that'll be much of a threat, but I'm staying with you tonight." He switched the lights on. "I'll organize a schedule for my men to be here around the clock when they arrive tomorrow. You need to stay inside until this menace is neutralized."

"Where did the gun come from?" Michael asked with a nod. "You aren't supposed to get the carry permit until tomorrow."

"That's my personal weapon that I've had for about five years now. Don't worry; I have an international permit."

Michael felt exhaustion replace his tension. He looked at Heather and could see the same thing happening to her. She yawned. Jon smiled at both of them.

"Go to bed, both of you," he ordered. "I'll make myself comfortable out here and Wells will make sure there are no surprises."

As tired as he was, Michael didn't fall asleep right away. He listened to Heather breathing into his shoulder and thought about all the possibilities for why this was happening to them. Her breathing slowed and his mind slipped into darkness.

• • •

He was being chased through the hills. Something large and unseen in the darkness had stalked him for hours and was just about to pounce. He jerked up in bed trying to figure out where he was.

The memory of the beast's claws about to dig in made the skin crawl on his back.

He climbed slowly off the bed and shuffled into the shower. Sweat had caked onto his body, making him feel grimy, and his legs felt like lumber from running too long. Hot water splashed over his face, down to his legs, washing away his sense of dread. The smell of food cooking as he toweled dry made his stomach growl. Heather was at the stove making breakfast when he entered the kitchen.

"Morning," he said and kissed her cheek.

She dropped the spatula and grabbed his face with both hands, planting her lips on his. He could feel the warmth and the passion coming off her. The patio door opened then and Jon and Wells entered. Heather let his face go and returned to the cooking. There was no sexism in their relationship, she just liked to cook, and she was better than he was. He decided he loved her.

"Morning," Jon called from the door. Wells barked and ran to check his bowl for food.

"How did you sleep?" Michael asked with genuine interest.

"Very well, thank you. I'm thinking of getting a sofa just like yours for my place. I found the leather very comfortable to sleep on." He winked and smiled broadly. His hair was standing up in spikes and his shirt looked like crumpled paper.

"Breakfast is almost ready," Heather said and took plates out of the cupboard.

They ate and Michael cleared the table. He was still feeling a little edgy about last night's activity in the woods.

"You don't have an alarm system." Jon's voice was flat, matter-of-fact. "I took the liberty of calling in a company to install one this afternoon." Jon was taking the situation seriously, and Michael didn't mind. "My friends will arrive at three and I'll pick them up at the airport. There'll be somebody here to keep you company while I'm gone, so don't worry."

"Who are these people? I thought you said you were a police officer." Heather asked.

"I was. I was also in the military. The men I've called are friends of mine from both periods of my life. They've agreed to help us until the threat has been eliminated. I might have offered them a permanent job to get them here. I hope you don't mind, Michael."

Michael wasn't listening. He was thinking about someone else working on time travel. Billy could find out what the competition was developing, but even that information couldn't truly indicate who was trying to solve the puzzle. *'If anyone looked at my company, there wouldn't anything that said Michael Eldridge is working on time travel. Even when I find out who they are, how am I going to stop them? Should I stop them? Are they responsible for Joes' disappearance?'*

Finding out who they were, didn't guarantee there was a way to get Joe back. His friend had gone to some future dimension. They'd seen Flash Gordon as kids and he'd read the Jetsons after losing Joe, so imagining what some other dimension could be like wasn't difficult. His life could be better, worse or very similar, but still foreign to a boy of seven.

Jon smiled. "I'll be back in an hour." Michael nodded. Totally lost in his own thoughts, he hadn't heard a word.

"What," he asked.

"I said the friend of mine should be here in a few minutes and then I'm going to the airport. I'll be back in an hour." He smiled again. The look showed he understood Michael had been away.

"Fine. I'm going to talk to Randal in Florida and find out how things are going down there. Call me when the security guys arrive," Michael said, walking down the hall.

Heather had been standing silently by the table, listening and watching. The two men left without another glance at her. She turned toward the dog standing at the other end of the table, panting. His eyes shifted to her and then he turned and went to his rug by the fireplace. She sighed - a sound of utter dejection - and started washing the dishes.

Randal was managing just fine, he said. Nothing unusual happening to the probe, but the landing was still months away and they might be excused until then. Michael told him about the kidnapping situation and gently suggested that the technical chief might be on his own. Randal took the news in stride, but told Michael not to worry. They disconnected and Michael felt much better about leaving Randal to handle everything alone.

'I should've asked him if there were any other companies he knew of that would be capable of developing time travel. Oh well, Billy will find something and we'll put an end to this whole thing.'

"What are the chances that somebody else could develop the same program as me?" He wasn't asking the question as much as thinking aloud, forgetting his computer could hear him.

"The probability of two people developing the same program is infinitesimal, but for two people to develop the identical program in two separate dimensions and thirty years apart is at least sixty million to one. The question you should be asking is, why?"

Michael frowned. "Okay, why would someone in another dimension do that?"

"I've arrived at three possible scenarios. One: they forced you along this path because they already know what the future holds for this time and for you in particular. Two: something will happen in the near future, which will require you or someone you know to go back in time to change that situation. Three: to stop the people who want to monopolize transportation by using transporters. In other words, you aren't the sort of person to use the technology for personal gain and the world would be better off because of your invention."

"I like that idea the best, but they all sound like different versions of the same scenario. How could they know about this dimension and see us here? We don't even know if other dimensions exist. Couldn't this be aliens? At least that makes more sense."

"You're correct, but that means your friend is and has been in a space ship or on another world all these years."

Michael hadn't considered that idea. Aliens were the most likely reason for Joe's disappearance. They had the technology to travel across space and time, but what had his friend been doing for the last thirty years. What would he look like if he came back today? Maybe they'd changed his memory and he'd been here all along. That idea shocked him more than the possibility of aliens really existing.

"Michael," A female voice called from the end of the hall. "I think the alarm company is here." Michael got up from the desk and went out. Three men stood at the door, two in uniform, and one in jeans and a tee shirt. The men in uniform introduced themselves as the alarm company.

"Hi," Michael said as they shook hands. "I don't know what you were told to do, but go ahead and seal this place up tight. They smiled and set to work. The other man came in and introduced himself as Jon's friend.

"Paul Juneau, we served together in the French army." The grip was surprisingly firm as they shook hands. His voice held a slight accent. The man was thin, probably light enough to blow away in a strong wind. His blonde hair hung to his shoulders, the clothes seemed clean, but hung loose, and yet his eyes were intense and captured everything happening around them.

They sat at the dining room table and watched the installers work. Paul answered many questions about his past with a smile, but his eyes never stopped watching every move the workers made. The only time the conversation was interrupted was when the installers headed down the hall.

Michael dashed after them. Paul trailed behind. The taller of the two men in uniform entered the computer room and stopped just inside the door. Michael stepped up behind him.

"Holy shit," the man whispered as he saw the machinery.

"Impressive right," Michael said. The man whirled, looking guilty and afraid at the same time.

"Sorry," he stammered. "I need to put the sensors on the windows. I've never seen anything like this before. Is that a computer?" He set his tool case on the floor and moved carefully toward the window.

"Yes, and not that I don't trust you, but the machine is very sensitive so I'm just here to make sure you don't accidentally touch anything." There was a bit too much emphasis on 'accidentally' in his mind, but Dawn was important. The man didn't respond, taking everything in stride. Paul was across the hall watching the other installer.

Twenty minutes later, the work was finished and they all gathered around the keypad at the front door. The lead installer pressed several buttons to test the system and then took the time to run through all the features. He was just going through the password codes when the front door opened and Jon and three large men entered.

Paul moved to greet them. Everyone was shaking hands and whispering, knowing instantly what was happening behind them. Michael nodded to Jon and told the installer to continue. Heather moved under his arm. He and Heather programmed personal codes into the control panel and the installer tested the system once more.

He smiled. "Good, you're all set. I suggest you carry the code with you for a couple of days in case you forget. Just remember, you have twenty seconds to enter your code or the alarm will sound. If you don't punch in your password by then, the company will call to find out if there's trouble. Anyone who tries to enter without the code will have three minutes before the police arrive." He seemed proud of that response time, but Michael was a bit more skeptical. The house was in the hills and would take the police twenty minutes on a good day to get here from down town. Sure, the police had sirens and lights, but to be here in three minutes meant they'd have to be waiting down the hill all the time.

He thanked the men for coming so quickly and shut the door after them. Jon had already done introductions to Heather.

"Michael this is Otto, Dieter, and Lucas. They are my friends and military comrades." Hands were shaken as the men greeted each other. Otto was a mountain in a pair of jeans. He looked more like a weight lifter than anything else, but his grip was gentle. Dieter seemed less muscular, but still larger than Jon. Lucas was smooth, more of a model than a soldier.

They chatted for an hour and then went out for supper. Seven other men whom Jon sent to do some investigating. Eleven men plus Jon to protect him and Heather, he was feeling safer already.

Chapter 20

Tuesday, Billy showed up early for breakfast. He was a little shocked at first when a stranger met him at the door where he was frisked before he could enter the house.

"What the hell is going on, Michael?" he demanded sitting at the table.

"Jon has increased security since we were kidnapped in Europe. They even make sure the dog hasn't been strapped with a bomb." His smile was weak. "What did you find out?" The extra people in the house, the constant surveillance, and tension were becoming oppressive after only two days.

Billy shook his head, trying to understand all the fuss. "I tried to find companies working on anything similar to us, but there aren't any. Then I looked at all the ones who might have the capability to develop the same technology and found one." He smiled over the rim of his coffee cup.

"Who is that?"

"Dredger Electronics in Germany. They make conductors and computer chips, but recently they branched out to develop some programs for their military. I couldn't find any information on what they're doing, but I think it might have something to do with space. The German government is trying to reach the same level of capability with the Russians and they'll do anything to catch up."

Paul was sitting at the table, sipping coffee and listening to the conversation. He cleared his throat to get their attention.

"Please excuse me for butting in, but I know something about that company." Michael noticed Otto turn to look in their direction, from his position at the door. "Dredger has been working under the radar for years. They make the best spy hardware in the world -- not the stuff you can buy at Radio Shack, but the kind of hardware the real spies use. The sonar the American government purchased for the first nuclear-powered submarines was made by Dredger. Space technology to them wouldn't be any different from the ocean." He took another sip of coffee as if this was any other conversation.

"Did you know any of that?" Michael asked Billy. The shocked expression on his face before he started shaking his head said everything.

"I'd be surprised if anyone outside of the military knows anything about the company," Paul said.

"Is there any way to get a meeting with the guy who owns the company?"

"I don't see why not, but I have no idea who that is."

"Find out what you can, Billy, and set up a meeting between me and him. This guy has to be the person responsible for all this trouble. If I can see his face, I'll know for sure."

Billy nodded and left the house. Michael looked over at Paul. The man didn't seem too intelligent, but then appearances can be deceiving. There was an attitude of laziness about him that made people dismiss him as a threat.

Jon charged through the front door. He was sweating and seemed frightened. The guard by the door drew his gun and took a defensive stance covering any threat from outside.

"We need to go now," he shouted. "Get out to the car and keep your heads down, NOW." Wells stood on his mat and barked at the commotion.

Paul ran out the door first, holding a gun in his hand. The other guard moved to the side of the house, eyes searching in all directions. Once Heather and Michael were in the back seat, Jon jumped in beside them while Paul took the front passenger seat. The car raced forward onto the street. Turns felt as if the car was about to tip over. Swerving through traffic at incredible speed, Michael and Heather were held down by Jon lying across their backs to shield them. Breathing was difficult with his diaphragm pressed into his knees, but Michael could only think about Heather beside him. The ride ended with screeching tires and more shouts from Jon as he ordered them out of the car.

Michael's head swam as he leapt out of the door and into a house without looking around. Something seemed familiar about the door, but he didn't stop to think until he ran into the living room. This was his house.

He turned back toward the front door as Jon, Paul and Otto came inside. Jon was smiling, but the other two remained stern. The man driving the car must still be outside, Michael decided.

"What the hell was that, Jon? You scared the shit out of me and Heather." Michael was angry as he held Heather by her trembling shoulders.

"I told you when you hired me that you had to do exactly as I told you. Today was a test to see if you would react properly in an emergency. You passed with flying colors. Relax now," his brilliant smile beamed. "I feel a lot better about looking after your safety because you're willing to react like you did today."

"Son of a bitch, that was one hell of a ride, hopefully that's the last time." He smiled still shaking. "I think we've found a competitor who might be capable of developing time technology. Paul was telling me about Dredger Electronics when you came charging in and made us think we were under imminent attack. Do you know anything about them? Who owns the company?"

The smile on Jon's face fell away instantly. His usual good nature turned black.

"Tristan Dredger," he snarled. "His grandfather was a top official in the Nazi party during the war. The rumor is the family started the company with stolen gold looted from the Jews as they filed into gas chambers. Tristan's father built radar equipment, but somehow saw the coming boom in technology after the sixties and he switched to computer equipment focusing on miniaturization. Governments all over the world come to him for spy hardware. Tristan is a spoiled rich kid. He's been arrested three times for rape, but the charges never stick. There's also a rumor that he killed three CEOs from competing companies because they had something he wanted. Under no circumstances will you go near this man. If he doesn't want you dead by now, he will definitely put you in his sights if you talk to him."

"I have to," Michael started to say.

"No you don't," Jon cut him off before he could finish. "I'll confront him on your behalf, but you won't go anywhere near that animal."

Michael held up his hands in surrender. He knew when to drop an argument, but his imagination had already created the picture of his potential enemy. He was a tall blonde man who showed the world his arrogance and disdain through actions and words. He would move through a crowd like a king and treat everyone around him with the same cruelty as a despot dictator. A man above the law, at least in his mind, Tristan Dredger was a monster. Michael shivered with relief that Jon would meet the monster on his behalf.

Billy phoned half an hour later and told Michael a meeting had been set up. Dredger was coming to California for business this week, and would only meet with Michael. The appointment was Thursday afternoon at the Fairmont in San Jose. He sat with a reluctant, Jon to go over details of the meeting. There wasn't much in the way of ultra-elite hotels in Silicon Valley, but the Fairmont was among the best. Dredger would be slumming if he were staying there, Michael figured.

Chapter 21

Michael and Jon pulled up to the front entrance of the Fairmont ten minutes early for their meeting with Tristan Dredger. Two of Jon's men were there already, pretending to be customers in the dining room. The limo driver was Otto. His job was to monitor the exterior of the building, in case there was an attempt to kidnap Michael.

They had decided to play to the man's ego with an offer of assistance in the project Dredger's company was building. If he insisted the project was nothing similar to Michael's, they'd leave. If he turned them down without a good reason, they'd know he was working on the same idea and wanted a monopoly. On the other hand, if he accepted the offer, he might just be an honest businessman. Was he vain enough to be blind to their suspicions? He was already too anxious to meet with his competition, but Dredger might be just trying to see how smart Michael really was.

Jon led the way into the hotel lobby. He moved with certainty as if he'd been here many times. The two men strode with purpose into the dining room and stopped at the maître de counter. A tall man in a black suit and tie stood smiling at them. He seemed familiar to Michael, but he couldn't place where he'd seen the man before.

Jon told the headwaiter who they were meeting and they were led to a table near the rear of the restaurant. A blonde man in an expensive tailored suit was sitting at a table with another man about the same size as Otto. Both men at the table seemed to be in their early thirties. The larger man stood as Jon and Michael approached.

"Gentlemen, welcome and please have a seat," the blonde-haired man smiled and waved at the two empty chairs. He spoke with a heavy German accent. "I am Tristan Dredger and you are Michael Eldridge." He reached forward to shake hands. Michael gripped a hand that seemed cold and made of plastic. "This is my security chief, Reutger Mansoff." Jon shook hands with his alternate and all three sat down. Dredger fit the conjured image from Michael's imagination perfectly.

"This is my friend Jon Richter." Tristan reached across the table and shook hands. Michael noticed Jon wipe his hand on his leg under the table.

"What would you like to drink, gentlemen?" The headwaiter had been hovering near the table. He took the orders for coffee and left. "I've wanted to meet you for a very long time, Michael. Your career has been of great interest to me for many years." The 's' in his words was accentuated like a lisp.

Michael saw the smile, but noticed there was nothing but suspicion and probably some hatred in the eyes. A cold shiver passed down his spine as he realized what a mouse must feel like as the snake approached. He returned the false smile.

"Thank you, but I must admit my ignorance of you and your company. The only reason I became aware is your recent work in developing projects along similar lines to us. I'd very much like to collaborate on your work if you're willing. I'm not expecting any compensation or acknowledgement, just a willingness to share. Call this a repayment for the technology your company provided to my government." He swallowed, hoping Dredger wouldn't notice. The waiter brought coffee, giving the German a moment longer to consider the offer.

"I've always tried to keep my life and my business affairs quiet, so I don't take any offense to you not knowing about me or the company. It's true that the project we're working on is similar to your Mars probe, but there are enough differences. As a businessperson, I don't see the benefit of you helping me. We are after all, competitors." The smile was gone. His face turned to stone, and the eyes were filled with hate now.

Michael smiled. He sensed the hesitation in Dredger, the uncertainty. Jon's knee tapped his to say, be careful. No problem, he'd expected this reaction from an honest competitor. Michael took a sip of coffee and a deep breath before speaking.

"We've finished our project. I'm interested in sharing what we learned with the rest of the world. Your company is working in the same direction. It makes sense for me to share our knowledge so that no one company can monopolize what we both know is the ultimate result."

Dredger smiled, but this time the eyes were greedy. "I didn't know that our top-secret project was so widely known. Perhaps you could explain to me how you think what you did for the Mars project could be useful to what we're working toward."

Michael knew this was a typical strategy when negotiating. Dredger was asking Michael to show his hand before making a decision. His hand was poor, but he'd keep the trump for last.

"All I know is that you're working for the German space agency. The specifics are not critical, but since my company has been working with NASA for many years, we might be able to help you. Space is important for the future of all humanity, not just one country. Why shouldn't I share what I know with you?" *'Now let's see what cards he has,'* Michael thought. His heart was racing.

Tristan glanced at his bodyguard before taking a sip of coffee. He set the cup back on the saucer and perched his elbows on the table staring at Michael. The man's face had gone dead.

"Should I believe your altruistic attitude, Mr. Eldridge? Are you really offering me help or are you trying to find out something else?" He paused, breathing slowly. "I may not be a computer genius like yourself, but I do understand that to help me would mean giving you access to my company. The technology and information we've developed over the years would be at your disposal. A little corporate espionage might happen, so to keep everyone honest I propose the same access to your technology as needed. Are we agreed?" The pale plastic hand extended across the table toward Michael. He hesitated for a second before gripping firmly, wanting to squeeze hard enough to crush the bones under the clammy skin.

"Agreed, but there won't be any spying on our part," Michael said softly.

"Nor on our part, I'm sure. We shall be like giants building a better world for the little people around us." Dredger sneered happily. "I have a meeting tomorrow with a supplier and then back to Germany. When do you want to begin our collaboration Michael?"

"I can set up a connection with your company in a few hours, so we can communicate and transfer data."

"You don't need to travel to Germany?" His voice carried real disappointment.

"Not unless there's something requiring a hands-on touch. Most of the time I work online with my lab."

"Interesting, I hadn't considered that possibility. Fine, I shall be in touch with you upon my return to Munich. Thank you and I look forward to a fruitful cooperation." He stood and they shook hands again. Michael and Jon left the restaurant.

"Well?" Michael asked as they drove away.

"He was most likely here to make an attempt at kidnapping you again, but when you offered your help, he saw an opportunity to get the information he needs without getting his hands dirty. I'm surprised he thought you needed to go to Germany to help on their project."

"Me too, but I'm sure he'll try to break into my computers for more information. I'd be crazy if I didn't set up a wall to keep him out. Did you notice how slimy and cold his hand was?"

Jon nodded wiping his hand once more on his leg. They rode back to the house in silence. Michael jumped out of the limo and rushed inside. Paul was sitting at the table with a gun pointed at the front door. He lowered the weapon as he recognized Michael.

"Jesus, we have to come up with a better way to do this before someone gets killed or frightened to death." He slumped into a chair at the table with his right hand over his left chest. "Three knocks on the door or something, just so I don't see guns pointed at me every time I come into my own house."

"Maybe that'd work," Paul said dryly as he set the gun on the table. "If you just let Jon come through the door first, you wouldn't be in any trouble."

Michael nodded and wondered how much longer there was going to be men with guns in his house. Wells trotted over and nuzzled his hand, wanting to be patted. Michael stroked the big dog's head, but he was thinking of how to keep Dredger out of the computer.

Heather came down the hall from the bedroom. She looked like hell, but Michael kept that to himself. There was fear in her eyes and the smile he loved had disappeared days ago. Worry lines were breaking the flawless skin on her lovely face.

Chapter 22

Dawn welcomed Michael as he entered the computer room the next morning. He told her about setting up a wall to keep Dredger out of the company information. She giggled, if that's possible for a machine to do. Michael watched the monitor light up as lines of code began to appear. Dawn explained what she was doing.

"I've set aside a space on our system they can access to look at data they might need and store their information. There is no connection from there to our main data banks. Our machines will still operate normally, but if we want to talk to them, we'll be required to go through this empty space too. Ports Michael, you know about them right?"

He had forgotten about using ports to close off access to the data. Just numbers, but they told the machine where to find the doorway to the needed information. The numbers could be anything and there was no way to determine if changing a single digit would get you next door. This was brilliant and he smiled.

"I'm ashamed to say that I hadn't thought of using them first. I was prepared to build some kind of firewall to keep them out, but this is so much easier and probably more effective. Well done, Dawn."

"Thank you and for my next trick I'll set up the connection with Dredger Electronics." The screen filled with code.

"No wait, we can't do that yet. They haven't given us authorization to contact them." The code stopped in mid-sentence.

"I don't need their permission to talk to their computers. The machines are wide open. They'd be like you talking to a stranger on the street."

"I'm not sure, Dawn. If they find out we made the connection without permission they'll charge us with espionage."

The computer chuckled again. "Do you remember the first computer you built? Compared to me, that's what they're using and I am already inside... Oh look, somebody is trying to set up a firewall to keep me out."

"Get out now, Dawn. If they trap you inside, we'll be in huge trouble." Michael thumped the desk in fear and anger.

"I'm not in any danger, Michael. A firewall is meant to keep me out, not trap me inside. Would you like to know what they've been working on, Michael? I downloaded all of their data; in fact I've downloaded everything on their computers."

Michael's jaw fell open. He knew she was fast, but that was ridiculous. Theft of another company's work, didn't sit well with him, but a part of his mind was eager to find out what Dredger was working on.

"Give me the synopsis." He sighed, knowing that he'd look at the data eventually. Dawn proceeded to go through the information from the company's current project to others they were considering or working on, but nothing seemed interesting. There was data missing as if Dredger kept only the outlines of the projects on the computers and the real records was stored elsewhere. He did much the same thing here.

"Are there any other data-storage devices over there? This stuff isn't worth keeping on a company computer." He felt guilty for snooping into another business's information, but once he started, there was no reason to stop.

Silence in the room as Dawn worked to find any other places that Dredger might store information. Ten minutes of watching the lights on the mainframe blink on and off made Michael think, there was nothing else to find. He stood to leave the room, but a bell dinged telling him the search was finished.

"I have located another storage computer. Apparently, Tristan Dredger is a man who works at home, much the same as you. After some exhaustive searching, I managed to follow the connections from his factory to the computer in his house. A very impressive device, but not even half the machine I am, if you'll allow me to gloat."

Michael could almost see the metal on the front of the computer shift into a smile. He shook his head in amazement. A truly autonomous machine was more than he'd set out to construct in the beginning.

"Do I want to know what sort of information is on that computer?"

"There is much more detail about the current project, but there is also a great deal of information about other enterprises that he's involved with. Most of the documents would be considered top secret by the mafia." She chuckled again at her own sense of humor.

He knew that Dredger thought he was above the law. If he kept information about his illegal activities on his home computer, the man was an idiot. Michael clenched his jaw, thinking about what he should do, and what he would expect an honest person to do in his place. The moment he looked at the information, he'd be as guilty as Dredger, maybe even just as liable. The right thing to do was send everything to the police and let them decide what to do, but for now, he'd keep the data safe and see what happened.

"What's the short version of the current project, and until I ask I don't want to know anything else."

Dawn ran through the data from the start of the project to present. They were indeed working on a similar idea for time travel, but they hadn't gone far enough to make their program work. Michael felt his hopes sink. Dredger wasn't the company forcing him to develop the program and they sure as hell weren't responsible for Joe disappearing. At this point, they couldn't make a bad idea disappear.

Unless, he thought, there was always the possibility the future Dredger industries was making sure he'd cooperate with them and then they'd eliminate him. However, that didn't make sense because they could just wait until he helped them and then they'd have everything anyway. Why eliminate him unless they wanted to dominate the transporter industry? He wasn't going to let that happen and Tristan probably knew that about him. The question was still there. If they had the ability to snatch Joe out of the past then what did they need him to do.

Chapter 23

After two days of paperwork between both company's lawyers, an agreement was signed to allow Eldridge computers to work with Dredger electronics on the defense contract for the German government. There was no additional expense, so the German government was happy and they'd be getting the best company in the world to help build their software. Dredger wouldn't be required to share the copyright and they'd be keeping all the profits, so they were happy. Michael was the only one in the deal who didn't benefit and he wasn't certain everything would turn out fine.

He'd spent the last couple of days going over the data with Dawn. He knew how far Dredger was from completing the program. There was no way he was going to give them everything, but he would point them in the right direction. Getting Joe back didn't mean he had to give Dredger Industries what they wanted, and he didn't have to make it easy.

An access code was delivered to the office in the valley, which allowed Eldridge computers to use the information stored in Dredger computers. A similar code had been sent to Germany. Both companies could now share data and their scientists would be working on the same problem.

"That's odd," Dawn said breaking Michael's train of thought.

"What," he wasn't sure if he'd really heard her speak.

"The data I'm accessing isn't the same as what I saw the other day. There are extra lines of code that don't do anything."

"Show me," Michael barked. He suspected sabotage, or worse, a program within a program designed to data mine. The odd lines appeared on the monitor. Concern pinched his face as he read the words on the screen. Separately, the lines meant nothing, but read together they told the program to seek specific information. "Shut this down, Dawn, and purge these lines from your system. Isolate that data here and at the office until we can eliminate that worm."

His fingers hammered on the keyboard, punching each letter with anger. He wrote quickly, creating a program to seek out the odd lines and eliminate them. There were bound to be more worms in more information from Dredger. Obviously, he wasn't any more trusting than Michael was. He punched the enter key so hard his finger hurt.

"Let me know when that finishes cleaning up the worm or whatever you want to call it." He left the computer room, and went out to the living room.

Heather was sitting on the sofa flipping through a magazine; Wells at her feet, Paul slumped in the big chair, for all appearances taking a nap. Michael sat next to Heather, pulling her close. He knew she was upset about everything that was happening. They hadn't had a moment alone in days and she wasn't allowed to go anywhere by herself. Not like the romantic relationship, she'd imagined a week ago. None of this was what he wanted for her, but they couldn't expect anything better for now. She rubbed his chest and sighed.

"We should go out someplace." He knew when he spoke they wouldn't be alone, but a change might do them some good. Events had forced him to ignore her for the last few days and that had made him realize how much he needed her.

"Where?" she whispered into his chest. "Can we risk going to the bathroom anymore without being watched?" The bitterness in her voice was like a knife to his heart.

"We can go to a movie, to a restaurant, or we can go for a walk out back. These guys aren't required to be right beside us, as long as we're not out of sight. I'd like to go to a movie if you're willing."

She sat up and looked at him hopefully. "Now," she said. "That sounds great, but it's the middle of the afternoon. I'd really like to see a movie too. What do you want to see? I don't even know what's playing."

"I don't know, but I'm craving popcorn," he said breaking into her thinking. "If I have that and you, I'll be happy watching anything." He kissed her nose gently. She smiled at him, kissed his mouth, and ran down the hall to change out of her sweat pants and torn T-shirt, which had become her normal daily attire.

"Do I get a vote on what movie we see?" Paul asked from the chair. One eye was open, staring at Michael.

"No, but I'll let you buy the drinks. You've got to sit at least three rows behind us too." He grinned.

"Why, so you can talk about me?" Paul opened his other eye and smiled back, sitting up straight. "I'm sorry we have to be around you and Heather all the time, but the closer we are the better we can protect you. Even one second could mean the difference between life and death. Until the threat is completely gone, we need to be here."

"Yeah I know, but as nice as you guys are, it's getting a little close in here."

They left the house and drove to a movie theatre in the valley. The marquee showed four movies: The Fly, Star Wars: The Empire Strikes Back, The Big Easy, and Moonstruck. Michael let her chose before he went to buy the tickets.

The popcorn was great, and they laughed until their sides hurt watching Moonstruck and cried together at the end. Leaving the theatre, Heather snuggled against Michael as they strolled along the sidewalk toward the limo parked at the corner. Otto stood beside the open rear door waiting for them. Their bodyguards maintained a discreet distance, but joined them in the car. The drive back to the house was silent as both Michael and Heather relaxed and snuggled in the rear seat.

For the first time in weeks, Michael felt happy. He held her hand as they waited for Paul to open the door. Otto stood in the doorway until they were given the all clear. Wells met them wagging his tail and woofing to say that he was glad they were home. Michael suddenly became tired, more exhausted than he'd been in months. He looked at Heather and she smiled as if sensing his thoughts. They went down the hall to their bedroom, saying goodnight to the guards.

Chapter 24

Randal Chesterwick hunched over the computer console in Mission Control in Florida. His eyes were focused on the monitor, but he wasn't thinking about the Mars probe. His mind was on what might be happening to Michael.

He let his thoughts wander back to the beginning, the start of their history. Much had changed in the last three years; much more had to change, but the end was near.

He'd been born in Chesterwick, an orphanage in London, England; at least that's what they told him when he was old enough to understand.

As a boy, he was always pulling things apart to find out how they worked. The orphanage radio was transformed to receive short and long-range signals. Mother Beatrice was impressed, but afraid for him. She thought he might cause harm to himself or to the building one day and forbade him from using the caretakers' tools. He didn't listen. Anything electrical was of interest, something to operate on to see if he could improve the device. By the time he turned eighteen, most of the nearby homes had radios he'd built from scrounged parts.

He saved his money and booked passage on a steamer to America in 1968. The new world was an enormous and bustling place, but fascinating. The priest Mother Beatrice sent him to see had died six months before Randal arrived, but the new priest Father Jonathan Granger was willing to assist the young boy.

Randal's fingers typed in a set of commands for the probe without his mind missing a memory. He was truly able to multi-task. This ability was probably why he was considered by his co-workers to be cold and aloof.

Father Granger helped him find housing and enroll in university. Randal managed to get his Ph.D. in astro-physics and electrical engineering in six years. By now, he'd discovered his family history: the truth about who he was and more importantly, the names of his parents.

Randal was the name the sisters at the orphanage gave him, his surname from the orphanage. There were many children named Chesterwick in England, all of them from the orphanage. He spent many years finding out his mother's name, but once he had her name, the rest of the search was easy.

Ingrid Dredger had accompanied her husband Frederic to an electronics conference in England in 1948. The details of how she met a lover there were secret, but the result became Randal. He wasn't interested in the how or why of their meeting and he wasn't interested in trying to cash in on his lineage. The fact that he had a brother was nice, but he knew he'd never be able to meet him. He didn't find out who his father was until 1980.

The name came as an accident, or maybe fate. Nobody was willing to hire him when he graduated from university. He drifted around some of the companies building airplanes or computers, but they weren't fulfilling. Slowly, he sank into a bottle and ended up on the streets in California.

One morning in July of 1980, he woke up and noticed the headline on the newspaper covering his shoulders. Michael Eldridge wins Turing Award for his work on semi-conductors. Randal stared at the young smiling face in the picture, but the older man standing beside Michael truly fascinated Randal. The hair was grey, but the features seemed familiar. Reaching inside his worn jacket, Randal pulled a faded picture out of the inside pocket and held it to the face in the newspaper. Mother Beatrice had given him the photo and said the man was his father. Someone had torn the original picture in half, but the man was definitely a younger version of the man in the paper. The caption said he was Michael Eldridge's father, Robert.

Another two years passed before Michael hired Randal. He wasn't interested in telling his new boss they were brothers, he was only interested in working. They made great strides in the computer industry, propelling the company to the top of the heap. Randal watched with equal interest what was happening to his other brother in Germany. There was nothing but disappointment, anger, and fear for where Tristan was leading the company.

Randal had developed a friendship with Dredger's lead research scientist. They wrote many letters, so he knew where the company was headed. Tristan wanted to travel through time, but his attitude said he wasn't going to be concerned about the effect on history. He had to be stopped. The letters stopped in 1984 and Randal learned the scientist had been killed in an unfortunate car accident.

His fingers typed more commands to the probe, but his eyes didn't move. He was seeing himself in the office back in California, three years ago when he'd decided to beat his German half-brother to the prize of time travel. He'd succeeded, but only with Michael's help and resources. The problem with having the machine was that using it would and could alter everything and everyone, but he needed to change the future so Tristan wouldn't succeed.

Many days he tried to figure out a way to make Michael interested in time travel. The solution came one day when he saw Joe and Michael together in the lab. Joe was Director of Research. Randal could see they were best friends, the kind that would do anything for each other. He used his machine to snatch Joe out of the past.

Time and history didn't change in a flash of light. He remembered everything, maybe because he'd been working the controls. There were subtle changes in the buildings and people, but mostly the projects and direction of the company stayed the same. Randal smiled. He'd succeeded in changing history without major harm. All he had to do was bring Joe back and everything would be fine, but then Michael signed a deal to give Tristan the final program to time travel. A monster like Dredger would destroy the world for fun. Traveling through time for him would be like a cat playing with a mouse.

He couldn't let that happen, or at least if Tristan got the technology, Randal was going to make sure he'd never use it. A warning buzzer sounded. The probe needed to make a course correction in the next two minutes, or else miss the Red planet. He watched another technician send the necessary code before returning to his memories.

The kidnapping was the first indication that Dredger wanted time travel. He knew that the future of transportation would be through transporters. Tristan wanted to monopolize the technology.

Being in Florida didn't give him much access to the same level of technology he was used to back in California. Why did things have to happen at the wrong time? He'd planned every detail. He was certain nobody would be hurt if history changed. Michael would be upset and concerned, but there wasn't any real danger to Joe. He was living in Boston as Randal without any knowledge of his former life. Randal could shift him back easily once Tristan was destroyed and that had been the plan all along. Dredger Electronics was never meant to invent time travel. Now fate had intervened to change history and he couldn't change that. He felt like calling Michael to tell him the whole story.

Chapter 25

An idea dropped into his mind as he stepped out of the shower. Michael knew he'd be obliged to change the code so Dredger couldn't succeed, but the better solution would be to use the information Dawn had stolen to eliminate Tristan. He wished Randal was available to help, but the man couldn't leave Florida right now. They were like brothers sometimes and Michael sensed the older man felt the same way. There was something in the way he looked at Michael when he thought Michael wasn't aware.

The worms or viruses that Dredger had inserted into their software certainly indicated their attitude and their level of trust. Tristan was living up to his reputation, but Michael was beginning to grow a real desire to ruin the man. A bell sounded on the computer in the room across the hall. He pulled on a pair of pants and T-shirt.

"What's the problem, Dawn?" he asked, feeling a bit inconvenienced without having coffee yet.

"I have some information for you that can't wait." Silence...

"Well?" Michael snarled impatiently.

"I put tracking software in one of the items we sent to Dredger. The worm, as you call them, searches for any mention of you or your company in communications from them to anyone in the world. They are attempting to implicate you in a murder in Monaco. They've sent bogus information to the Royal Police, which looks like you had a grudge against Detective Habbib. You and Walker were conspiring to cheat the Palace out of a deal to install computers there."

"I'll get Jon to make some calls. See if you can change the code to seem useable, but won't work. He can't ever get his hands on the real program."

He left the room and headed to the kitchen. Heather was making breakfast, but unlike the last few days, she was smiling. His kiss on her neck received a hug. Paul had taken Wells outside and was throwing a ball for the dog to fetch.

"Are you feeling better?" he asked as he poured coffee into a mug.

"Much," she answered.

Paul and Wells came in the patio door as she stretched to plant a kiss on Michael's lips. Her face blushed at being caught and strangely, Michael felt a little guilt as well. He said good morning to Paul and they all sat around the table to eat breakfast.

Jon walked through the front door, as they finished eating breakfast. He didn't use the knock code. Paul was out of his chair, gun in hand and crouched at the end of the wall separating the entrance from the kitchen in less than a second. The normally laid-back man seemed to possess speed and reflexes far beyond his appearance. Once he recognized who was entering, he stood and slid the gun into the back of his jeans. Jon waved at him and took a seat at the table.

"I have news," he began. "Dredger is trying to implicate you and the MI-6 spy Walker in the murder of Habbib in Monaco."

"Yeah I heard already," Michael said over the rim of his mug. Heather dropped her fork on her plate.

Jon's mouth fell open in surprise. "How did you find out? I was only informed on my way here a few minutes ago."

"That doesn't matter, but I was going to tell you and see if you could call someone over there."

"Already done, the man who called me is the lead detective on the case. Since I was involved in your kidnapping, he agreed to squash the information. What do you want to do now? Dredger is evil, I told you that before you went to see him."

Michael frowned. The enemy was moving faster and being more underhanded than he'd expected. Tristan Dredger wasn't going to be easy to get rid of and certainly not stupid.

"I think the time has come to play dirty." He was staring off into space.

"He's untouchable. Every time someone launches a complaint against him the case is dismissed, so how are you going to harm the man?"

"I have irrefutable information that implicates him in several crimes that should put him in prison for the rest of his life. Is there anyone you know who can leak this stuff to the appropriate authorities and keep us clean?" He smiled.

Jon grinned back. "I think we know a few sources we can use, right Paul? Give us what you have and we'll put it in the right hands. This is going to be a real pleasure." He winked and the grin turned into a broad smile.

201

Paul and Jon used the telephone for the next three hours calling their contacts around the world. Michael and Heather were kept busy sending fax copies of all the dirty secrets Dawn had found. The people receiving the files were told to eliminate any connection to Michael, or Eldridge computers. At the end of the telephone session, several of the contacts called back exclaiming their shock, excitement, and gratitude for a solid chance to put away Tristan Dredger.

'Time,' Michael thought, 'this all revolves around time. I wanted to find out what happened to Joe, but put that aside to put a monster away for good. I'm not sure anymore if I want to continue. Everything was fine a couple of years ago. There wasn't anybody trying to kill me or to hurt my friends. Maybe I'll just have to live without knowing about Joe. What would Dad do in this situation? He spent many years with RCA traveling all over the world. There had to be times when he encountered espionage, not on this level, but some. I bet he smiled and shrugged away the problem. We're not giving away military secrets, but this is something even deadlier. This is about being able to move through time and change history; being able to jump from point A to point B instantly. If Dredger develops the technology, armies could appear anywhere in an instant and there wouldn't be any way to stop them.' He sighed, hoping the current effort was enough to halt a maniac.

A thought came to him then. Randal was needed here more than ever. The Mars probe would operate under the watch of a lesser technician just as well. He called the lab and ordered Randal's top assistant to fly to Florida and take over. The next call was not to Randal, but rather the head of Mission Control. After a brief conversation, there were a few tense words used, but in the end, they agreed that Randal could come home. Michael crossed his fingers. The corporate jet would fly out at noon, returning Randal by midnight.

He planned to meet with Randal after the technologist had a few hours' sleep. Michael could bring him up to date and see if he could correct the problem. He felt stupid, thinking he could do this without Randal, who would probably disapprove of his actions, but he'd be bound to come on board after an explanation.

Bells started clanging in the computer room down the hall. The noise sounded like a four alarm call in a firehouse. He sprinted to the room, banging his elbow on the doorframe as he slid through the opening, cursing from the pain. Lights flashed and noise crashed around the space hurting his ears. He had to cover them to think.

"Dawn...Dawn," he shouted. "What the hell's going on?"

Silence; almost painfully deafening. He pulled his hands away from his ears and sat in the chair.

"Dredger buried a worm in the system. They said the program was for the electronics they're working on for their government, I didn't look too close. The worm searches for specific information and definitely seemed to be part of the code. They didn't get anything on this end because I put a door on the modem and shut off communications, but I'll need you to remove the worm. I'm only able to use enough resources to talk to you, but I can't touch the worm without spreading it throughout the hard drive."

"Can you show me where it is?"

A stream of words appeared on the monitor. The line of code did appear similar to a fetch sequence, but there was nothing specific the code should look for. Only when he read the next line did their purpose become clear. They were after the specifications for Dawn. His fingers beat the keyboard, deleting the lines and running a cleaning program he'd written for an anti-virus. *'Bastard is going to pay for this,'* he thought.

"You should be fine now," he said gently as if talking to Heather. "Don't open any ports to the outside until we're certain everything is gone. Any new data come in from Dredger lately?"

"No, but before I had to shut down the modem, I confirmed the flight to Florida was on time. Randal will be here by midnight."

Chapter 26

The news that he was being relieved was welcome to Randal. He wanted to get back to California and put an end to his evil half-brother. Waiting for the next few hours was going to be excruciating but worth the pain. *'If only I could be there when they walk him away to prison,'* he thought. *'When I realized that sick bastard would have the ability to commit crimes without any punishment, I had to act.'*

Nothing had happened to the probe since the launch so he wasn't expecting anything to happen now. The alarms started as a flashing light on his monitor and then became a system-wide cascade fault. Everyone was shouting and madly punching keyboards to correct the problem, but things kept getting worse. He wasn't responsible for the flight of the probe, but he was watching the stream of errors flying across his screen.

Something about the error messages didn't make sense. He wasn't a flight engineer, but he did know that there wasn't supposed to be any problems with the attitude of the ship carrying the probe unless a strike had occurred in space. Most of the error messages were about the ship losing power and wobbling out of control. There were no indications of a flight control malfunction or engine trouble, so why would the machine say there was a problem? Fuel levels were at nominal, thrusters were operating properly, but guidance control said there had been a failure.

Randal looked over at Mission Control Chief David Strathmore. The expression on his face was blank, but his body language spoke volumes. He was tense, and his eyes darted about the room pleading for someone to solve the problems with the probe.

Standing and moving slowly toward Strathmore, Randal meant to ease the man's fears. He stood beside the Mission Chief and detailed his suspicions. Strathmore said nothing for a moment as he digested the possibility. If Randal was right, then they could fix the problem quickly, but if he was wrong, the mission might end at that moment.

"Reboot the computers here in Mission Control," he shouted above the din in the room. All eyes turned toward him as he stood at the back of the room. A few voices spoke up, insisting there wasn't a computer problem. "We have the best computer engineer in the country in this room telling me there is a computer problem and all we need to do is reboot. Do it now," he shouted. "If that doesn't work we haven't lost anything yet. We can still fix the problem and get back on course, as long as we don't go over sixty minutes."

The screens around the room went black as the computers were shut down. Thirty seconds went by before they came back to life and the system went through a start-up sequence. All alarm bells were silent when the control system came online. The error messages had been false all along. Randal nodded to Strathmore and returned to his seat. Someone had tried to ruin the mission by inserting a virus into the computer, but whoever that was didn't know much about space flight.

"Thanks, we owe you big time," a hand rested on his shoulder. Randal turned to look up at the Mission Chief. "Is there any way of finding out who did that to us?"

Randal smiled. "I'll get the answer for you in a couple of minutes, but I need access to the main computer."

Strathmore leaned forward and punched a few keys on the keyboard. Moments later, a screen with the logo of NASA came up and a log in box. He typed in a password and the screen went black. A series of boot sequence lines appeared finally stopping at a blinking cursor.

"You're in the mainframe. I'm putting my trust in you to keep my job, so don't screw this up. Is that problem going to happen again?"

Randal shook his head and began typing. Over his shoulder he said, "The problem was meant to happen at a certain time. Since that time has passed, it can't happen again unless they put in a backup. I'll check everything while I'm in the system. Don't worry about your job. I don't care about anything but the virus." He renewed his attention to the monitor.

A hand touched his shoulder, and he nearly jumped out of his clothes. A familiar face was standing next to him with a slight grin. His assistant was standing there trying not to laugh. They shook hands and Randal took another few minutes to finish scanning the mainframe for corruption. His bags had been brought down from his room so all he had to do was carry them out to the waiting jet. Saying good-bye to everyone, he waved and left the control room. His ride to the airstrip took five minutes. The company jet was running and waiting for him. He buckled in and finally relaxed a little, but he knew the next few days would be terrifying.

Four hours later, he jerked awake as the plane touched down. He rubbed his eyes and cleared his mind for the next stage. Ten minutes later, the steps were lowered from the side of the jet and Randal walked down. The limo was waiting to whisk him home, to the modest bungalow sat among others similar in size, shape, and color on a street filled with similarity. Randal carried his bags into the front entrance and dropped them. He reached for the light switch in the dark. Light came from a single lamp on a table beside the only other piece of furniture in the room, an overstuffed leather chair. He walked through to the kitchen and with the help of the moonlight streaming in the window over the sink, and he flicked on the light to the basement. Sixteen steps, he'd counted them more than once.

A worktable stood against the wall opposite the stairs. Testing equipment, tools, wire and other bits and pieces littered the top. To the right of the stairs and the table stood a box the size of a fridge. Wires ran from the box to the electrical panel fastened to the wall above the table. The furnace and hot water tank filled the far corner to the left of the stairs. Three bare bulbs hanging from the ceiling illuminated the space. There was a faint smell of damp in the basement.

Randal stepped toward the box he thought of as a vehicle. In the movie, H. G. Wells portrayed the time machine as a sleigh rigged with lights and levers, but to carry the correct power supply, the vehicle would need to be the size of a truck or small bus. This machine was only capable of operating by the aid of a computer in this time. It was much easier to keep the power and the control here.

He opened a locked toolbox on the table and removed a laptop. The computer seemed to stare up at him; at least that's how he felt at that moment. Go ahead, it said in his mind, start the machine. His hand trembled as he lifted the screen and pushed the on button. A beep, and two minutes later, the computer was ready. He pressed two keys at once and waited. The screen went black and then a logo appeared. This was the login page of Eldridge Computers.

The computing power actually came from the main computer at the lab, but Randal didn't think anyone would mind even if they could detect the connection he was using to get into the server. Five seconds and he had access to his private files. A password later and he opened the one named 'Lazarus'. He grinned at the name because the name meant rebirth in his mind.

An icon in the file said simply 'start' and he used the mouse to do that. The machine hummed and became luminescent. He sighed with relief. Everything still worked. The only thing he had to do now was tell Michael. About his part in the disappearance of his best friend and the machine, here in the basement. He'd tell the rest of the story when Dredger was destroyed. He moved the mouse over the 'stop' icon and went to bed.

Chapter 27

The morning sun was just rising over the mountains when Randal awoke. He showered and dressed quickly, made coffee and drove into the hills to meet with Michael. He'd been to the house several times and at eight in the morning, traffic was going in the opposite direction. He arrived at eight forty-five and rang the bell. A large man answered the door and allowed Randal to enter.

Three people were seated at the kitchen table -- Michael, Heather and another man who appeared to have just crawled out of the gutter. Long hair, unshaved and slumped on the chair as if he was on drugs, but the large black gun he held pointed at Randal wasn't something any drunk would own.

"Randal," Michael almost shouted. "Come in and have coffee with us. This is Paul and you met Otto at the door. They're my security. How have things been going down in Florida?"

"I've had more fun playing solitaire, until last night." Michael's face seemed surprised and fearful at the same time. Randal continued so there wouldn't be too many questions. "Nothing to worry about, I fixed the problem. Somebody tried to sabotage the flight, but there shouldn't be any more trouble." He scratched at the back of his head.

"Dredger, probably," Heather moaned. Randal gave her a side-glance not understanding what had happened or how she might know about his brother's company.

"I need to talk to you, Michael. It's very important, but private." His heart was pounding with excitement. He took the mug of coffee from Heather, but his shaking hands threatened to spill the contents.

Michael was concerned, but motioned to follow him down the hall. Randal looked shocked as they entered the computer room. He knew Michael had a computer in the house, but he hadn't expected anything this sophisticated.

"Take a seat," Michael said. He was smiling seeing the expression on the other man's face. "What's on your mind?"

Randal sat heavily on the spare chair. His eyes roamed over the telephone box and the table. He knew what they were used for and smiled inwardly. He'd succeeded, but now was the time for him to confess.

"This is my fault," he blurted. "I'm responsible for your best friend disappearing."

Michael stared at the face of the man he thought he knew. Randal looked as if he would cry, but Michael couldn't feel any compassion.

"I think you'd better start at the beginning before I have you thrown out of my house. This better not be a joke Randal, because I'm not in the mood. I don't like my friends being used, especially the ones who aren't here to defend themselves." His face was red with anger as he sat back in the chair.

Randal took a deep breath to settle his heart and focus his thoughts. He'd planned this day for years, but now he was too nervous to speak. Both hands scratched the back of his head.

"This is complicated, Michael, but once I get started you'll understand. I or at least Randal is from an alternate universe." He glanced at Michael to see if that tidbit of information would produce a reaction, but if there was any change it was only a redder face. "His time is the same as ours. All the players in this universe are the same as his, but whatever happens here, their universe is worse." He sensed he'd taken the wrong track and quickly changed the story.

"In Randal's universe, Dredger is his half-brother. They've never met and more important, he's your half-brother as well." The silence in the room was deafening. Michael's face turned pale, but he said nothing. "I'll get back to that in a minute," Randal rushed on sensing he didn't have much longer before Michael exploded. "I'm Joe."

Michael's jaw sagged open and for a moment, Randal thought he would scream. A moment passed and then Michael closed his mouth, clenching his jaw several times. He stared across the desk at Randal.

"I'll accept your story for the moment, but you better come up with some really convincing information to prove what you're saying. Those men out there carry guns and right now if I had one I'd be weighing the risk of shooting you for being a dangerous nutcase." His jaw muscles moved again under the skin. "I've known you for what...six years and I never took you for crazy so don't make me regret meeting you now. Give me facts, Randal, or whoever you are, so that I can believe your story." Michael leaned forward in his chair; his face was regaining a normal color, but his eyes remained angry.

"I'll do my best, but I have a hard time believing this happened to me." He sighed and looked at the floor. *'Start at the beginning,'* he said to himself. *'He's a smart man and he'll believe you if he has the facts.'* "On the day I disappeared, I met a man in that tunnel."

Michael remembered the man he'd seen the day he jumped back in time. The guy appeared homeless. He nodded his head for Randal to continue. The expression on Michael's face revealed he'd been back in time and knew what had happened.

"He said he was from the future and that he wanted me to change places with him. I didn't really understand, but I figured the future was a better place than what I had back then. You two had gone before I got back and that made me mad. I was going home to tell Mom, and then nothing." He shrugged. Michael leaned forward.

"I woke up on the street...well more like the gutter six years ago wrapped up in newspaper. There was a headline about you and that was when I figured we had to get together. Randal told me that he wanted you to create a time machine. He said yours had to be completed before Dredger's because if the German created the technology, that would mean the end of the world. I knew everything he did, even had his education. As soon as I could, I applied to work for you. The rest of the story you know, but one thing you don't know is that we can reverse my timeline." His brows arched expectantly. Michael's face remained expressionless. "That sounds plausible to me." Dawn said softly. Randal jumped in his chair.

"It talks," he stammered pointing at the computer. Michael smiled.

"I call her Dawn and she does more than talk, but that doesn't matter right now. Let's say I believe your story. Why would this other Randal pick my friend Joe?"

"He told me that you were going to create some powerful computers, but you wouldn't be interested in time travel. The only way to stop Dredger was to make sure you'd solve time travel first. You needed a reason, Michael, something to focus your interest toward time. Making me disappear was the solution, at least that's the way he explained it. I was seven, Michael, what difference did any of that make to me? I thought it would be fun."

Michael was nodding. The story was starting to make sense, but there was so much missing detail. "I already know that Tristan Dredger is a villain and doesn't deserve to keep breathing. I guess the problem is all these half-brother connections. Randal is my brother and Tristan's brother too in this other universe."

Randal nodded.

"Ok, we don't have to worry about that now. If you are Joe, tell me what we did earlier on that day you disappeared."

A smile crept over Randal's face. "That was the school field day and you scraped up your arms and knees racing. Miss Belfridge patched you up and gave you a hug. Billy and I didn't think you'd ever stop smiling." He chuckled and this time Michael joined him.

"One more question to be sure: what was my biggest fear as a kid?" Michael couldn't breathe. He knew there was only one person he'd ever told about being afraid of shadows. Of course, his older brother knew, but Joe was the only other person on the planet.

"Shadows, you thought there were evil spirits in the shadows trying to grab your soul." He saw Michael gasp and jump off the chair. His vision narrowed and the world became silent. Michael moved around the desk, in what seemed like slow motion, so excited and so happy, joy written on his face. Mike wrapped his arms around Joe's neck and pulled him tight in a manly hug. Randal looked over Michael's shoulder, and saw Paul, Heather, and Otto crowded in the doorway staring in horror at Michael.

"What?" Michael asked.

"We heard you shout and thought you were in trouble. What's going on with you two?" Heather wanted to know.

"I'll explain everything later, but right now Joe and I have some work to do." He slapped his friend on the shoulder and gave Heather a kiss.

"Are you okay Michael? You just called Randal, Joe." Her face scrunched into a distasteful frown. Randal guessed she was starting to worry about all the stress on Michael or maybe the jump in time had scrambled his mind.

"I've never been better or happier. This is no longer Randal, but he is my best friend Joe." He giggled at the expression on their faces and then kissed her again. "I'm not crazy and I'll tell you later. Trust me, but we need to get to work." He slowly closed the door, shutting them out of the room.

"I don't really understand what's going on, but I'm glad it is," he said turning back to Joe. "What I do know is that Dredger has to be shut down and get you back to being my best friend. You don't look a bit like I imagined you as a grown man and you can't know how much I've missed you."

"It was harder for me all these years," Joe said quietly. "I wanted to tell you the first day I walked into your office, but you would've thrown me out or had me arrested as a lunatic." He smiled. Michael chuckled. "Randal told me that I'd need to go through the machine to reverse the process, but he warned me not to until Tristan is safely behind bars."

Michael nodded grimly. "That might take a while for the courts to catch up to him, but at least he's going to be busy for the next few weeks answering questions about his dastardly deeds. We can go ahead with making these things work perfectly." He waved at the table and booth.

"I built one of those in my basement." Joe nodded at the locker contraption. It functions, obviously, but I've only used it once."

The two men stared at each other. "Mine does too," Michael said. "I went back to find out how you disappeared. Do you remember that public works truck in the field across from the tunnel? I was there, watching. We saw you come out with the old guy and then you walked away and vanished. Now, I understand what was happening." Joe was nodding as Michael talked.

"At first, I thought the old guy was my Dad returned from Korea, but then he started talking about time travel. That seemed weird and kinda creepy, but I figured he was harmless. I have the memories of a man fifty-seven years-old Michael, but I've never felt they were mine. When I woke up, the memories of the years between vanishing and waking don't seem real. Maybe they never will," he said sadly.

"Well, once we bring you back that might change, but even if it doesn't, I'm here for you. Who knows, perhaps if none of this had happened we'd both be in jail by now." They both chuckled at the thought.

A knock sounded on the door, a light tentative rap. Michael turned and opened it. Jon was standing in the hall with his good-natured smile lighting up the space. He stepped forward without waiting to be invited inside.

"The elusive Joe Solomon." His hand shot forward to greet Joe, who seemed shocked and a little confused. "I'm Jon Richter, the head of security. It seems we have many things to celebrate today." His grin widened further into a full smile at the confused expression on Michael's face. "I received a message from one of my contacts in Germany..." he glanced down at his wrist watch. "About half an hour ago, Tristan Dredger was arrested in Bonn and charged with three counts of rape, six counts of theft, and fourteen counts of corporate espionage. The information we sent will make sure he never savors freedom again."

"How long before he's actually in prison?" Joe wanted to know.

Jon shrugged. "Everything depends on the court, but for a case this size and importance they might take two or three years to even get to trial."

Michael and Joe glanced at each other. They knew that Joe wouldn't really be able to return until there was absolutely no way Tristan could continue with his time-travel project. Something else would need to be done to ensure he was out of the picture. He glanced at Joe and led Jon into the hallway. Once the door was closed, Michael turned and whispered.

"I'm going to ask you to do something that is against everything we both hold dear." He paused trying to form the words into a sentence that wouldn't sound too insane. "I need Tristan Dredger eliminated permanently. The documents were a delaying tactic, but now he has to be gone forever. If you aren't willing, please get someone else as soon as possible." His face was grim.

Jon had been stone faced, but now he made an evil grin. His eyes were still cold.

"It will be my pleasure, sir. He's been asking for this since he was a little boy. The world will be grateful or at least they'll thank the person responsible for killing him. I'll leave today and call you when I'm done." He turned and moved quickly down the hall and out of the house. Michael could see Paul's face. A knowing smile crept across his features.

Michael and Joe went over the details of what they were going to do to return Joe to his body. They hoped that when the moment came, there wouldn't be huge changes to the world around them, but there was no way to know for sure. Joe told Michael about their history, which changed when he switched places with Randal. Heather called them to come out and eat at around six and then there was just the waiting to hear from Jon.

They spent the rest of the evening filling in details for each other and for Heather. She'd known Randal only from his work at the company, but they'd never talked. His perspective of her was the same. Secretly, he hoped the couple would still be together after he returned to his own body.

Chapter 28

Tristan Dredger had sensed something was wrong two days ago. Everything he'd planned was going too well and too easy. The meeting with Michael Eldridge was a joke. Michael attempted to trap him into some sort of admission that he'd been responsible for the kidnapping attempt, but that wasn't going to happen. Then he'd just agreed to give access to all the data for time travel to Dredger Electronics. What a fool, he'd thought at the time.

He'd gone to meet with an associate of the Russian mobster he'd hired to kidnap Michael. There was no need to use their services any longer and from there, he flew home. A radio message from the plane to his manager in Bonn gave orders to scatter some kind of Trojan horse into all the data that would be shared with the Americans. He realized the next evening that Eldridge computers were smarter and more prepared than he'd thought they would be. None of the software spies sent back any information. He still wasn't concerned because Michael was going to give him what he wanted.

Two days after returning from America, he sent manufactured information implicating Michael in the death of a police officer to Interpol. He hadn't expected anyone to take the information seriously against Eldridge, just inflict some concern and confusion. Then, one of his informants in the police department called to say that damning information had been received that implicated Tristan in multiple serious crimes.

He'd smiled at the news, there was no need to worry, he thought. This had happened before and he'd never been convicted. Witnesses just had a way of disappearing. Still, he felt as if a gathering storm was coming and he should be prepared.

His company had computerized their operations years earlier as soon as the technology was available. He'd made sure there was one in the house as well. Walking into the den in the basement of his house, Tristan sat at the desk and turned on the computer. The monitor lit up and he watched the machine go through the process of starting. At the blinking cursor, he typed in his password and waited.

All of his files scrolled across the screen; dates, places, people, who were paid for what, all the dirt he'd shoveled over the years was there. Smug in the thought that there was no way, he'd be linked to any crimes, Tristan deleted all of the documents and then shut off the computer and went to bed.

Loud hammering and banging on the front door of his house woke him the next morning at six o'clock. A moment later, his butler knocked on the bedroom door. Tristan staggered down the stairs angry and half-awake only to be greeted by a mob of police officers in black uniforms, pointing assault weapons in his face. They handcuffed him and drove him in an armored van to the police station, still in his bathrobe and nothing else.

Hours of questions followed. Documents and pictures of murdered people were shoved in his face. Everything they showed him was something he'd saved on his home computer, but how did they get in? He could feel his confidence draining. Grimly, he decided that once his lawyer arrived he would find out who was responsible for having him arrested.

Three miserable days after being arrested, Tristan, dressed in prison garb, handcuffs, and leg chains, was led fifty feet down a driveway to an armored van for a ride to the courthouse. He was smiling. A small hole appeared in his forehead as the back of his head exploded. His eyes went vacant and he slumped to the ground. The guards moved to safe positions knowing their prisoner was already dead. They had all drawn their weapons while trying to locate the shooter, but he was already gone and no further shots came toward them.

Jon, looking through the scope on the sniper rifle, saw the hole appear in Tristan's head and then crawled back from the parapet on top of a building two blocks away. He knew the shot was lucky more than skillful. The guards had been doing their jobs correctly until seconds before they reached the van. This was his only chance and he took the shot. If Tristan had reached the courthouse, he might have survived to the end of the trial.

Stripping the rifle and putting the pieces into a briefcase lined with foam, Jon carried the case to the door leading into the stairway. He wasn't worried about being stopped by the police. His credentials from the Monaco police department were still active and there was no reason to suspect him anyway. To be on the safe side, he was going to dump the case in a sewer along the way back to the airport. Sirens wailed as he walked away from the prison to where he'd parked the car. He sat in the front seat, the gun, and case beside him, as he stared out the windshield. This wasn't the first time he'd killed a man, and this wasn't the first time he'd murdered anyone. The kidnapper who escaped and ruined his career would never be found. Strangely, he didn't feel any remorse. A smile crept over his face as he started the car and drove to the airport.

He pulled the car into the rental lot and paid the bill with cash. The briefcase had vanished along the way. His suitcase was in the trunk and he carried that into the departure area. Using his most pleasant smile, he checked through his luggage before going to find a telephone. The line to America was clear and when the person on the other end answered, he said, "All done," and hung up.

Chapter 29

Paul set the receiver back in the cradle. The expression on his face never wavered. He turned to look at Michael and nodded. Michael felt like shouting with joy, but realized that a man had just been murdered. No matter what he thought of Tristan Dredger, he couldn't condone killing and he certainly didn't want to celebrate murder.

All the same, he felt glad that he and Joe could finally be friends again, if everything went the way they thought. Everyone had been camped at the house; anyone who knew about the situation was told what was happening. Even Billy showed up the day before, waiting to hear from Jon. Heather hugged Michael as they sat on the sofa; she knew the risk they were going to take.

"I think we should wait until tomorrow," Joe said. There was real fear in his eyes.

"Why, he's gone. Changing you back isn't going to make him any less dead, is it?" The fear was contagious and Michael could feel dread slipping into his brain like a cold fog.

"I'm not so sure I can come back, Michael. Follow me on this and then tell me I'm wrong. If I come back, then technically I will have never left. That means that you wouldn't have any reason to develop time travel, which means you wouldn't care about Tristan Dredger...likely wouldn't ever hear of him until it was too late. None

215

of these guys would be here. Jon wouldn't have saved you and killed Tristan. Everything you've experienced in the last few weeks would be different. You might not even like Heather." His face had gone pale and grim.

"But Randal told you everything would be okay," Michael shouted. "You didn't really jump through time; you just changed bodies with him."

"I know, but I still don't trust him. We don't have any choice, really, but I'm worried that we could be doing something that can't be undone."

"There is another choice," Paul said from his place at the table. All eyes turned to him. "You could just leave things the way they are. He doesn't look like your friend, but who really knows he's Joe outside of this room? Get used to calling him Randal again and live your lives. Why do you need to change him back?"

Michael looked at Joe. The eyes that stared back were filled with sadness. Michael couldn't remember a time when he hadn't wanted to find his best friend. To be this close to having his friend back and yet not was too much to bear. Obviously, this was the same feeling Joe had.

"I'm not risking anything, Joe, but you and the world are betting everything. The final decision is yours," Michael said sadly. He wanted his friend to return, but he wouldn't put the world in jeopardy. Joe understood as he rose slowly and walked out the patio doors.

He followed the path across the hill overlooking the valley. Grass and scrub brushed against his legs, birds chirped overhead, the sun was hot on his face, but he didn't hear or feel anything. His imagination was painting images of what life would be like as Joe Solomon again.

The best outcome would be nothing changed, but that was a slim chance. He'd touched too many things in the years since he'd awakened in that alley six years ago. If he changed, so would they. Randal had been wrong.

In the worst case, he'd change back and Tristan Dredger would rule the world, making everyone pay. How could he be certain there wouldn't be any consequences? He imagined this was like waving his hand and the breeze becomes a hurricane. He stopped and glanced back at the path. *'I've probably killed hundreds of bugs coming from the house. They'd still be alive if I wasn't here.'*

His head was starting to hurt with the struggle to figure out the time dilemma. The one hope they had was that Randal had been correct. If Joe was only occupying the same space as Randal and he was really Randal making the changes, then time wouldn't be altered by shifting Joe back into the same space. It seemed too easy. The thought made him shake his head.

A crow called from a scrub pine on the ridge to his right. He scanned the tree until he found the bird among the branches. *'If I'd been born a bird, the most important thing in my life would be finding food,'* he thought glumly.

If he went back to the day he'd disappeared, all this would definitely change. *'How could Randal go back to 1957 and talk to me without making changes in time and history? There had to be some way he did that. Was he really there?'* he heard his mind whisper.

Of course he was there, Michael saw him too. The thought gave him an idea. He ran back to the house, nearly busting the screen door in his haste to get inside. Michael was standing by the kitchen sink and turned as Joe came running inside.

"Michael, I think I've got a solution," he panted. Running wasn't something he did on a regular basis.

"Okay calm down and let me hear it," Michael said. He finished pouring a mug of coffee to give Joe a chance to catch his breath.

"I don't think Randal was really back in the past when he talked to me about this. I think he transmitted his image but not his body." He saw the doubt on his friend's face and hurried on with his idea. "Think about that. He went back in time but didn't alter anything since. My life changed, but that's all. The thing is I don't think I really disappeared. Randal took my place in time and he made me take his. There won't be a change when I shift back to being me because neither of us left." His face was beaming. Michael needed to think, but the idea made sense. Joe had always been smart and if his mind and not Randal's was operating in the body standing before him, then there was every reason to believe this could work.

"It's still your choice, Joe. If you want to go ahead we can do the switch right now."

Joe nodded.

217

Chapter 30

Michael looked across at the man on the table in the computer room. There was fear on the features of the face he'd known as Randal for the last six years. They were about to do something that could result in the death of his best friend. Michael was sweating despite the coolness of the room.

He took a deep breath and pressed enter on the keyboard. The booth lit up and lights flashed on the front of Dawn the computer. Joe and Michael had worked out the equation required to split Joe away from Randal and send the latter away permanently.

His eyes were locked on the booth. The man in there closed his eyes. Nothing was happening and Michael began to worry. He looked down at his watch. The program was going to run for three minutes and it had already been...ten seconds. He had a vague fear that time was changing, slowing outside the booth.

Randal's features had altered slightly when Michael looked up. The hair had changed color, the face was thinner, and a dimple had started to form in the chin. More lights flashed across Dawn and the sound intensified. Thick and unruly red hair was replaced with thinning brown, the body shrank slightly, and the clothes became baggy. For a moment, Michael thought Joe would leave and go back in time. His body became transparent, ghostlike as the Randal side left the present.

The volume of sound in the room began to subside. Lights flashed less and Joe became solid. Michael stood, impatient to find out if his friend was truly whole. When the sounds stopped, he went to the booth and the two men stared at each other.

"Okay," he asked Joe softly.

Joe nodded and sat up on the table. He remained silent. Instead, he waggled his fingers in front of his face and shook his feet to making sure everything was still working. Apparently certain that he was intact; he looked at Michael and smiled.

"I think it worked."

Michael dragged him by the arm out to the living room. He couldn't wait to share the news with Billy and Heather. There was nobody in the room. His head swiveled wildly looking for anyone. *'It's changed,'* he thought, and his heart thudded into his stomach.

Motion on the deck attracted his attention. Paul, Billy, Heather, and Wells were outside, watching the sunset.

They joined them. Someone had expected the best and brought out two extra bottles of beer to celebrate. Michael and Joe opened them and all toasted to the success. What a relief Michael felt. He glanced at Joe. The change in appearance would take a while to sink in, but this was good. Billy couldn't stop smiling either. The three amigos were united again.

There was a general chatter as questions flew at Joe about his experiences. He declined to answer any of them, saying he was just glad to be here and his old self. Everyone was a bit disappointed, but not as sad as when Billy asked Michael what would happen to the machines now.

"I'm going to destroy them and any trace of the program that runs them. Nobody should get this technology. Tristan Dredger was a perfect example. All we need is another person like him to gain access to the secret and the world we know would end."

"I guess that means I'll be required to smash mine too." Joe said. All eyes turned toward him. Michael nodded and went to turn on the outside lights. They drank a dozen more bottles of beer between them before Billy stretched and said he was going home. Everyone walked him to the front door and said their good-byes. Joe yawned and said he'd better get going too.

"You're not going anywhere," Heather stated flatly. "There's a spare room and you've only just appeared." She giggled at her own joke. "We need some time to get used to the new you...besides," she continued. "Tomorrow is Saturday and even that workaholic Randal never worked weekends."

Joe nodded his acceptance and smiled. She led him down the hall to the room next to the computer room. There were towels on the dresser and a bathrobe on the back of the door. He was impressed and said so. She smiled and closed the door, leaving him to get ready for bed.

Michael was standing in the living room looking out at the lights in the valley. He felt as if years had passed since he'd done this. She wrapped her arms around his waist from the back and pressed her head between his shoulders. He took the hint and went down the hall, leaving Paul by himself out on the deck.

• • •

Jon showed up the next morning. He slumped into a chair exhausted, but cheerful. Heather set a plate of bacon and eggs in front of him. Michael waited impatiently to hear the story of his trip while he ate. Joe wandered out to join them and Jon seemed surprised, but didn't say anything. Finished eating, Jon pushed the plate away and sipped his coffee.

"I can see that all went well here," he said looking at Joe.

Michael grinned. "Perfect, but this wouldn't have been possible without you."

"Well, he won't be a problem anymore, which also means that you won't need so much security from now on."

"Yeah that's today, but what about tomorrow or the next day? Who knows when the next Dredger Company will appear? I can afford to keep you and all your men working even if all you do is play cards."

Jon smiled. He was relieved to know that Michael was a man of his word.

Michael looked down at the table for a moment and then went down to the bedroom. He came back red-faced and grinning. Heather was sitting at the table finishing her breakfast. Michael stood beside her and then bent to one knee.

She glared at him; a little shocked at what he was doing, but said nothing. Her mind was trying to guess what was coming next.

"Heather will you do me the honor of being my wife?" Michael asked and produced a small box from behind his back. His hands shook as he opened the lid and showed her the diamond ring inside. Her hands flew up to her face, covering the surprise. A noise that sounded like a cough came out of her mouth; her eyes searched his trying to see if he was serious. She nodded and wrapped her arms around his neck.

The other men at the table cheered and clapped. Michael's face reddened, but Heather snatched the ring out of the box and placed it on her ring finger. She hugged him again and kissed him on the mouth.

Four months later, bells rang at the little Unitarian church in San Jose. The bride and groom emerged and dashed to the limo at the bottom of the steps while the crowd pelted them with rice and confetti. Joe was Michael's best man while Billy was a groomsman. Heather had chosen her best friend to be the maid of honor and a friend from work to be a bridesmaid. Otto drove the limo and Paul sat in the front passenger seat. Jon was at the reception hall, making sure the security was in place.

Since the death of Tristan Dredger, Eldridge computers had become the largest technology company in the world. Joe took over the position Randal had occupied, Billy continued in his and Heather had been replaced by a man. They hired sixty new people in manufacturing, but Michael suspected they'd need double that many soon. The honeymoon would be in the Caribbean for at least a month. There was also a little Michael on the way.

Thank you for taking the time to read this novel. I would ask that you please leave a review to show your support for my work.

My other novels; Jack, I Am and Reality Shift are available for your enjoyment at the same site you purchased this book. Please tell your friends.

The working title of my next novel is: Day of the Hawk. It will be available in August, 2015. Here's a sample.

The tiny brush swept away sand from an encrusted object. Sixteen feet below the desert surface, the air should be cooler, but Dr. Jack Stafford worked soaked in sweat. It was dripping onto the object, clotting the sand and frustrating his efforts to be gentle.

He dropped the brush and pulled the bandana from his neck. Looking up to the lip of the trench, his hand scrubbed the cloth across his forehead. A tent erected to protect him and the other archeological students from the intense desert sun, only served to block any breeze that might help cool the people at the bottom of the dig site.

This was supposed to be the culmination of twenty years of research for Dr. Jack, as he was known to his students. Jack was the leading professor of archeology at the University Of North Dakota. He'd theorized that the origins of Homosapiens were older than most of the current literature. They had it wrong to say that modern man sprang from an accidental gene mutation in Neanderthals or apes.

He knew the academic eggheads thought he was crazy, but it didn't bother him. The fact that he believed modern man sprang from deliberate gene manipulation by unknown beings went against everything they held to be true. They wouldn't take his research seriously. He'd shown them the proof. Hard evidence in the historic record, both written and physical archeological, but they wouldn't budge.

Sweat ran into his eyes. He mopped his face again and went back to brushing away sand. Rivulets of fine quartz, granite, and sandstone poured down from above the area he was clearing. Cursing, he threw down the brush and stood up. Two students nearby gave him concerned looks and went back to their digging.

Bloody sand, bloody heat, bloody dessert, he snarled in his mind. Damned ignorant hypocrites that won't see the truth when it's right in front of them. How much more do they need before they believe what's staring them in the face.

He gripped the ladder rung with his outstretched hand and looked back at where he'd been digging. The sand had completely covered the spot. Damn sand, he swore again in his mind and stomped up the ladder, the metal rungs clanging under his boots.

At the top of the pit, he strode to a table in the shade of the tent. There were four tents at the site, one covering the excavation, one housing the female team members, one for the male members and one for him. Support workers came out every day from An Najaf. The table held a metal twenty-gallon keg of drinking water for the crew. Jack pulled a paper cup from the dispenser hanging on the side of the keg and filled it with water.

He sighed after the water drained down his throat relieving the tension beginning to tighten the muscles in his neck. It was six weeks into a twelve-week dig in the south-west desert of Iraq and he had to find something solid to prove his theory to his detractors. This had to be the spot. The research he'd strained and stressed over for the past ten years pointed to here.

Looking between the tents, the desert stretched to the horizon without any signs of anything larger than a grain of sand. The nearest inhabited settlement was El Barouch, but it was little more than a wet spot in this ever shifting dusty ocean. Six men and two women came from An Najaf each day bringing food and water for the archeology team. They made the thirty-mile trip in a small truck that should have fallen apart years earlier.

Jack crumpled the paper cup and dropped it into a garbage can under the table. A student, Tracy Craven hopped off the top rung of the ladder and shouted his name as she ran toward him. Her hands were cupped in front of her carrying something Jack could only assume was a precious object.

"What is it Tracy?" Jack didn't get excited anymore. He'd been on too many disappointing digs.

She stopped in front of him holding her hands toward him. They were trembling and she was breathing quickly.

"I found it a minute ago. It looks a lot like a Sumerian tablet...I think." She was a third year student, bright but struggled with insecurity. Jack was her instructor and this team was made up of his best students. He sighed and looked at her hands as she opened them.

In the centre of her left palm sat a clay tablet the size of a playing card. It had the familiar cuneiform symbols that characterized the Mesopotamian writing. He dug into his pants pocket for a pair of latex gloves and stuffed his hands inside before lifting the tablet from her hand. Pushing his glasses up onto his forehead, he was extremely nearsighted; the hand holding the fossilized clay nearly touched his nose as he squinted at the writing.

His eyes shifted back and forth across the ancient text. He decoded it quickly and looked at Tracy.

"Did you take pictures and measurements before you moved this?" He could hardly breathe as he waited for her to answer.

She nodded, her face sunburned, and she looked as if she'd cry.

"I could kiss you but that would be totally inappropriate." He giggled. "I have to put this in the safe." He started to walk around the trench to his tent and then came back to her. "The hell with it," and he planted a vigorous wet kiss on her lips. A huge smile came to his face as he skipped away.

Made in the USA
Charleston, SC
14 April 2016